Letters from Ruby

LETTERS FROM RUBY

Adam Thomas

a novel approach to faith

Letters from Ruby

Copyright © 2013 by Adam Thomas

ISBN-13: 978-1-4267-4137-1

Published by Abingdon Press, P.O. Box 801, Nashville, TN 37202

www.abingdonpress.com

The persons and events portrayed in this work of fiction
are the creations of the author, and any resemblance
to persons living or dead is purely coincidental.

Library of Congress Cataloging-in-Publication Data

Thomas, Adam, 1983-
Letters from Ruby / Adam Thomas.
    pages cm
 ISBN 978-1-4267-4137-1 (binding: paper / trade pbk. : alk. paper) 1. Clergy—Fiction.
2. Older women—Fiction. 3. West Virginia—Fiction. I. Title.
 PS3620.H6245L48 2013
 813'.6—dc23

                                                                2013006948

The scripture quotations unless noted otherwise are taken from the New
Revised Standard Version of the Bible, copyright 1989, Division
of Christian Education of the National Council of the Churches of
Christ in the United States of America. Used by permission. All rights
reserved.

The scripture quotation on pages 259-60 is taken from The
Authorized (King James) Version. Rights in the Authorized Version in
the United Kingdom are vested in the Crown. Reproduced by permission of the Crown's patentee, Cambridge University Press.

The quotations on pages 34 and 295 are taken from the Book of
Common Prayer.

The poems on pages 7, 54, 130, 261, 310 are from Walt Whitman's
Leaves of Grass (Boston: Small, Maynard, & Co., 1904).

The lyrics on page 44 are from "Danny Boy," by Frederic Weatherly
(1913).

Printed in the United States of America

1 2 3 4 5 6 7 8 9 10 / 18 17 16 15 14 13

For the real Ruby
(1927–2012)

When lilacs last in the dooryard bloom'd,
And the great star early droop'd
    in the western sky in the night,
I mourn'd, and yet shall mourn with
    ever-returning spring.
Ever-returning spring,
    trinity sure to me you bring,
Lilac blooming perennial
    and drooping star in the west,
And thought of him I love.
                        —Walt Whitman

Joy, shipmate, joy!
(Pleas'd to my soul at death I cry,)
Our life is closed, our life begins,
The long, long anchorage we leave,
The ship is clear at last, she leaps!
She swiftly courses from the shore,
Joy, shipmate, joy.
                        —Walt Whitman

Prologue

Calvin Harper pulled the nail from between his teeth and centered it on the penciled X. He gave the nail an experimental tap with his hammer and then drove it home with five sharp knocks. Bending down, he retrieved a frame from its resting place against the base of the wall. He slipped the wire onto the nail, eyeballed the levelness of the picture, and stood back to admire his work. The frame held a crisp and yellowed newspaper clipping: a grainy image of a damaged World War II–era cruiser beneath the headline, "News from the Pacific: Longest Ship in the World Stays Afloat, Makes Port." A hand-written note in the margin read, "Calvin, here's the ship Whit told you about."

Calvin studied the frame for another minute, then tilted it ever so slightly to make it more level. "Though there's no need," he said to the empty room. "I'm just going to shake it out of place when I hang the next one." The clipping was the ninth piece he had hung that morning, and as he looked around the living room he realized just how many more were lying against the wall below pencil marks.

"Time for a break," he told the frame.

Setting down the hammer, Calvin wove around half empty boxes and stacks of books, squeezed into the dining room, and spied his break time occupation, a glass of lemonade sweating in the late June heat. He gulped down the better part of the lemonade in one go and placed the cool wetness of the glass against his own sweating forehead.

None of the dining room chairs was free of boxes, and the only unoccupied spot on the dining room table was the one that now bore a sweat ring from Calvin's lemonade. Using his shirttail as a rag, he wiped the water off the dark, handcrafted tabletop. As he touched the table, the memory of how he came by it stole into his mind, and he smiled a faraway kind of smile. He shifted the boxes off one of the chairs and sat down.

"What have we here?" he asked himself, as he unfolded the flaps of the topmost box. It was full of books for the most part, but slid into the space between one stack of books and the side of the box was a collection of envelopes held together by a rubber band. With the same eagerness and gentleness of an archaeologist excavating a piece of ancient pottery, Calvin drew the envelopes from the box, pulled off the rubber band, and placed the letters on his lap.

The envelopes were the color of tea after a liberal helping of milk has been added. Calvin rubbed the top one between his fingers: the weight and craftsmanship of the paper was surely a relic from before the age of e-mail. He ran his fingers over the familiar postmark: "March 17, 2010, Victory, West Virginia," it read.

The flowing cursive script came from the same era as the stationery. Calvin read the return address under his breath: "Mrs. Ruby Redding, 817 Lilac Court, Victory." His own name on the address line looked quite proper and official in the graceful hand. Even after three years of priesthood, seeing

"The Reverend" affixed to the front of his name still made him wonder at the mysterious ways of God.

Calvin pulled a single sheet of cream-colored paper from the envelope, and the faraway smile returned. "Dear Reverend Calvin," read the salutation, which was written in the same flowing script as the envelope and the note on the framed newspaper clipping.

"Dear, dear Ruby," said Calvin as he began to read.

Dear Reverend Calvin,

I hope you are settling nicely into your new home in Boston. I didn't have your address, but I did have the lovely letter you sent to the whole congregation about taking your new position. Church of the Transfiguration. Now that's a mouthful and no mistake. I could say "St. John's" four times over before you get that name out! You remember Cooper, my grandson? Well, he got on the computer and found the address to the church before I could finish stirring the sugar into his tea. He even showed me a picture of the church building and took me on a "virtual" tour through the insides. It's a lovely church.

I hope you are enjoying Boston, though I expect it's still cold there. I had a bit of a stay outside of Boston once, a long time ago. Once I rode the swan boats all day long, just round and round the pond, on the lookout for ducklings trying their hardest to stay afloat. (I think the driver was a little sweet on me, so he let me ride for free. No harm in that, right?) Have you been on the swan boats? No, I can't imagine you have, it being winter, after all. Make sure you try them in the spring. There's something so peaceful about that little circuit of the pond, like your worries aren't allowed aboard. You can pick them up when you get off, but during those few minutes on the water, worry just doesn't exist. You'll see what I mean.

It's still quite cold here in Victory as well. You moved right after the blizzard, and a month later some of the snow is still here—mostly the remains of the huge piles in parking lots. The ladies and I haven't been quite as regular at Morning Prayer as we usually are because of all the ice. Esther Rose slipped on it last week and broke her wrist. Thank God that's all she broke. A hip would have been much worse. It's a good thing she's already had both of hers replaced. We visited her at home yesterday and prayed with her there. We brought over the red prayer book and everything.

Today the MMs put on their yearly St. Patrick's Day lunch for us old timers. They really do it up right in the parish hall. Everything was green, even the food. Avis made a great big gelatin mold in the shape of a shamrock that the lot of us barely put a dent in. And, of course, Josie came in full leprechaun costume, complete with a stringy yarn beard, oversized top hat, and buckles on her shoes. She was the life of the party, as always. We all had our picture taken with her. I'll send one to you as soon as they are developed.

We miss you here at St. John's, but we are still plugging away. I hope your new start in

Boston leads to so many wonderful things for you that you can't keep track. I especially hope you meet that young woman who makes your toes curl. I imagine Boston's a better place for that than Victory!

Wishing you all good things,

Ruby

⎯⎯⎯ ⟁ ⎯⎯⎯

Calvin traced the loops and lines of Ruby's signature. It was graceful and beautiful without being ostentatious. Like its owner, thought Calvin. He ran his finger along the signature a second time. *Wishing you all good things too.* He looked at the stack of letters on his lap and then glanced into the living room where all those pictures still needed hanging. "They can wait."

He replaced Ruby's letter in its envelope and moved it to the back of the stack. The next one was written only a few days after the first. As Calvin pulled out the second letter, he thought back to those days in Victory. "Dear, dear Ruby," he said again. "All of them, dear to me."

He took the last sip of his lemonade, rocked the chair back on two legs, and waded out into the depths of memory.

1

Calvin Harper exchanged the highway for a two-lane county road that stumbled down into a valley between two Appalachian peaks, or what would have been peaks millions of years ago, but which were now more like exaggerated humps in the terrain. They were not imposing like the Rockies. They didn't pierce the sky like mountains do in pictures from scenic calendars. Rather, they lay comfortably on the earth, like the lumps a sound sleeper makes under the covers. Evergreens and deciduous trees carpeted both squat mountains, and a hundred shades of high summer green painted on them a kind of contented, venerable majesty that the adolescent Rockies will not match until wind and time have scrubbed away their rough edges.

Calvin followed the winding road down into the valley, which fell north to south between the two slopes. Calvin could see dozens of houses peeking out from the dense cover of trees on the opposite slope. As he descended, the density of houses on his side of the valley grew thicker until there were enough of them for a generous person to collect them with the word "neighborhood."

A weathered sign, which had skipped its last three or four repainting appointments, greeted Calvin at the spot in the county road where the slope gave way to level ground. He stopped for a traffic light, the first he had encountered since leaving the interstate, and read the sign. "Victory—Established 1781—B&O Railroad 1842—State Football Champions 1981, 1982, 1994." Beneath the sign hung half a dozen plaques announcing the local societies: Rotarians, Elks, the VFW, and some he couldn't read.

Calvin's eyes passed over the rest of the plaques and fell on a rusted metal sign hanging at the bottom. A shield dominated the sign: red cross on a white field, a patch of blue in the northwest corner. The once bold colors were now pastel, and the once bold writing was now faded nearly to illegibility. But Calvin knew what the sign said without reading it: "The Episcopal Church Welcomes You."

He smiled at the familiar words, knowing people all over the country were driving into towns and seeing similar signs. But the smile drooped as he strained to read the particulars below the message: "St. John's—across the railroad tracks— two blocks—on right." Calvin put the car in gear as the light turned green and ventured into Victory, wondering how true the cheerful message of welcome was in a small town nestled between two demoted mountains.

The car bumped over the railroad tracks, and Calvin looked down the row of old buildings for a first glimpse of St. John's. He could tell the downtown area of Victory, which straddled the tracks, had thrived in years past. There were too many buildings down the main drag and clustered near it along the side streets for Victory always to have been a small, tired town.

But now many storefronts were shuttered and dark. Calvin couldn't tell if they were out of business or simply closed, though it seemed strange local businesses would be closed in the middle of a weekday. Some locations were obviously vacant: windows hid behind hastily hammered plywood, upon which was spray-painted, "4 Sale," and a phone number to contact someone named Wally.

Three buildings on the block past the railroad tracks had names carved into the stone of their lintels: Town Hall, Firehouse #2, Williams Inn. But the building displaying the words "Town Hall" also sported a banner announcing it as the location for the summer semester of a local community college. Firehouse #2 was a Chinese restaurant named Year of the Dragon. Williams Inn had a collection of mailboxes tacked to its grimy brick wall and a small forest of satellite TV antennae sprouting from its patch of front lawn, and Calvin realized it was no longer a hotel, but what must be tiny apartments.

By no means a ghost town, Victory bore all the hallmarks of being left to its own devices when the town's main industry fled. Calvin didn't know what that industry was exactly, but it was the same story all over the state—plants closing, mines cutting back, aging workforce, young people choosing to live anywhere but there. What saved Victory from falling off the map entirely, Calvin's bishop had told him, was the elderly population. Fifteen years ago, there had been a single nursing home in the town. Now there were five, plus another half dozen assisted- and independent-living facilities for seniors.

"And what comes along with elderly people?" the bishop had asked. Before Calvin could respond, the bishop answered his own question. "Doctors. Nurses. Orderlies. Lab techs. Paramedics. Janitors. Estate lawyers. People at the Y who teach water aerobics." He ticked off each one on a finger. "And those folks have families." The bishop picked up a magazine from his desk and tossed it to Calvin. "In that issue, the AARP rates Victory as one of the top ten retirement communities in the country. And you're their new priest."

Calvin parked his car on the street half a block past St. John's. He was surprised and pleased to see the church stood out from the rest of the buildings on Washington Street. The steeple was easily the highest point this side of the railroad tracks, and the bricks of the church's exterior seemed shinier than those of the surrounding buildings. The mortar in between bricks crumbled only here and there, and the bell, visible in the tower above, gleamed in the midafternoon sun. On first glance, the only things Calvin disliked about the exterior of St. John's were the windows. A layer of Plexiglas protected each window, but the outside panels were so caked with the filth of years that Calvin had only a vague impression the church owned stained glass at all.

He walked up the three steps to the front door and pulled. It was a massive, iron-studded oak thing that would look more at home on a castle keep. And it was locked. Calvin looked at his watch. It was only 2:30 in the afternoon. He looked left and right, hoping to see a sign with hours or directions to the church's office. With no sign in sight, he circled the building and found the door to the office three-quarters of the way around, also up three steps. This door was locked too. He peered in the small window set in the door only to see a dark hallway and several more closed doors.

Calvin continued his circuit of the grounds, and as he was about to turn back onto the sidewalk, he spied a small door set into the side of the church. He walked up to it and was surprised to find the door was much smaller than any door had a right to be. He couldn't possibly understand what this door was designed to accomplish, but he tried it anyway. Locked, of course. Or was it? He tugged again and realized the door was locked only by a crossbar, like the kind you'd find on the door to the castle keep he had imagined earlier. He stood at the door for a few moments, thinking.

Now, in the ensuing minutes, Calvin made three mistakes. First, he decided it was a perfectly good and normal idea to force open the small door. He cast around for something thin enough to slip through the gap between the door and frame and strong enough to lift the bar without breaking. There was nothing in the churchyard but sticks and twigs. Then he snapped his fingers and ran back to the car. As a going away present, his parents had given him a set of pots and pans along with various other cooking implements. Calvin had stored them in the passenger seat because he had already packed the rest of the car. He rummaged for a moment and then pulled out a brand new chef's knife. He jogged back to the small door and began maneuvering his makeshift lever into place. This, of course, was his second mistake.

"What in the world are you doing, boy?"

Calvin froze at the sound of a clipped voice behind him. As the question hung in the air, he took a single moment to wonder the same thing. What *was* he doing?

"Turn around slowly with your hands where I can see them."

Calvin turned around slowly with his hands where the police officer could see them. He looked up and was mildly surprised to see the knife clutched in his right hand. So too, it seemed, was the police officer, who took a step back and put his hand on his holster.

"Drop the weapon."

Calvin dropped the weapon. It spun gracefully out of his hand and buried itself in the soft earth of an unkempt flowerbed bordering the church's wall.

"You must be some kind of stupid, boy, breaking into a church in broad daylight."

And this is when Calvin made his third mistake. He laughed. It began as a grin and then a chuckle escaped between his teeth and, before he could catch it and pull it back in, another followed and soon the absurdity of the situation was spilling from his lips in waves of unbridled hilarity.

By the fact that Calvin ended up in the back of the police cruiser, he could tell the officer did not agree with his assessment of the situation.

"So you weren't breaking in, you say?" asked the officer after Calvin had calmed down.

"No, sir," said Calvin. "I mean, I was breaking in, but it's not a crime."

"Oh, it's *not* a crime. Perhaps I missed the day they taught 'Breaking and Entering' at Police Academy, then?"

This time a chuckle escaped between the officer's teeth, but it held no mirth.

"I apologize. I'm not explaining this right, sir."

"Then. Try. Again."

"This is my church. I'm the priest. Well, I will be. Today's my first day. I don't have a key yet, and there's no one here, even though the administrator is supposed to be in the office. I just wanted a look inside, and I guess I wasn't thinking straight. I've been driving all day."

It all came out in one breath. Deflated, Calvin slumped forward and placed his forehead on the grill between the front and back seats of the police car.

"Aren't you a little too young and a little too stupid to be a priest?" asked the officer.

"Well, sir, I'm not too young."

The officer chuckled again, and this time a hint of amusement crept in. Then he laughed a single time. It came out like a bark, and as he laughed, he toggled his radio. "Dispatch. This is 127. Got a kid here. Caught B&E in progress at St. Jack's side door. Says he's the new priest."

"Copy 127," hissed the radio. "Hold on a sec, Carter."

Officer Carter eyed Calvin, who gave him a weak, defeated smile. Carter answered the smile with a look that said, "Wait till I tell my wife about this one." A long moment passed. Then another voice spoke from the tinny radio.

"Yeah, 127, this is the Chief. What's his name?"

Carter shot Calvin an inquisitive look.

"The Reverend Calvin Harper," said Calvin.

Carter thumbed his radio again. "Says his name is Calvin Harper."

The Chief's own laughter crackled over the radio. "He is the new priest at St. Jack's, Carter. Cut him loose."

Carter put down the radio and stared at Calvin. Calvin's smile widened, until the look of defeat turned into one of triumph.

"Oh, and Carter," said the Chief. "Help him get that door open."

The sound of Officer Carter's police cruiser roaring down the street faded as Calvin closed the small door behind him. He found himself on a square landing about a third of the way up a staircase, which made its curling ascent to the choir loft. The shadowy narthex below him looked uninviting, so Calvin took the stairs in the direction of a soft, purple light emanating from what he guessed was the circular stained glass window set high in the west wall of the church. As he took the first step up, his head brushed the ceiling, and he noticed just how narrow the staircase was. At a hair less than six feet tall, Calvin wasn't used to stooping to go up stairs, but these stairs in particular seemed peculiarly shrunken.

His steps echoed in the empty church until he reached the loft. An old oriental rug muffled his footfalls as he navigated a jumble of folding chairs that might have once been arranged in a semicircle around the organ's console. The purple light was, indeed, coming from the rose window, which adorned the wall behind the loft. Seen from the street, this window was a dirty hole in an otherwise clean brick exterior. Seen from within, the window sparkled with story. The dove of the Holy Spirit stretched its wings from the central pane of the window. The spokes springing from this central pane displayed vines that twisted their way outward and bore fruit in a dozen different colors, all of which stood out gleefully against the soft, purple background. The vine of each spoke ended in a word: faith, meekness, temperance, love, joy, peace, longsuffering, gentleness, goodness.

Calvin smiled at seeing the King James language and wondered how many people over the four hundred years since the translation's birth had been told their gift of the Spirit was "longsuffering." The modern translation, "patience," just doesn't have the same ring to it, he thought.

He continued surveying the window until his eyes landed once again on the word that had first caught them: faith. What was it that Hebrews said about faith? Things hoped for. Something about "unseen." Calvin scanned the patchy Bible in his mind and was surprised when he remembered the verse for which he was searching. "Faith is the assurance of things hoped for, the conviction of things not seen."

He slumped down onto one of the folding chairs near the organ's console. Assurance. Conviction. If there were two things Calvin had less of concerning his coming to Victory, he couldn't think of them. He looked out from the loft to the darkened church below. The soft light from the rose window fell on his back, but it did not extend past the edge of the loft. He could see the edges of the pews outlined in the faint light of the other windows. He could make out the shapes of the lectern and pulpit and rail and altar. But everything was dim, leeched of color, as if Calvin were just waking up in the hour before dawn and couldn't quite understand all the shapes of the perfectly ordinary things in his bedroom.

The bishop had sent him to Victory as Priest-in-Charge. Calvin could have refused to take the assignment, but that was never really an option—not for a priest fresh from seminary, which was partially paid for by diocesan funds. The *assignment*. He turned the word over his tongue. When priests go to new churches, they are supposed to be *called* there, called by God and by the people of the church. Not assigned. Not tossed in the ring because no one more qualified would take the position.

Calvin crossed his arms over his chest and allowed a wave of self-pity to wash over him. He was a stranger in a strange land. He was alone. No one had even come to the church to welcome him. He nursed the pity until it mutated into full-fledged self-satisfaction. He had taken one for the team. No one else wanted the job, but he had done his duty. He was Jonah if Jonah had gone straight to Nineveh like a good little prophet. A smug grin began at one ear and played across his face, but it turned sour before it reached the other side. The Ninevites listened to Jonah, but he still ended up alone on the hillside.

The pity returned and mingled with the satisfaction, and Calvin sank into the depths of self-righteous lamentation. He didn't deserve this. He had always done everything everyone had asked of him, and he still got banished to the radar station in Alaska? How was that fair? He should be on the staff at some big, suburban church, not the hospice chaplain at this backwoods church on life support. Calvin stopped for a moment and looked for more reasons to lament his situation. He remembered the small door and the shrunken staircase. And to top it off, I don't even fit inside the building.

And then he remembered more of his conversation with the bishop. "It's one of the oldest churches in the diocese, son—both the people and the building. Built way before the railroad went through. You know, there wasn't even a West Virginia yet." And all at once Calvin realized why the door was so small and why the staircase was so shrunken. The side door was once the slaves' entrance. The choir loft was once the slaves' balcony. There must have been enough fertile ground in between the low mountains for some sort of farming operation. Tobacco, perhaps? Calvin didn't know the history of the area, but he knew he was right about where he was sitting. When he looked around the loft and imagined dozens of enslaved people huddled close together listening to a white preacher using the Bible to justify the slaves' dehumanizing servitude, the pity and satisfaction and self-righteous lamentation fled from him.

He sat there, hollowed and ashamed. "What am I doing here?" he said aloud to no one in particular, except perhaps to God, though if he was praying, he didn't realize it at the time.

March 22, 2010

Dear Rev. Calvin,

The snow is finally gone from Victory. I've been watching one last pile shrink by the day in the grocery store parking lot. A month ago it was an iceberg. Yesterday it was what someone would have emptied from a cooler after a picnic. And today it's gone—just in time for spring. It has been a long winter, longer than any I can remember, and I can remember more than eighty of them. Perhaps next year I'll go somewhere sunny and warm. I told myself the same thing this year, but I couldn't bear the thought of leaving this old house, what with its fireplace and piano and all the pictures in the hallway. Imagine that! When I was young, I fancied myself the grand world traveler (though, to be honest, anything outside of Jericho, Pennsylvania, felt like "the world"), and now heading down to St. John's for Morning Prayer is adventure enough. I know I sound wistful, but don't you dare pity this old lady. My friends are there, waiting for me when I cross the tracks, and they are my joy, as were you when you were here.

You think you have all the time in the world to get to know someone, but a year, two years, fifty years—it's never enough. There is always something you never said out loud, although you always meant to. It hides somewhere in your heart waiting for the right moment to be said. Sometimes you miss the moment. Sometimes you don't realize there was anything still hidden until it's too late to uncover. I know I've told you many silly stories about my life— hiding under the house in the rain, receiving the rose in Hyde Park, Margaret's first day of school—but, until you were gone, I never realized how much I wanted to tell you the whole story. This story would never make the news or be turned into a motion picture, but it's ours— Whit's and mine—and that makes it special.

You are special young man, Calvin. I know you don't like me saying so because you think I'm partial. But my partiality doesn't make me wrong. You are a special young man, and you deserve a special young woman. That's why I'm glad you left Victory, even though I'm sad you are gone. Victory's not a place for—Lord, how young are you—a twenty-six-year-old? Even so, eighteen months is too short a time to get to know a person. Perhaps at twenty-six, a year and a half feels like forever. I know it did when I was that age, and it wasn't even a year and a half. Korea is a long way from Pennsylvania. Now don't get me wrong. I didn't sit on the porch all day waiting for Whit to come walking up the driveway in his dress uniform with his duffel slung over his shoulder. But still, the days are long and the nights longer when your sweetheart is half a world away. The whole time he was in Korea, he kept a picture of me nearby. He used it as a bookmark, and his favorite book was never far from his side. As for me, I kept a photograph of him framed on my bedside table. I still do, of course.

That reminds me: the pictures I promised in my last letter are in here. You can barely recognize Josie in that leprechaun costume, except for her infectious smile shining out from under that funny yarn beard. It has been a year since she met Donald Pennyworth. Those two, oh my. They are just now becoming a couple—and we've been waiting for a year for it to happen. The photo of Mary is my favorite. She couldn't get over Josie's costume, and the look on her face is just priceless.

One more thing. Do you remember when you rearranged all the wires behind our television? I think you did it when you first moved to Victory. The TV hadn't been working, but you unplugged something and plugged it back in somewhere else and *voila*! it was working again. Well, Pumpernickel—that's Margaret's cat, who's living with me while Margaret and Cooper are away—she got behind the television and must have loosened a wire or two because I can't seem to get more than PBS right now. Not that I'm complaining! That is the station I watch most often anyway. Ah well. If that's the least of my worries, then I'm doing just fine. I really can't complain. The sun is out, the snow is gone, and the air is fresh.

Wishing you all good things,

Ruby

P.S. You be sure to be on the lookout for that young woman who makes your toes curl. It wouldn't do to be wasting all this praying we ladies are doing for you if you don't have your eyes open.

2

Calvin awoke the next morning in an unfamiliar room that smelled of old cigarettes. The room had probably been a non-smoking one for years, but the stale odor had lain low, hiding in the carpet's fibers and resisting all forms of carpet care. It was an odor Calvin tasted more than he smelt, and he rose wondering if someone had made him swallow a pack of Camels in his sleep.

He stumbled into the bathroom and surveyed the wall for a light switch. A confused minute later, he found the switch on the wall outside the bathroom and squinted his way through a teeth brushing he hoped would neutralize the taste of decades-old tobacco. When his eyes finally adjusted to the harsh light above the vanity, Calvin rummaged for his glasses, and inspected himself in the mirror. His dark hair was still too short in the aftermath of a disastrous haircut he received the day before his graduation from seminary. The usually limp hair now stood up in every direction following a night of tossing and turning. He tried in vain to push the wayward hair flat and settled instead for turning on the shower. While he waited for hot water, he gathered breath for a final slumber-filled yawn, exhaled, and tasted cigarettes in the back of his throat. Sighing, he reached once again for his toothbrush.

Half an hour later, Calvin left the motel, a squat building with dirty siding and fake plants hanging from the eaves. He squeezed himself into his car and glanced around to make sure the pile of stuff that filled the backseat sat undisturbed following a night in a seedy parking lot. Nothing seemed to be missing. Well, he thought, if something had been stolen, at least I know a police officer in town.

The motel was on the county road a few miles inland from the interstate, and Calvin retraced the path he had taken the day before. This time, however, he turned off the main road at the intersection next to the sign announcing the town of Victory (and a supposedly welcoming Episcopal Church). Taking a right at the traffic light, he followed a winding road until he came to the crest of a short rise. Another right took him back down the hill and past an abandoned construction site.

Calvin parked the car on the street and surveyed the idle apartment complex. Seven buildings encircled what one day would be an oval parking lot, but was currently a mud pit the size of a football field. Several faded, yellow construction vehicles littered the pit, their sunken treads covered in caked mud. Pallets of bricks and two-by-fours sat in stacks adjacent to each building, and a trio of portable toilets lay on their sides at the edge of the lot. Calvin looked from building to building. Only one seemed close to completion, but he guessed the interior was still all plywood and exposed wiring. Down the line, each unit was less finished than the one before, as if Calvin were looking at the seven-step Darwinian evolution of the apartment building. The final unit was simply a slab with the beginnings of a skeletal structure protruding skyward.

Calvin counted to the fourth building, which was wrapped halfway around with insulation, and looked to a square opening on the top floor, which was ready to receive its window. There's my apartment, he thought.

He was supposed to have moved into that top floor apartment yesterday. The model he had seen at a complex a few towns away had cathedral ceilings and a gas fireplace, and he had decided an extra hundred bucks a month was worth those amenities. But some time after Calvin signed the paperwork and paid his deposit, the housing market drove off a cliff. By all the empty new construction he had noticed just in the day he had been in town, Calvin could tell Victory had been hit badly. During the housing boom, the town was just barely close enough to Washington D.C. to qualify for commuter status. For some with jobs in the District, a big, cheap house was worth six soul-sucking hours in the car every day. But then gas prices skyrocketed, the housing market collapsed, and Victory's renaissance was over before it began. Now the town had hundreds of brand new, single-family homes standing empty—ghost neighborhoods, which never had the opportunity to acquire any ghosts.

Calvin gave one more regretful look at the top floor window, got back in his car, and, like the developers and contractors and construction workers before him, left the unfinished complex for good.

━━━◦◦◦◦━━━

Ten minutes later, Calvin parked once again in front of St. John's, and this time he was heartened to see a faint glow escaping through the grime-covered windows. He tossed the remains of a fast-food breakfast into a garbage can on the curb, skipped up the smooth, stone steps, and tried the massive door. It was either locked or too heavy to open for someone like Calvin, who had only a passing acquaintance with weight training.

Frowning, he walked backwards down the steps and surveyed the door. And then he noticed something incongruous for a door that happened to be three stairs from the ground—a plate-sized silver button to the right of the door, upon which was drawn a blue stick figure in a wheelchair. Calvin pushed the button. For a moment, nothing happened. Then Calvin heard a motor wheeze to life, and the monstrosity creaked open, sweeping him back off the stairs as it swung outward.

"Well, at least I know my church is safe from invading barbarians," Calvin told the door as it closed again. "Just disconnect your motor and no one's getting in."

He pressed the button again, and, prepared this time, jumped back off the steps before the door could swat him. As the door reached the zenith of its circuit, Calvin doffed it an imaginary cap and vaulted into the church. He found himself in the dark narthex, which is what church people call entryways in order to confuse newcomers, he thought, grinning to himself. The stairs to the choir loft ascended to his right. Another set of stairs, which he hadn't noticed the day before, descended to his left. He turned around and saw a second silver button. So it's just as hard to push as to pull, he thought. Recessed into the walls on both sides of the door were large, segmented brass cabinets. In the semidarkness of the narthex, they looked to Calvin like post office boxes, though he knew their beloved, powdery cargo was much more precious.

"You must be Calvin," came a voice from within the church. Calvin turned around and saw a foursome of cardiganed ladies smiling at him. The light from the nave backlit them and gave each a faint buttery aura. "Come on out of that dark narthex."

"We never use that door anyway."

"We've been expecting you, sonny. We're about to start."

"Oh, and welcome to St. Jack's-across-the-tracks."

Each lady spoke in turn, and each began speaking just as the one before finished. They stood arm in arm like a barbershop quartet who have just finished their encore. The two on the ends each had a purse over one forearm; one had a brooch the size of a baseball pinned to her chest; and one was wearing pearls with her cardigan sweater. Add a few grandchildren or an interesting shop window, and Norman Rockwell could have painted the scene. As he stepped into the light to greet the quartet, Calvin couldn't help but reflect their smiles.

He reached out his hand and was halfway through, "Hi. I'm Calvin Harper," when the Brooch cut him off.

"Prayer first. Introductions second," she said. Then, looking at her watch, she sniffed and said, "It is, after all, 8:17." And with that, she turned, processed up the aisle, and knelt in a pew in the snug side chapel.

Purse One and Purse Two gave Calvin sheepish grins and followed the Brooch to the chapel. But the Pearls took Calvin by the arm, winked conspiratorially, and whispered, "Esther Rose is a sweetheart, but she can be a bit, shall we say, regimented. I think if Morning Prayer starts at 8:17 her whole day will be two minutes off schedule." She patted Calvin on the hand as they walked arm in arm up the aisle. "Don't tell her I told you before prayer was over, but I'm Ruby. Ruby Redding."

Calvin returned Ruby's conspiratorial wink: "Calvin Harper. It's very nice to meet you, Ms. Redding."

"Likewise. And 'Ruby' will do fine. None of this 'Ms. Redding' business."

"Yes, ma'am."

There were only four pews in the chapel, and they were configured in pairs facing each other on either side of the altar. The pews were the color of honey, a late spring vintage with a deep autumn grain tracing patterns over the wood. The fair-colored furniture partnered with a faded blue-gray carpet to give the chapel (and the rest of the church, for that matter) a light, airy quality, which was much more inviting than imposing. The chapel altar was set against the wall, and a short, silk frontal hung from it, proclaiming with its several brilliant shades of green the long season between Pentecost and Advent.

The Brooch, whose name was evidently Esther Rose, and the two Purses had taken up residence in three of the four pews, so Calvin followed Ruby into the fourth. As they knelt, Calvin glanced at his watch—it still read 8:17. He thumbed through the red Book of Common Prayer, found the correct page, and waited. At 8:18, he checked his watch again, and wondered why no one had begun the opening sentences. At 8:19, Calvin looked up to find Esther Rose staring at him from the facing pew. Her expression was the special one a person wears when she is ready to leave the restaurant but the server has failed to bring the check.

As 8:19 threatened to turn into 8:20, Ruby nudged Calvin with her elbow and pointed to a line on the open page of his prayer book. He leaned over and whispered in her ear: "I was hoping one of you would lead this morning, so I could, you know, learn the house rules."

"Oh, you'll do fine, dear," she whispered back. "God will be delighted either way, even if Esther Rose isn't." She tapped his book again. "Just go for it."

Calvin looked at the stony-faced woman across the aisle, cleared his throat, and read, "I was glad when they said to me, 'Let us go to the house of the Lord.'"

"Let us bless the Lord," said Calvin.

"Thanks be to God," responded Ruby, Esther Rose, and the two Purses.

"May the God of hope fill us with all joy and peace in believing through the power of the Holy Spirit."

"Amen."

Calvin snapped his prayer book shut and slid it home in the pew rack. He checked his watch and was pleased to find the time was only 8:40.

"He reads a bit too quickly, and I don't think we've ever done that second canticle he chose."

Calvin looked up to see Esther Rose muttering to herself in what she apparently thought was a whisper only she could hear. Well, she's not wrong, he thought. He had sped through the readings to try to make up those lost minutes, and how was he supposed to know there was an approved list of canticles?

"Pay her no mind, dear," Ruby said. "Esther Rose would find fault with a lilac that bloomed a day early." She looked across the chapel toward her elder. "But there's a real stalwart sweetheart underneath all that regimen and gruff critique. You just need to know where to look."

The ladies led Calvin through a door set in the east wall of the sanctuary, which opened onto a fluorescently lit hallway with cement walls and a flecked linoleum floor. The dark and empty church offices stood opposite the door to the sanctuary. Ruby once again took Calvin's arm, and he allowed himself to be escorted down the hallway to the left and into the parish hall. The hall was about the size of a tennis court, with half a dozen fans hanging from cords of various lengths attached to a high, A-framed ceiling. Sturdy, hard-plastic tables covered the same flecked linoleum, and old metal folding chairs encircled each table. One of the Purses broke off from the group, weaved her way through the tables, and poured coffee, which Calvin accepted gratefully. When all had a beverage, they sat down around the table nearest the coffee machine, and Calvin recognized he had intruded upon a ritual several decades in the making.

Esther Rose blew on her coffee, took an experimental sip, nodded, and then fixed Calvin with an appraising look. "The older I get the younger everyone else seems to be—my doctor looks like a high school cheerleader, and now my priest is barely out of diapers."

Calvin started to sputter an unintelligible rejoinder, but she waved a hand saying, "Ah well, we were all fresh-faced at one time or another." The matriarch took another sip of her coffee and gestured to one of the Purses. "Even Avis here still seems like a pup to me, and she became a grandmother last year." She rose heavily to her feet and adopted a formal air. "My name is Esther Rose Lincoln. It is a pleasure to make your acquaintance, Reverend Harper."

She held out her hand palm down, and Calvin, sensing this woman valued propriety, leapt to his feet. She curled her fingers into his hand, and he made a short bow. "Calvin Harper, the baby priest, at your service, Ms. Lincoln," he said, deciding it was better to make light of her assessment of his age rather than retort. Unlike Ruby, she did not correct his usage of her surname.

As Calvin straightened from his bow, he noticed the ghost of a smile flit across Esther Rose's face, and he knew he had retrieved a few points he had lost earlier. She tapped the woman on her right, who stood and grabbed Calvin's hand in a vigorous shake. "Avis Noon, Reverend Calvin, but you can call me Avis in the . . . "

". . . morning and evening, as well," the other three ladies finished for her.

She looked around at them and grinned. "Well, anyway, it is so nice to finally meet you."

36

Esther Rose gestured to the other Purse, who remained seated. "Excuse me for not getting up, Father, but these old bones would rather stay put until I must needs rise," she said.

A trace of an ancient Irish brogue surfaced when she said the word "father," and Calvin wondered how long she had been in the United States. Since childhood, probably, he thought. "That's quite all right," he said as he walked over to shake her hand.

"Mary Williams. My husband Arthur was the sexton here for over thirty years. Knows every nook and cranny of these old halls."

"That's great. If I can't find something I'll know just who to ask."

Mary chortled into her coffee cup. "Ah, sonny, he's been retired for nigh on fifteen years. I expect nothing is in the same place anymore."

"Could be so," said Calvin. "But churches have a way of not changing much over the years. At my church during seminary, they had a shelf of computer program manuals from the late eighties. No one ever thought to throw them away."

Avis piped up, "You could have brought them here. I think one of the computers in the office is about that old."

Esther Rose cleared her throat. "Yes, well, shall we continue," she said, and she gestured to Ruby.

"Oh, Calvin and I go way back. We're old friends."

"You are?" said Esther Rose, taking the bait.

"Oh yes," said Ruby. "We met more than half an hour ago."

Mary, Avis, and Calvin laughed aloud, and after a short pause, Esther Rose seemed to make up her mind, and she chuckled briefly too. Ruby beamed.

Midway through his second cup of coffee, Calvin was still answering questions about himself as the four ladies took turns interrogating him. Where was he from? What did his parents do for a living? How many siblings did he have? When did he know he wanted to be a priest? How old was he again?

"I'm twenty-five," said Calvin, and he was surprised to find none of his usual defensiveness in his tone.

"Oh my," said Avis. "I've got forty years on you, and I'm the youngest gal here."

"Good Lord," said Mary. "When I was twenty-five, I used to . . . " She paused and for a moment her eyes were distant. Then she smiled. "Well, best not for mixed company."

Ruby patted Mary's hand and said, "Come now, Arthur's told us some of your old stories, and none is too sordid. Don't hold out on us now."

Mary put her other hand atop Ruby's. "Ah, but Arthur didn't meet me until I was twenty-six."

And once again the group dissolved in a fit of laughter. When all had recovered, the grilling resumed in earnest. What did Calvin study in college? What was his favorite subject in seminary? Did he have a sweetheart?

"I have had. But no, not right now," he said.

"Ah, sonny," said Mary. "You're young yet. No reason to be getting ahead of yourself."

Esther Rose had been silent for a while, but now she spoke: "My Ted and I were married a week after we met. We didn't have much time because he was steaming for France the next day." The same faraway look that had come over Mary appeared on Esther Rose's face.

"Go on, dear," coaxed Ruby.

"We were way ahead of ourselves," said Esther Rose, returning to the present. "But I don't think either of us really expected he'd come back to me. When he did, it was like we had done everything backward. We were already married when he finished courting me."

"But then you had, what, fifty-one good years?" asked Avis.

"We had fifty-one years," said Esther Rose. "I'd say forty-seven were good. The first two he was overseas, and our Eleanor was born with her daddy gone. She was toddling about when he first saw her. I remember the day he came home like it was yesterday. He limped into my parents' house, and we squashed Eleanor between us as we embraced."

"And the other two years?" asked Calvin.

The four ladies grew quiet, and Calvin realized he had brought up a forbidden topic. Finally, Ruby broke the heavy silence with a pat on Calvin's hand. "He was very sick, dear."

The silence descended again, only to be broken by a soft sniffle from Avis Noon. Calvin looked at her, and saw tears tracing pathways down her lightly wrinkled cheeks.

Ruby rose and walked around the table to Avis. Putting a hand on Avis's shoulder, Ruby said, "Come, my love. Let's go see him."

Avis, Mary, and Esther Rose stood up and followed Ruby back to the sanctuary. Calvin walked a few steps behind, trailing the ladies as they shuffled down the aisle of the nave and into the dark narthex. What had he said? How had he upset Avis when they had been talking about Esther Rose's husband?

Mary found the light switch, and the cabinets that had looked to Calvin like post office boxes gleamed in the soft light. With Ruby supporting her, Avis approached the columbarium and ran her fingers over the raised letters of a plaque affixed to one of the small doors. Then her hand went to her mouth, and she turned to bury her face in Ruby's shoulder.

"There, there, my love," said Ruby. "There, there."

Calvin looked at the plaque Avis had been touching and read: "Alexander Noon." Then Calvin shook his head in disbelief as he read the date of death—less than three months ago.

Esther Rose and Mary encircled Ruby and Avis, and the four of them stood in a huddled embrace as Avis heaved and sobbed into Ruby's cardigan. Calvin backed against the wall and watched them and only after several minutes remembered to pray.

—ᚑᚉᚑ—

Ruby and Calvin stood on the curb and waved as the car carrying Mary, Esther Rose, and a freshly grieving Avis turned the corner onto Washington Street. "I can't believe I did that," said Calvin, slumping against the warm brick of the church's exterior.

"Did what, dear?" said Ruby.

"Was so insensitive to both Esther Rose and Avis. I just had no idea."

"Of course you didn't. And you best not go taking credit for other people's grief, especially in your line of work." Ruby moved to Calvin's side. "Ever since Alex passed, she's been hit a couple times a week with a fresh wave. There's no telling what will bring one on." She reached up and squeezed Calvin's shoulder. "You just be on the lookout for it from now on."

"Yes, ma'am," said Calvin.

"I already told you: none of that Ms. Redding nonsense. And you can keep your *ma'ams* too."

"Yes, ma'am," said Calvin.

Ruby seemed to be trying to frown at him, but she appeared unable to work her mouth into one, so she settled on a thin smile instead. "Ted's there too. In that columbarium. But he's been there near fifteen years. My husband and I already have our niches bought and paid for. There's a peace that comes with knowing where your remains will be."

Ruby gave Calvin another of her signature conspiratorial winks. "And where are your remains staying since you've come to Victory?" she asked.

"Oh, I signed a lease for an apartment out Plantation Drive, but it fell through because they halted construction. I'm at the Victory Arms Motel at the moment."

"Oh, dear, that won't do at all," said Ruby. And then without hesitating, she added, "All right, get in your car and follow me."

And with that, she marched down the street as fast as she could and eased into her car, leaving Calvin bewildered on the sidewalk. She put the car in gear and pulled into the street. Rolling down the window, she called out, "Can't follow me on foot, son."

Calvin dashed to his car, and five minutes later they pulled onto Lilac Court. Ruby parked in front of a one-story home with a faded burnt sienna brick exterior and recently bloomed lilacs flanking the stoop. Calvin parked behind her and got out.

"Welcome to my home," said Ruby. "You'll be staying here until you get your situation settled. Now come inside. I'd like you to meet my husband, Whit."

March 25, 2010

Dear Rev. Calvin,

This morning, Mary reminded us today is a holy day on the church calendar called the Feast of the Annunciation. I'm sure that's not news to you, but it was to me. At my church growing up, we didn't talk about this or that feast. We sang songs and listened to sermons and that was that. But Mary grew up Roman Catholic, so she remembers all these holy days, and this one is special to her because of her namesake. Can you even begin to imagine what that Mary was thinking and feeling when Gabriel came to her in her little room? It's a wonder she was able to get out any words at all. She must have been very sensible and very brave.

We read her song—the Magnificat—as one of the canticles this morning. "My soul magnifies the Lord and my spirit rejoices in God my savior." I can't think of a better prayer than for my soul to magnify the Lord, because the Lord is there all the time, but sometimes I need something deep inside to make God clearer for me, to bring God into better focus. Do you know what I mean?

Anyway, I think it's funny how the church calendar puts the Annunciation exactly nine months before Christmas, as if Mary had a perfect gestation time. I imagine with all the stress of traveling to Bethlehem, she'd have gone into early labor.

Speaking of that, my own parents were a bit like Mary and Joseph. (No, I'm not comparing myself to Jesus—how silly would that be!) My mother got pregnant before the wedding, and they tried to hide it. But it was one of those—what do you call them—open secrets? Everyone knew, but no one said anything. My brother was born just five months after the wedding. If you hadn't heard the whisperings in our small town before then, you certainly could have put two and two together.

My mother didn't tell me any of this until Whit and I announced our wedding plans. We only had a month-long engagement, so you can see what my mother was thinking. But in our case, we had known each other for years, and there didn't seem to be much point in putting it off for propriety's sake. Besides, if I had gotten pregnant before our wedding, that would have been a whole other can of worms considering Whit was in Korea for an entire year before our engagement. He proposed the week he returned from the war, and I think he had been working on what he was going to say for his whole deployment. My poet. He wrote it all down and memorized it.

What was I on about before? Oh yes, my mother's secret forbidden pregnancy. My brother, Daniel, was born just five months after the wedding. Everyone in town called him "Early," and I never knew why until my mother told me. Early Winslow they called him, and the name stuck. But I always called him Danny Boy or D.B. for short. He was only three years older than me, but he always seemed so grown up. I adored him, naturally. D.B. always included me, his kid sister, in the adventures he and his friends wove in the woods behind our little house. Sometimes I was the damsel-in-distress, though I didn't fancy that too much. Most often I was the crew and had to swab the poop deck. But every once in a while, I was the hero in the story built by our collective imaginations. It's amazing to me how much I can remember as I start to put it down on paper. Recalling these ancient memories is often easier than remembering if I went to the grocery store yesterday.

It's good to think of D.B. He's not often in my thoughts these days, seeing as he passed on near thirty years ago of a heart attack. It was the same day John Lennon was shot, and I remember dreaming of John singing "Danny Boy" as he and my brother walked away together into the distance. Whenever I hear that song now, I hear the echo of that dream:

> *Oh, Danny boy, the pipes, the pipes are calling*
> *From glen to glen, and down the mountainside*
> *The summer's gone, and all the roses falling*
> *'Tis you, 'tis you must go and I must bide.*

D.B. wasn't but 58 when he died. Even in death, he was Early too.

Oh my, look at me running on about my big brother. He was a dear heart. You remind me of him, Calvin, in the way you weave stories into your sermons. I always loved how you used the pulpit as a prop. I expect D.B. would have approved. It's odd to think neither of you ever shared this earth with the other.

By the way, the snow is finally gone here in Victory. Here's hoping spring remembers it's supposed to produce flowers.

Wishing you all good things,

Ruby

3

Calvin awoke Sunday morning in a familiar room that smelled of old potpourri. It was his third morning waking up in Ruby and Whit's guest room, and yesterday he decided the smell of potpourri must have been coming from the floral print wallpaper. Perhaps the wallpaper was a special scratch-and-sniff variety, he mused at breakfast. Whit just chuckled and said if such a product existed, then Ruby would have done the whole house in it.

A contented smile played across Calvin's face at the memory of his hosts laying out a breakfast that would have broken a less sturdy table than the one in their dining room. He had been embarrassed at the amount of work Ruby had gone through to lay such a board, but, of course, she said "Pish" and "Nonsense" until he retracted his embarrassment. Besides Margaret and Cooper, few people visited Ruby and Whit, so it was her pleasure to cook for someone other than her husband, she reasoned.

Calvin's smile arched into a yawn, and he reached for his glasses. He lay in bed for several minutes and watched dust motes float and dance in the hazy morning light, which streamed through the lacy curtains in the window. Today was his first Sunday at St. John's. Two services and the parish's annual picnic were ahead of him. Well, he thought, as long as I don't get arrested or make anyone cry, I'll be ahead of the game.

Half an hour later, Calvin parked in his spot behind the church and licked his fingers. The pastry with which Ruby had sent him out the door was as delicious as she had promised. He entered the church by the door to the hallway, which led to the parish hall, and put his bag on the chair in his empty office. Pulling his sermon's pages from the bag, he mumbled it to himself as he walked through the church unlocking doors and looking for light switches. He found enough to provide illumination, but there were still a few stubbornly dark pockets in the nave.

Returning to his office, Calvin began pulling vestments from a black hanging bag. First, he donned his white alb and tied a cincture around it. Then he made two loops in the cincture, settled a stole over his neck, and dropped it through the loops. In the restroom across the hall from his office, he checked himself in the mirror to make sure his stole hung evenly over both shoulders. The stole was a gift from the church at which he trained during seminary. It was dark green—the color of leaves just before the sun sets. Throughout the stole in no discernible pattern, gold thread was worked, but subtly, so you could only see the thread up close. From a distance, it made the green shine. This was the first time Calvin had put on the stole since being ordained a priest.

He took several deep breaths and looked in the mirror again. He looked like a priest, but so young, even he had to admit. If people saw me on the street they might think I'm just wearing an eerily accurate Halloween costume. But Timothy was young. Jeremiah was young. And that didn't stop God from using them. Calvin looked down and fingered the ends of the colorful ribbons that marked pages in his prayer book. So how are you going to use me, Lord? He prayed in silence for a minute and then looked in the mirror once more. "It's not a costume," he said to his reflection. "It's who I am." Or at least who I hope I am.

He exited the restroom, turned the corner, and headed back into the sanctuary. A handful of people had arrived since he had unlocked the doors. They were scattered all over the church, as if a sower had thrown his seed willy-nilly across the nave. No one sat in the same pew with anyone else, and, of course, the front pews were empty. And all the lights were on. So someone must have the secret knowledge of the light switches, thought Calvin.

Twelve people attended Calvin's first service. Of course, he wasn't sure if twelve was many or few at this particular church. Did the fact that the service began at 7:30 a.m. keep people away? Or perhaps people skipped church during the summer? Or maybe a dozen was a large number, and they turned up to get a look at their new priest. Whatever the case, at 8:15 a.m., Calvin stood at the back of the nave and shook twelve hands.

The first four belonged to a foursome of gentlemen wearing khakis and brightly colored polo shirts. Each could be retired if he wanted to, but Calvin deduced from their spry energy that these fellows still worked because they enjoyed it, not because they had to.

"Fantastic sermon," said the one wearing robin's egg blue. "Clocked in a few seconds over ten minutes."

"Uh . . . " said Calvin.

"In fact," said the one wearing lemon yellow. "You could shave a minute and still be okay. But a fine job, sir."

"Uh . . . " repeated Calvin.

"Keep them like that, and we won't ever have to rush," said the third man. His shirt was a hideous alternation between mustard and salmon colored stripes.

The fourth took Calvin's hand in a vise-like grip. His polo was ever so slightly pink, as if he had washed a white shirt and a red sock in the same load. But Calvin could tell by the logo of an expensive brand that the color was no accident. "Welcome to St. John's, young man," he said, continuing to shake Calvin's hand, which was rapidly losing its supply of blood. "I'm Carl Sinclair, the mayor of Victory." He gestured to the other three. "Here we have Harold, Phil, and Phil."

Calvin tried to break free of the handshake, but Carl Sinclair, the mayor of Victory, held firm. "I'm sure we'll get to further introductions later," said Carl, and Calvin could tell he was being dismissed. "Right now, we have an engagement."

The mayor relinquished his grip, and he, Harold, Phil, and Phil left the church through the mammoth front door. As they emerged into the sunlight, Calvin could see golf gloves sticking out of all four back pockets.

The rest of the parishioners ambled toward the back of the church and introduced themselves to Calvin. He met each person's eye and filed each name away, though he knew it would be several months before he could recall everyone at a glance. That first Sunday, he was most aware of their hands. Many were lined with age, some were bony and frail, a few were strong, and one trembled as its owner fought through the Parkinson's to grasp Calvin's hand. The final person in line had a hand Calvin had shaken before. Once again, Esther Rose held her hand out to him palm down. Calvin grasped her fingers and made a shallow bow. "Ms. Lincoln, it's good to see you," he said.

"Come with me, Calvin," she said, and she steered him back up the aisle toward the sanctuary. "I see you have met the mayor."

Calvin could tell by the way she said "the mayor" that Esther Rose didn't think much of Carl Sinclair, so he attempted a neutral response: "Yes. He's got quite a handshake."

"I'm sure he does. He's had a lot of practice, the old fraud."

"Fraud?" Calvin wasn't a fan of gossip, especially in church, where he himself would be a ripe topic, but he had trouble keeping the curiosity out of his voice.

"Oh, never mind. He's harmless really." She gave a forced chuckle. "But I suspect people keep voting for him simply because his campaign signs rhyme."

Calvin could picture the signs dotting the roadsides: "Sinclair for Mayor. That's catchy."

"I'll say one thing for Carl," sighed Esther Rose. "He's very good at getting elected."

As they walked up the steps to the sanctuary, Calvin thought he heard her whisper "the old fraud" again under her breath.

"Coffee?" Calvin asked, attempting to change the subject.

"Yes," said Esther Rose. "But first, let's go over the things you did wrong during the service."

She handed Calvin a yellow legal pad, upon which were listed seven bullets in elegant cursive.

Calvin filled the time between services drinking coffee, unpacking the rest of his vestments, and going over Esther Rose's list (which included "prays too quickly" and "makes too much eye contact while consecrating communion," among other things). The second service came and went, and Calvin was glad to see closer to three-dozen people in attendance.

After the second service, everyone went out to the small yard attached to the side of the church. It just so happened that the day of the annual parish picnic coincided with Calvin's first Sunday. A table laden with fried chicken, casseroles, vegetable trays, and pie stood against the side of the church. Balloons rose from other tables set up around the courtyard. The parishioners began queuing up at the food table. Most of them were seniors and middle-aged couples, but one pair drove down the average age considerably. They couldn't have been more than a few years older than Calvin, and the woman was just beginning to show.

"Brad Stewart, and this is my wife Rebecca," said the young man when Calvin went over to introduce himself.

"So good to meet you both," said Calvin. "When are you due, Rebecca?"

Upon further reflection later that day, Calvin realized that was not the best question to ask a woman at first meeting. He might just have made someone cry after all, but luckily for him, Rebecca did happen to be pregnant. She put a hand to the slight bump in her sundress and said, "Sometime around Thanksgiving."

"That's wonderful," said Calvin. "Well, it sure is good to meet people who couldn't possibly be my parents or grandparents."

"Hey, my parents are right over there if you need some," said Rebecca, pointing across the courtyard. Her mother waved and began making her way to them. "Calvin, this is my mother, Emily Lincoln."

"I was just saying to Sandra over there how handsome our new priest is in all those vestments," said Emily. "And up close too."

Calvin blushed deep red. Brad laughed. Rebecca put a hand on Emily's shoulder. "Come now, mother. Do you want to scare him off on his first Sunday?"

"Oh, sweetheart, I'm just being friendly," said Emily. "But don't you think he and your sister would make a nice couple."

Calvin's deep red turned to deep purple. Brad laughed again and clapped him on the back.

"Mother!" Rebecca said breathlessly.

"I don't know," said Brad. "Carrie is pretty cute."

"Of course she is," said a new voice. "She is, after all, one of my daughters."

A tall man with thinning hair and what once was a muscular physique strolled up, put his arm around Rebecca, and kissed the top of her head. "As is this one," he said, and he looked Calvin up and down. And then, noticing Calvin's puce cheeks, he said, "Oh, Emily, did you embarrass the boy?"

"I didn't say anything that wasn't true," said Emily, and she gave Calvin a reassuring smile.

"My wife has a special way of telling the truth," said Emily's husband. "It usually ends up in people's faces looking like yours does right now." He extended his hand to Calvin. "Theodore Lincoln, Jr." They shook. "But everyone calls me T.J."

"Theodore Lincoln, Jr.?" repeated Calvin. "So you're Ted and Esther Rose's son?"

"That's right."

Calvin plunged his hand into his pocket, pulled out the sheet of yellow legal paper, unfolded it, and handed it to him.

"Ah," said T.J. "I see you've met my mother."

"Yes, sir."

T.J. counted aloud. "Hey, only seven. She must really like you."

Calvin raised his eyebrows.

"You should have seen the list she gave me right after T.J. and I got engaged," said Emily.

"Me too," said Brad.

Calvin moved through the line at the buffet table with the Stewarts and was getting ready to sit down when he felt a tap on his shoulder. Turning around, he found himself face to face with a uniformed police officer. Calvin jumped backwards and dropped his paper plate, which flipped over and released its contents of fried chicken and macaroni and cheese. "Honestly, officer," he stammered. "I was allowed to be in the building. I wasn't breaking and entering. Ask anyone here. This is where I work."

Calvin bent down to retrieve his now soiled lunch, all the while ordering his defense in his mind. There's bound to be a lawyer or two in this church who could represent me, he thought. If only I had grabbed the spatula instead of the chef's knife, I wouldn't be in this mess. He straightened up, and as he did so, his thoughts moved from his mind to his mouth. "Spatulas are much less threatening, after all," he said in the direction of the cop.

The Lincolns and Stewarts overheard this verbal end to Calvin's internal monologue, and Brad spoke up. "Spatulas are less threatening than what?"

"Than sharpened cutlery," said the policeman. He had close-cropped, graying hair and a square jaw, which remained impassive despite Calvin's spluttering.

"But officer, I didn't do anything wrong," said Calvin. He waved a macaroni and cheese-encrusted hand in the air, as if calling for aid from a lifeboat.

"That's for the courts to decide," said the policeman. His voice was clipped and full of gravel, and his jaw and hard eyes looked chiseled from stone.

"But, but," was all Calvin could think to say.

"Put the plate on the table and turn around."

Calvin put the plate on the table and turned around.

"Reverend Calvin Harper. You are under arrest for the attempted breaking and entering of St. John's Episcopal Church in Victory, West Virginia."

"But, but," Calvin tried again, but his vocabulary had fled him.

"You have the right to remain our priest. Anything you say can and will be used by us for the building up of God's kingdom. You have the right to a senior warden. If you can't afford one, that's okay because I am he, and I'm a volunteer."

"But, but," Calvin said one last time. Then the words the officer had said caught up to him. "Hey, wait a minute." He had heard the Miranda rights a hundred times on TV procedural dramas, and they definitely didn't sound like that.

The family at the table couldn't suppress their glee any longer. Brad let out a roar of laughter, and T.J. banged the table. The granite look vanished from the officer's face.

"Police Chief Harry Stern," he said, holding out a massive hand to Calvin.

Calvin looked from the chief's hand to his face. He had heard that voice before. Comprehension dawned, and Calvin joined the laughter, though his was filled with queasy relief. "You let me go on Wednesday. It was you on the radio."

"That's right. I'm sorry for missing the service this morning, but we had a scheduling problem, and I had to go to the station." He looked down at his clothes. "Hence the uniform."

Calvin sat down heavily on the bench next to Brad. "Wow. You had me for a minute there. I told myself when I woke up this morning that if I didn't make anyone cry or get arrested, I'd be ahead of the game."

"Well," said the Chief. "When you reacted the way you did to my uniform, I couldn't resist. Now why don't we get you a new plate and have a chat."

The buffet line had been nearly picked clean by the time Calvin returned to it, but he managed to assemble a passable lunch with the remains of the macaroni and cheese and some broccoli and cauliflower, always the last survivors on vegetable trays. Chief Stern directed him to a table with only two occupants, who turned out to be Ruby and Whit Redding.

"Do you have a verse or two for me today, Whit?" said the Chief.

"Always do, Harry. Have a seat," said Whit. "Now let me think."

Calvin smiled at Ruby. It was good to see a familiar face on his first Sunday, especially one who wasn't planning on giving him lists of his faults.

"Here we go," said Whit. He put his hands behind his back, cleared his throat and intoned:

> Not I, not any one else can travel that road for you,
> You must travel it for yourself.
> It is not far, it is within reach,
> Perhaps you have been on it since you were born and did
>   not know,
> Perhaps it is everywhere on water and on land.
> Shoulder your duds dear son, and I will mine, and let us
>   hasten forth,
> Wonderful cities and free nations we shall fetch as we go.
> If you tire, give me both burdens, and rest the chuff of
>   your hand on my hip,
> And in due time you shall repay the same service to me,
> For after we start we never lie by again.

"Fantastic," said the Chief, and he clapped Whit on the back. Calvin could tell this was something of a ritual between these two. He wondered what the significance of those lines was.

54

"So how did our young priest do this morning?" asked Chief Stern.

"Oh, he did quite well," said Ruby, turning to look at Calvin. "And the more you lead services, the more comfortable you will get, I'm sure."

Calvin smiled again. In fact, he hadn't done "quite well" at all. He had announced the wrong page number twice, spilled wine on the pristine linens on the altar, and entirely forgotten to say the absolution. It hadn't been a train wreck exactly—more like a train fender bender. Do trains have fenders, he wondered. Either way, a church veteran like Ruby would have picked up on his flubs. But he could tell that Ruby was trying to build up his confidence, and he appreciated it.

"Well, I'm looking forward to next Sunday, then," said the Chief.

The conversation turned to small things: how long Chief Stern and the Reddings had been attending St. John's, what the church population was like in non-summer months, where Calvin might find a place to live since his apartment was likely never to receive windows or drywall.

"If I were you, I would look only on the other side of the railroad tracks," said the Chief, gesturing down the street in the direction of the old train station. "This side of town is . . . " He paused and glanced up in the air as if expecting to find the word he was looking for floating above him. "Unsavory," he concluded.

"Unsavory?" repeated Calvin.

"Most of the abandoned buildings are on this side of town. People are poorer. The farther from the interstate, the more degraded are the neighborhoods. There's a drug problem, of course, especially prescription. We have our share of robberies to deal with—users or dealers breaking in to homes of the elderly to raid medicine cabinets. You wouldn't believe the number of break-ins that leave the rest of the house untouched. It's sad to say, but we track most of the drugs back here to this side of town. Statistically speaking, my patrol cars cover this side of the track much more than the other, even though the other side is much larger."

"Wow," said Calvin. "I had no idea Victory was like that."

"Every town is like that, son," said the Chief. "But most people ignore it." He tapped his badge. "I can't."

Ruby chimed in, "And we don't ignore it here at St. Jack's either, Harry."

"True," agreed the Chief. "AA and NA meet four times a week in the parish hall. We started the local food pantry about twenty-five years ago and still support that. But it's never enough, is it?"

"Well, it's something," Ruby said with finality.

Chief Stern turned his attention to his plate. The grin he had worn after the mock arrest was gone, replaced by the worries of a dedicated man fighting a war that would never end. But Calvin could see conviction and strength etched into the lines of his chiseled face, and Calvin knew that here was a stalwart ally.

Silence descended on the table, only to be broken by the happy sounds of picnickers enjoying the late June sun. Calvin searched for a less weighty topic of conversation, but something was nagging him, something that Ruby had called St. John's when they had first met.

"So you call the church 'St. Jack's-across-the-tracks' because . . . ?" asked Calvin.

"Oh, it's just a silly nickname for the church, dear," said Ruby. "Most folks who attend here live on the other side of the rail line."

"The church predates the railroad by several decades," said Whit. It was the first time that he had spoken since his and Harry's ritual exchange. Whit, it seemed to Calvin, was a listener, only contributing to a conversation when he had something worthwhile to say, never just to fill space. "The town boomed during the heyday of the railroad and spread out in both directions from the tracks. But when the rail was rerouted, downtown businesses shut down, and this side of the track withered. Hence Harry's policing dilemmas."

"So most folks who come to St. John's live on the 'good' side of town," Calvin summed up.

"You got it," said the Chief.

"But they come to church on the 'bad' side of town."

"Yes."

"Why didn't you just move the church to the good side of town?"

At this question, Ruby and Chief Stern began speaking at the same time, and it took a minute to sort out who said what.

The Chief said, "This building is 200 years old. People's great-great-grandparents got baptized and married here. You don't mess with history like that."

Ruby said, "The better idea would be to build up this side of town so there would be no good or bad sides at all."

Calvin could tell that his search for a less weighty topic of conversation had failed, so he tried once more. Surely this new effort would be more suitable for picnicking on a sunny day.

"I've looked at all the windows in the church this week and read through some of the parish history, and I can't for the life of me figure out which John this church is named for."

Chief Stern looked at Ruby, who looked at Whit, who looked back at Chief Stern. Then all three burst out laughing.

Calvin knew they weren't laughing at him, but still a bit of heat rose in his face. "I'm serious," he said. "Is it John the Baptist or John the Evangelist?"

Chief Stern was the first to regain his composure. "Look at him. First Sunday and he's already questing after the deep mysteries."

"Maybe you can tell us," said Whit, still chuckling.

"Oh, you two, don't make fun," said Ruby.

"I'm very confused," said Calvin.

"The truth is that we don't rightly know," said Whit.

"No one does," added the Chief.

"You don't know who your patron saint is," said Calvin.

"Well, we know he's John," said Ruby.

"You just don't know which one," confirmed Calvin.

"That's right," said all three together.

Calvin smiled, and this time he began the laughter that spiraled around the table. Once they had all caught their breath, Whit told Calvin the whole story.

"Back in the late seventies, the rector was a man named George Grayson. Now Father George looked like a no-nonsense kind of fellow—military haircut, thick horn-rimmed glasses, always impeccably dressed in suits with his collar and black clerical shirt. But Father George was really an old softy, and when it came to contentious issues, he trod the middle ground rather than taking one side or the other. Such was the case we are presently discussing."

As Whit spoke, Calvin began to generate a mental picture of him as a younger man. Ruby had mentioned that Whit had been a college professor, and Calvin could hear Whit slide into a comfortable, didactic tone as he spoke. All he needed was a tweed jacket with elbow patches and a blackboard for the transformation to be complete.

"For some reason, around that time, the parishioners of St. John's began trying to figure out which John was our patron. Personally, I think this became our pet issue because we didn't want to fight about the new prayer book or women's ordination to the priesthood. Those were the hot topics of the day, after all. So we deflected our energy onto something that was, ultimately, unimportant. But for some reason, at the time, it seemed to matter more than most things.

"There were two camps, one for each John, and the congregation was split down the middle. I still don't know why people picked the sides they did. There was evidence dug up in the archives for both saints, but none of it was conclusive. The offices of the diocese were no help. So Father George did what he always did. He tried to find a way for both sides to claim victory."

"So what happened?" asked Calvin. He had forgotten all about his macaroni and cheese as Whit's story unfolded.

"Rather than declare which John was our patron, Father George simply instituted two parish picnics each year rather than one. They were scheduled on the Sunday closest to the feast day for each John. A brilliant solution, right? Well, in the moment, we all thought so. It turns out that John the Baptist's feast day is in late June, hence the picnic we are attending right now."

Whit gestured to the buffet table and the balloons that were spinning in a light breeze. Calvin felt the warm air blow across his face, and then he realized Father George's folly. "But John the Evangelist's feast day," said Calvin, "is in late December."

"Right," said Whit. "And no one wants to have a picnic indoors the week after Christmas."

"So what did the parish do?" asked Calvin.

"Father George stuck to his compromise until he left a few years later. We had two parish picnics a year. This one in June was wonderfully well attended. The one in December? Father George and a few staunch members of the John the Evangelist camp. When Father George left, today's picnic kept going and the other died. So if you ask newer parishioners who the patron saint is, most will say John the Baptist."

"Just because his picnic won?"

"Yes."

"There are, of course, some diehards left in the congregation," said the Chief. "We still think that John the Evangelist is our patron, but the issue rarely comes up. Since his feast day is two days after Christmas, we almost never get a chance to celebrate it."

"Though you can see the influence of the Evangelist's contingent in a few places in the church," said Ruby. "The MMs for example."

"The what?" asked Calvin.

"The Mary Magdalenes—our ladies' fellowship. We do the cooking for events and funerals and such. We put on a monthly luncheon for the old timers. We take the summer off, so the next one's in September. It's quite a good time."

"And now you know all of this church's secrets," said the Chief. "Really, there aren't many. We are a small church that used to be bigger, like most churches nowadays. And with the economy the way it is, we have to do more with less. Last year, I had to cut the parish secretary from thirty hours a week to twenty."

"So that's why the church was empty and dark when I got here in the mid-afternoon," said Calvin. "The website still says that office hours are nine to three."

Chief Stern sighed. "That website hasn't been updated in ages. I think we lost the password or something. Anyway, I hope this picnic makes up for the fact that we didn't have a welcoming contingent the day you arrived in town."

"Oh, but you did send me a welcoming contingent, Chief," said Calvin.

"I did?" said a surprised Chief Stern. "Who?"

"His name was Officer Carter."

April 2, 2010

Dear Rev. Calvin,

I expect you've had a busy week up there in Boston. Remember last year when you collapsed on Easter Sunday? I remember checking your office the week before Easter to see if you had a cot and a sleeping bag in there because you seemed to be at St. John's every hour of every day. Perhaps you're getting a little more rest this year, what with you not being the only priest at your church. You won't get this letter in the mail until next week, at which time it'll be too late for you to know that I've been praying for you this Good Friday. But prayer is prayer whether you know I'm doing it or not, right?

Last weekend, Cooper pulled some boxes from the attic for me and put them in the dining room. I haven't had time to go through them yet, so I pushed them under the dining room table. I'll get to them soon, I'm sure. Cooper opened one in the attic to make sure they were the right boxes, and he pulled out an old hymnal that my mother gave me when she was teaching me piano. I played through some of the songs this morning before going to church for the Good Friday service. There's nothing quite like old hymns: "In the Garden," "The Old Rugged Cross," "Blessed Assurance."

My mother—Priscilla Potter Winslow was her name—played piano at our church, and she always seemed to know the hymns by heart. I don't think I ever saw her look at a hymnal on a Sunday morning. The songs were just inside

61

of her, waiting to spill from her fingers onto the keys.

At home, she taught me how to play on an old upright. It was a dreadful piano, really. One of the front legs was missing, so it wobbled any time I played a low note. All three strings that made up the E-flat above middle C were gone, so whenever that note came up in the music, there was a rest whether you wanted one or not. And the poor thing couldn't stay in tune. It was a blessing that my mother had a tuning wrench and knew how to use it. No roosters or alarm clocks woke me up as a child, but the sound of my mother hammering away at the keys to tune the strings sure did. But, in the end, that old piano was ours and we loved it.

Truth be told, there were plenty of times when we should have sold the thing. Times were lean. My mother kept a stew going, and everything she could get her hands on went into it, whether it was a traditional ingredient or not. The resulting mixtures wouldn't have won any awards, but anything tastes delicious when you're hungry enough. D.B. and I called her stew "Priscilla's Pot," and we ate it four or five times a week, especially in winter when the stew warmed our insides enough to make us forget how cold our outsides were.

I wasn't quite four years old when the stock market crashed, so I never could recall times that weren't lean. My mother would use that as her reason for every small hardship we had to bear: "I wish we could adopt that kitty, Ruby, but times are lean. I wish we could have a cake on D.B.'s birthday, Ruby, but times are lean." I didn't quite understand what she meant, but I could see the sadness in her eyes when she said it, and I knew that sadness and lean times were linked somehow. I tried to work out their connection, but I had no point of reference as my parents and D.B. had, so I just got along with no kitty and no cake. I did have a doll though. She was my only possession, but I didn't think of her that way. You don't possess your friends. I remember having tea parties with her and telling her that I wished we could have more than one imaginary biscuit, Dilly, but times are lean.

Of course, times weren't just lean for us in the Winslow household. Even if we had wanted to sell the old piano, I doubt there would have been anyone within a day's walk that could have afforded it. There were families in our town that were more well off than ours, but it was all relative. In Jericho, Pennsylvania, if you didn't have to eat Priscilla's Pot four or five times a week, you were doing just fine indeed. But at the time, I was unaware of any disparity. Life in the Depression was...life. It was the only one I knew, and that made it normal. I had Dilly and I had D.B. I had what my mother called a "Sunday" dress, but I wore it all week just the same. And I had no reason to compare myself to others—to, say, the girls who had a Sunday dress and another one. I was happy because I didn't know that I shouldn't have been.

Despite it hovering behind her eyes, my mother hid her sadness well. She worked so hard those first few years of the Depression to put ingredients in the pot. She did any odd domestic job that cropped up around Jericho. She played piano at church, dug up roots, and picked berries in the woods behind our house. She even taught D.B. how to shoot the rifle that my parents kept under a floorboard in their room. Since the rifle was as tall as I was, I wasn't allowed to shoot it, though that suited me just fine. D.B. went hunting on many an afternoon, but I don't remember him ever coming home with an animal. He was a fine fisherman though, and he would let me hold the net for him when he caught fish in the slow river that bordered the other side of the woods. Priscilla's Pot often had a fishy flavor.

You might be wondering where my father was in all of this. We sure were. I never rightly knew what Mortimer Winslow did for work before 1929 because he never spoke of it. There weren't too many options in Jericho, but whatever his job was, he lost it when I was still too young to know what work was. The Depression had the opposite effect on Mort (everyone called him that, even D.B. and I) than it did on my mother. While she scurried around Jericho sweeping, cooking, and cleaning, he sat on the back porch all day long. He just sat there, sucking on a pipe with no tobacco in it. And whittling. D.B. would bring him sticks from the woods, and Mort would slash away at them until they weren't sticks anymore, but tiny birds or foxes or angels. Then he would keep whittling until there was nothing but shavings.

I suspect we called him Mort along with everyone else because he never felt much like a father when we were young. I didn't understand at the time how worthless he must have felt not to be able to provide for his family. And I think my mother's grim determination to be the provider made him feel even more useless. But she did what she had to do. I can almost hear her say, "I wish you could have had two functioning parents, Ruby, but times are lean."

I'm still not rightly sure why I'm telling you all these things, Calvin, but it feels good to remember; even if the memories aren't all nice and shiny. It's a wonder that I stayed so happy in those years considering everything that was happening. Or not happening. The past is friendlier than the future. Well, mine is anyway. I imagine that, young as you are, your future is all sunrises and shooting stars.

It will be if you find that girl who makes your toes curl.

Take care of yourself.

Ruby

4

On the last Thursday in September, Calvin finished moving into a cavernous townhouse that was situated on the Police Chief Harry Stern–approved side of the tracks. He had started moving in the day after the Fourth of July, but that one final box had become part of the décor of the kitchen. He didn't remove the last few items until a severe bout of procrastination had triumphed over his regularly scheduled sermon preparation. A couple days worth of Ruby's cooking had made Calvin's search for his own housing happen with perhaps less urgency than a long stay at the Victory Arms would have. But no matter his love for starch-laden breakfasts, he knew that 817 Lilac Court was nothing more than an extended pit stop.

The townhouse managed to look run-down even though it was brand new. Construction during the housing boom had been hasty and less than precise, so while the units that formed Calvin's row were up to code, he often observed a general sag in the building, as if it were frowning. The yard, which was blanketed with rolls of scrubby sod, had about the same square footage as the new queen-sized mattress that Calvin and Brad Stewart negotiated up the stairs on the day Calvin signed the lease. The landscaping consisted of a single bush and a miniature fir tree that hid the terminus of the gutter and the electrical meter, respectively. There were no shutters.

Calvin slid his pocketknife through the tape on the bottom of the box, flattened it, and stacked it on top of a leaning tower of pizza boxes in the coat closet, which doubled as a recycling center. And with that, he was officially moved in. Of course, since he had carried all of his earthly possessions with him in a compact car and had bought only the bare minimum of furniture since arriving, the townhouse still looked rather bare, like a monk's cell—if the monk were allowed a flat screen TV.

"I finally unpacked the last box," Calvin told the Morning Prayer Ladies over coffee the following Monday. "I must have been unpacking it piecemeal over the last few months because it only had three things inside when I got around to it."

"You spent three months unpacking that little car?" said Esther Rose. She was on the far side of ornery that morning.

Calvin had begun to learn the shades of Esther Rose's attitude, but he was still a rookie. "No, ma'am. I unpacked the car the first day."

And he knew the moment his response left his lips that she was writing "sasses his elders" on the yellow legal pad in her mind.

Avis Noon came to Calvin's defense with a nervous laugh and said, "Three months would have been some sort of record in our house. We moved several times when the kids were growing up, and we always had boxes that stayed packed the whole time. After a while, Alex made a rule that if a box were not opened between moves, we got rid of its contents."

Only in the last few weeks had Avis started to talk about her husband without breaking down. Tears brimmed in her eyes, but they did not fall. Ruby still instinctively took up Avis's hand in her own, and Avis held on tight. Ruby's hand was a life preserver as the wave of grief washed over Avis. She stayed afloat.

"My folks have the same system," said Calvin. He glanced over at Esther Rose, who was studying her empty coffee cup. He knew his rookie mistake had taken her out of the conversation for good. Esther Rose seemed to be in the Emergency Department every other week with a sprain or sinus infection or gallstones, but she always emerged good as new, which was something of a feat for a woman her age. It was wounds to her pride that were deadly.

"So, sonny," said Mary Williams, "are you finally going to let us throw you that housewarming party?"

"Oh, I don't know," said Calvin.

Ruby teamed up with Mary. "You said you'd think about it when you finished moving in."

Avis made it three against one. "Single men your age don't realize all the things that you should have in your cabinets."

This conversation had been a monthly fixture around the table in the parish hall following Morning Prayer. Until now, Calvin had been able to hold them off with the excuse that he wasn't finished moving in. The truth was that he didn't want them to know that his dining room suite was patio furniture or that the second bedroom upstairs was bare from wall to wall. Brad Stewart had come over to watch college football a few times, and Calvin had sworn him to secrecy. As another man Calvin's age, who didn't realize all the things that he should have in his cabinets until Rebecca put them there, Brad had understood.

"All right," said Calvin, "if you really want to throw me a housewarming party, you can, but you have to do it here at church."

Good ideas often have their genesis in bad ideas, such as having a housewarming party at a separate location. Calvin knew his suggestion fell into the latter category when 75 percent of the MPLs protested and the other quarter continued to study her empty coffee cup.

"Okay, okay," said Calvin when the clamor died down. "New plan: we don't have a housewarming party for me." Rumblings began, but he quieted them with a shake of his hands. "We have a church-warming party for St. John's and all presents go to Bethany House."

Bethany House was the local food pantry that St. John's had started several decades ago. The pantry was now a separate entity, but the church was still its main contributor. When Calvin first heard of this particular ministry, he'd had to suppress a smile because Bethany means "House of Figs" in Hebrew. From then on, in his brain he called the food pantry "House of Figs House." He suppressed his smile now as he watched the protest melt away.

"We could invite people to bring what they would have brought to your housewarming," said Mary.

Once again, Ruby teamed up with her. "Staples like sugar and flour and baking powder and salt."

Avis made three, but now Calvin was on the team too. "And then Calvin will know what should be in his cabinets, but the food will go to Bethany House."

The four of them turned to Esther Rose, who looked up from her coffee cup and gave a ringing endorsement: "It's not the worst idea I've ever heard."

⸏⸎⸏

They set a date for the Church Warming Party, finished their coffee, and got up to leave. But Calvin had another idea brewing in the back of his mind, and he needed an accomplice, so he asked Ruby to hang back as the others made their way down the steps into a bright early autumn day. "Ruby, will you come downstairs with me for a few minutes?" he asked. "I need to pick your brain about something."

"Of course, dear," she said. "But I better take the elevator or you'll be waiting all day for me at the bottom."

Calvin began defending Ruby's ability to take on flights of stairs, but he sounded like a coach giving a pep talk. She waved him off. "Know your limitations, son. I don't have wings, so I can't fly. And I don't have knees that bend too well, so I can't take stairs. Let's not make a federal case out of it. I've still got my mind and that's more than I can say for some, make no mistake."

Part of Calvin felt ashamed for what he realized was a patronizing tone, and he thanked God that Ruby didn't take more offense than she did. But that was not her way. The other part of Calvin just didn't want Ruby to get in the elevator.

The elevator looked like a high school science fair project. There was no sleek metal door that slid into the wall, no carpeted interior, no panel of buttons. There was, on the other hand, a rusted metal gate, a plywood floor, and a light switch hanging from an electrical wire and sporting the numbers 1 and 2 in permanent marker.

"Are you sure you want to ride in that thing?" said Calvin. He himself had not been sure in his three months in Victory and had yet to venture one foot onto the plywood.

"It works just fine, you old worrywart," said Ruby. She shut the gate with a screech and flicked the switch. "You do realize," she continued as she began to descend, "that this is what all elevators look like beneath their shiny trappings."

"Thanks a lot," said Calvin, turning to the staircase. "Now I'm never riding an elevator again."

Despite its junkyard appearance, the elevator deposited Ruby unscathed on the bottom floor. Two hallways spread out in an L-shape, one running under the sanctuary, the other under the parish hall. They walked halfway down the latter and entered a large room dominated by a large piano. Calvin could have stretched out and taken a nap atop the instrument with no danger of rolling off the sides. The surface was an oily, reflective black, like the wooden equivalent of a designer leather jacket. Dozens of fingerprints marred the exterior, but one wipe of a dust rag would make the piano gleam. Ruby and Calvin sat down on the bench and lifted the lid. Curving tendrils of golden filigree spread out from the name of the manufacturer, which was embossed on the underside of the lid.

"Steinway and Sons," Calvin read.

"This is a beautiful piano," said Ruby. "I would play it, but I always forget that it's down here in the choir room."

"You've read my mind," he said as Ruby played an experimental scale on the upper reaches of the keyboard.

Ruby didn't respond, and Calvin decided to let her have a few minutes with the Steinway. He rose from the bench and sat in a chair on the first level of the choir's risers. Ruby scooted to the center of the bench and hit a deep sonority on the low keys. "Delicious," she said under her breath, and Calvin knew he had her.

When she was done tinkering, Ruby asked, "What do you mean, 'I've read your mind'?"

"I want to move this piano upstairs into the church. There's no reason to have such a fine instrument gathering dust and fingerprints in the choir practice room."

"Mmm," said Ruby. It was the universal sound of thoughtful noncommittal.

"It's such a waste down here. In the church we could use it during worship, we could have concerts." He reached for the personal. "You could play it whenever you want."

"I don't deny I would enjoy that." She smiled at Calvin, whose passion for the idea of moving the piano had begun to show scarlet on his cheeks. "I think it's a fine idea," she concluded.

Calvin relaxed. He had been turning this idea over in his mind since he had stumbled onto the piano during his first trip downstairs back in June. He then shelved it while he got his feet wet in the St. John's pool, but three months in, he figured now was the time to propose the move. The symbolism was just too good not to pursue. A beautiful instrument in the basement is like a wonderful church with nothing going on. So let's move the instrument. Let's enliven the church. He could see the whole campaign, the renewed vitality, all represented by the Steinway . . .

Ruby interrupted Calvin's scripting of his legacy with a pertinent question: "But where are we going to put it?"

"Simple," said Calvin. "We just need to take out a couple pews in the front of the nave."

"Mmm," said Ruby. With a different inflection the universal sound of thoughtful noncommittal becomes the universal sound of thoughtful disagreement.

"There we might have a few people to convince," she said.

———

Calvin escorted Ruby back to the science fair project and once again chose the stairs for himself. Back on the main level, they ambled to the entryway.

"So you think there may be some resistance," said Calvin.

"No, dear," said Ruby. "I know there will. But that doesn't mean it's not worthwhile. Just keep your chin up."

"I will."

Ruby put her hand on the doorknob. "Wait," said Calvin. "One more thing. Why was Esther Rose in such a foul mood this morning? I mean, I know she can be a bit . . . " He searched for a kind word.

"Rough around the edges," Ruby finished for him.

"Yes."

"Oh, I don't know. The weather turning colder. A pain in her hip. Loneliness. Pick one."

"I didn't mean to poke fun at her."

"You can't take responsibility for how other people react to what you say. But you can think about how they will hear your words." She took her hand off the doorknob and put it on Calvin's arm. "Remember, we're all rough around the edges. This life is about sanding us down and polishing us up."

She squeezed his arm. "I think heaven is full of sea glass."

"Sea glass," he repeated. "I like that." He turned the image over in his mind.

"Of course," said Ruby, "Now that I think of it, Esther Rose was probably extra rough today because it's campaign season."

"I don't understand."

"Oh, I'd bet a steak dinner and a soda pop that she saw one of Carl Sinclair's ads on the TV this morning. That would get her good and riled."

Calvin remembered Esther Rose calling the mayor an old fraud. "She doesn't like him much, does she?"

"Carl's not a bad sort. He's done quite a lot of good for this town, though circumstances aren't so good. But he beat her Ted in three elections in a row back in the eighties, so there are bound to be sour grapes. Though they've been sour for quite a spell now."

"Well, that solves a minor mystery," said Calvin, whose imagination had convicted the mayor of secret kickbacks and embezzlement.

"By the way," said Ruby. "I'm going to have to leave right after Morning Prayer tomorrow. Whit has an appointment with the dermatologist, and I'd like to go with him."

"Is everything okay?" asked Calvin.

"Fine, fine. But it seems with every decade, we add another doctor to our entourage."

Ruby made to put her hand back on the doorknob, but at the same moment, the door flew open.

"Oh, Ruby Redding, darling, my gorgeous saint, come here, come here, come here, I must simply kiss those cheeks of yours."

A whirlwind of scarves and purse and sunglasses surged past Calvin and pulled Ruby into a maelstrom of an embrace. For a moment, Ruby's arms stuck out straight on either side of a tall, slender woman, whose chemically enhanced platinum blonde ringlets exploded in all directions from her head. A leather coat the same shade as her lipstick fell to her knees, where her boots began. The boots ended in four-inch stilettos, which added to her already impressive height.

Once over her initial shock, Ruby bent her elbows and returned the hug, laughing all the while. "Josie," she said. "You're back."

"I went. I saw. I conquered. And I have returned," said Josie as she pulled from the embrace and righted a dizzy Ruby back on her feet. Ruby's cheeks and forehead bore the evidence of a dozen scarlet kisses.

"Josie has been in Europe for, what, five months," explained Ruby to a rather stunned Calvin. All of the light in the entryway seemed to be radiating from Josie's curls.

"Six," corrected Josie. "And what amazing, wonderful, spectacular months they were." Each time Josie spoke, everything came out in one breath, and the words tumbled after one another as if they each wanted an earlier place in the sentence.

"And who do we have here?" asked Josie, looking Calvin up and down. "Don't tell me. White collar, black shirt, star-struck expression—I know, aren't I fabulous—and young, young, young, he could be my son."

Before Calvin could defend himself, the platinum maelstrom had engulfed him, as well, and planted a solid kiss on each cheek. "You, cutie pie, are the Reverend Calvin Harper, and I am Josie Temple-Jones, recently returned from London, Paris, Prague, and Venice, where I bought this coat, isn't it grand?"

She stood back to be admired. Calvin, who was a bit star-struck, could only manage a single word. "Grand," he agreed.

"Hmm," said Josie. "Not much of a talker, but that's okay with eyelashes like those." She turned back to Ruby, who had sat down on the steps to recover from her laughter. "Where'd you find him, Ruby? The J. Crew catalogue? I mean, honestly. How's a woman of my years and situation supposed to pay attention to his sermons?"

"Ms. Jones," began Calvin, who had found his voice. But she cut him off.

"Temple-Jones. I have been and always will be a Temple, and Mr. Jones died of a heart attack a decade ago, God rest his soul." She crossed herself and kissed the faceted boulder attached to a ring on her left hand.

"Ms. Temple-Jones," began Calvin again.

"Say no more, darling. My network of spies in Victory" (and here she winked at Ruby) "has written me across the pond and told me all about you. I understand you are single and are in need of a young woman—or is it young man?—no, judging by those shoes, a young woman in your life."

Calvin shot Ruby the same look Caesar gave to Brutus, but Ruby's paroxysms of laughter had returned, and she was wiping tears from her eyes.

Josie Temple-Jones continued, "My late husband, God rest his soul, had a business partner in Victory named Doctor Dennis, who was a dentist, and we can laugh about that coincidence another time because now you must attend to the joyous serendipity that has brought you to Victory at the same time as Doctor Dennis has begun to retire, and his daughter Monica has started to take over his practice. And if there's one thing I know about Miss—or should I says Doctor—Monica Dennis it's that she wants a different last name."

Calvin tried to interrupt, but Josie seemed to have the lung capacity of an operatic tenor. "She's a lovely, lovely, lovely girl—nice eyes, great laugh—who just graduated from dental school and moved home to Victory. Calvin, I've already taken the liberty of making you an appointment to have your teeth cleaned two weeks from today."

She finished her speech with a flourish of both hands, like a conductor cutting off an orchestra.

Calvin opened and closed his mouth several times. His voice had fled once again.

Ruby stood up from the step and put an arm around Josie. Her head came to Josie's shoulder. "You sure do work quickly, my dear. But all I said in my letter was that he was single."

"Ah, but do you recall what Jane—I read her books every year, such a kindred spirit—says at the beginning of *Pride and Prejudice*?"

"It has been years," said Ruby.

" 'It is a truth universally acknowledged, that a single man in possession of a good fortune must be in want of a wife,' " recited Josie.

"But I am not in possession of a good fortune." It was Calvin's first complete sentence since Josie had erupted into the entryway.

"Here, flash me those pearly whites," said Josie, and she dazzled Calvin with a smile of her own. He couldn't help but reflect it.

"There's your fortune. Go get her, cutie pie."

———∞∞∞———

April 5, 2010

Dear Rev. Calvin,

They say that if March comes in like a lion, then it will go out like a lamb. But we had two lions this year. Victory was wet and cold every day last week. Then, yesterday, spring arrived just like that: brilliant sun, blooming flowers, everything green and fresh and scrubbed to a shine by all that rain. I don't think it's a coincidence that yesterday was Easter. I think the weather knew when to change. St. John's was packed as it always is on Easter Sunday morning. I recognized about one person in every four. I wonder what all those other folks are doing on every other Sunday morning if not coming to church? The church looks so different when it's full. Usually people sit on their own little islands with oceans of pews between them. But on Easter Sunday, you can't even see the pews.

The bright colors inside the church matched the flowers blooming outside. Everyone was dressed to the nines. There were ladies in hats (yours truly, included—I borrowed one of Josie's), girls in sundresses and colorful sandals, little boys in blue blazers and loafers. Seeing

78

small boys in formal wear has always tickled my funny bone—ninety-nine out of a hundred look about ready to shake themselves free of the khaki confinement, but there's always one who finds a serious dignity in his fine clothes. He keeps everything tucked in and smoothed down.

Your friend Natalie Stewart was wearing a precious floral-printed dress and matching bonnet. But you know how toddler girls are. She kept fluffing the skirt of her dress and half the time she wound up pulling the dress over her head. It was all Rebecca could do to keep her daughter's dress on her body. T.J. suggested they tie it to her shoes, but I don't think that plan went anywhere. I don't know if you've heard (maybe you have through the computer), but Rebecca is pregnant again! She's due in October, Esther Rose told me yesterday. It was good to see those four generations of Lincolns together in their Easter best.

When I was a girl, my Easter best meant that my dress got an even more thorough scrubbing than normal. Like St. John's yesterday, our church in Jericho was always full on Easter, but since it was full every other Sunday as well, no one mentioned it. I went to church because that's what we did on Sunday mornings. There was never a question about whether or not to go. We would leave Mort on the back porch with a fresh stack of branches, and the rest of us would walk up the dusty road to town. I suppose the only difference between Easter and a normal Sunday was that my mother dragged Mort along.

Like I said, the church was always full, Easter or no. Perhaps folk in Jericho were especially religious. Or living in a town named after a doomed place made people feel like a little extra Bible reading couldn't hurt. Or maybe all those downtrodden, broken people came together because when they did they turned into one whole person, and folk needed to feel whole.

I think that wholeness happened most when we sang. The piano at the church was in better condition than the upright at home, but only just. My mother pounded out the melody, and all those voices rose in unison. Up until I was too big, I sat on the piano bench with her and played an imaginary piano on my knees. She started teaching me when I was five or six, though I had to perch atop an apple crate set on the bench to be able to see over the keyboard. I never wanted to learn to read music because I never saw her look at a note. But she made me practice with her old hymnals just the same. The melodies were easy because I already knew the tunes. I would pick them up in a tick and then learn the left hand. But I'm lying a bit. You know I've always faked the left hand. I'm sure my mother knew I did too, but she never said boo about it. I think she was just happy that I enjoyed playing.

And I did enjoy the piano, but I enjoyed getting lost in the woods more. I was quite the inquisitive child, though my mother called me antsy. I couldn't sit still at the piano for too long, and there weren't enough books around for me to lose myself in. So I read nature. I read the footprints of animals and imagined myself a trapper gathering pelts to sell upriver. I read the birds' nests and wondered what it would be like to live in the waving topmost branches of trees. I read the anthills and beaver dams and mushroom colonies. I ran all over the countryside discovering things that had been discovered many times before, but that didn't matter because I had yet to discover them.

Times were lean at home, but nature's bounty knew nothing of the Depression. Maybe that's why I spent so much time in the woods, especially as I got older. In a way, I was just like Mort. He escaped to the back porch, and I escaped to the forest. The difference was that I didn't know I was escaping from anything, and he did. But that changed when I was eleven or twelve. I don't rightly know what my mother did to land him a job (though I'm certain he had nothing to do with it). But one day he put on his cap and walked out the front door instead of the back. He was going to work for the WPA up near Erie, my mother told us, and we would see him around Christmas time. I don't know why hearing that made me cry, considering Mort was far away even when he was home, but it did. I went to my bed to cry into my pillow and found on it a tiny wooden angel, carved from a maple branch. Turned out that Mort didn't turn all of his creations into shavings after all. Seeing the angel made me cry even harder.

We learned about the WPA in school, about how the president had saved the economy with his New Deal. I didn't know much about deals, new or old, but I did know that Priscilla's Pot was a less frequent delicacy at suppertime when Mort was away. My mother still worked hard as ever, and what little money came back from Erie went straight into dinner. When Mort came home at Christmas, he was still the same man—sort of caved in, like the weight of the world had collapsed his bones somehow—but he was different too. He held his head up a little more. He talked a little more. He even held my mother's hand. I remember that clear as day. I remember thinking I wouldn't have traded that moment for all the wooden angels he had ever carved. Then he was off again, this time to Philadelphia or down into Maryland. Between 1937 and 1939, Mort was home a grand total of three weeks.

In those same years, I did some growing. My mother kept adding material to make my dress longer. Then she gave up and made me a brand new one. D.B. was three years older, and he hit his growth spurt about the time I did. I don't know how my mother managed to keep both of us clothed. But by the time I was thirteen and D.B. was sixteen, he was big enough to fit into the clothes that Mort left behind. In the ironbound chest at the foot of my parents' bed, we found a moth-eaten suit, and D.B. started wearing it to church every Sunday. Folk were wondering why Mort decided to start getting religion. Then they realized it was just Early Winslow all grown up.

That was the same year the Germans marched on Poland. D.B. was grown up indeed, and I think my mother saw the writing on the wall because whenever she looked at him she started crying. But to us, ensconced in the backwoods of Pennsylvania, the maneu-

vers of European armies were just more fodder
for our games and explorations. We saw newspaper reports and read about the ghettos, the
bombing of Britain, the U-boat attacks, but it
was all so far away. We couldn't see the faces of
the soldiers dying on battlefields or the devastated streets of London or boats sinking in the
Atlantic.

But there were some changes at home. For
one, Mort stopped working for the WPA and
went to work at a steel mill in Bethlehem with
just about every other man in town. Bethlehem
wasn't but a couple hours from Jericho by bus,
so we saw more of him after the war began.
I guess I was thankful for that, but it seems
a silly thing to thank God for when all those
innocent people were dying.

D.B. and I used to sit by the railroad tracks
north of Jericho and watch the trains loaded
with steel beams lumber by on their way to the
coast. We would pick which car carried the
beams that Mort had worked on, and I always
imagined that he etched a tiny angel in each
one. Whatever ship was built from the angel
beams would be safe from harm. Watching
that steel go by, I never thought that I would be
building those ships soon. But you know your
history, Calvin.

It happened on my sixteenth birthday. It
happened farther away than any of those atroc-
ities in Europe, but it was so much closer all
the same. Because it happened to us. American
steel sunk to the bottom of the bay. American
boys trapped inside. American boys my brother's age. My mother had seen it all two years
before. The day after my birthday, the day the

president declared war, D.B. joined up. And so did Walter Redding, whom everyone called Whit, but I didn't know that at the time.

Oh my, I'm getting to the end of my fifth sheet of paper. I just get going and there's no stopping me. I guess thinking on these things helps, especially at the holidays. Calvin, I haven't wanted to burden you what with all your duties and new folks to take care of. But if you can find time to stick me in your prayers now and again I would be grateful. Times are lean for me right now. I think one of the reasons I've been writing these letters to you about my youth is that the past is a much happier place to be than the present. But I promise to get to those boxes in the dining room soon.

Get some rest,

Ruby

5

Calvin Harper reclined in the chair and stared at the penetrating eyes of Doctor Monica Dennis. Besides her landscaped eyebrows, her eyes were the only feature he could see, considering a mask was covering the rest of her face. He was trying to decide whether Monica's eyes were glacier blue or stained glass blue. (He had already started calling her by her first name in his mind, even though she had introduced herself as Dr. Dennis.) Or, he thought, perhaps they are dentist mask blue.

I wonder if she's trying to figure out the color of my eyes too, he mused. By the fact that she was staring into his mouth and scraping his teeth one by one with a hooked metal probe, he decided not. Odd first date, thought Calvin.

A month had passed since Josie Temple-Jones had scheduled Calvin's dentist appointment without his knowledge or consent. The original date was two weeks from Josie's whirlwind return to St. John's, but Calvin rescheduled to give himself more time to stoke his courage. Instead, he gave himself two more weeks to fret. He had never been a smooth talker where the opposite sex was concerned. He tripped over his words and over his feet sometimes. Oh, Calvin was good looking and polite. He paid for dinner without giving off an air of chauvinistic smugness. He held doors open. But he knew that he was stricken with the dreaded curse of certain men in their twenties: he was safe. The mothers of the women he had courted always liked him better than their daughters did. The daughters wanted to ride a motorcycle at least once before they settled down. Calvin owned a sensible, four-door sedan.

At the moment, however, Doctor Monica Dennis's hands were in Calvin's mouth, so he had not had a chance to trip over his words. He was sitting down when she entered the room, so he had not had a chance to trip over his feet either. All in all, things were going well. Perhaps she'll see my fillings and think I'm a rebel, he thought.

As she moved from his top teeth to the bottom, Calvin decided once and for all that her eyes were glacier blue, and then turned his mind to the successful Church Warming Party that had taken place the night before. Recounting a success in my professional life will give me courage in my personal life, he tried to convince himself.

<hr>

The Morning Prayer Ladies scheduled the Church Warming Party for the first Wednesday in November. They reasoned that with the holidays coming up, the folks who frequented Bethany House would need to replenish the staples in their cabinets. The annual Thanksgiving food basket drive was also in a couple of weeks, so the Church Warming Party would serve as a great kickoff. And since no one puts a bag of flour or canister of baking powder in a food basket, the two events would not overlap.

The MPLs thought of everything. They were especially proud of the signs they made to advertise the event. "If you think Rev. Calvin needs it in his cupboard, bring it to the Church Warming on November 5." They asked Calvin to take a photograph of a bare cupboard at his townhouse for the sign. Considering his cupboards held little more than a few boxes of pasta and a tub of peanut butter, this was not difficult to accomplish.

The evening of November 5 came, and the MPLs arrived early to set up. The three younger ladies scurried about while Esther Rose directed traffic from her usual seat near the coffee maker.

"Avis, put the plates on the other side of the table so people don't pick up their cookies before they have something to put them on," said Esther Rose.

"Well, maybe Mary should put her cookies on the other side of my plates," said Avis.

"But I've already set them out," shot back Mary.

"Why don't we just put a stack of plates on both sides of the table," said Ruby.

Calvin grinned. While watching the four of them plan the Church Warming, he had begun to notice the pattern of a family unit emerge, especially as the stress had built to the night of the event. Esther Rose, as the matriarch of the group, played the mother—critical, exasperated, long-suffering. He wondered if her yellow legal pad had made an appearance. If anyone had received a folded piece of paper, it would have been Mary, of whom Esther Rose expected the most, which made sense considering Mary was the eldest of the three younger ladies. Ruby filled the role of the classic middle child, playing peacemaker between Mary and Avis. As the youngest, Avis expected to get her way.

"You know," said Calvin, "sometimes you all bicker like siblings. Are you sure you weren't separated at birth?"

87

ADAM THOMAS

"Ah, sonny," said Mary as she rearranged the cookies. "Avis is just a wee lass. I would remember if she had shown up in a bassinet."

"We bicker because we love," said Ruby. "Here, Calvin, carry this coffee urn for me."

"I'll get it," said a new voice, and Calvin turned to see Chief Stern in the doorway to the parish hall. He placed a bag of groceries on a table near the door and strode to the silver urn, which could have held enough coffee for the entire population of Victory. The urn must have been secreted away in a closet because Calvin hadn't seen the massive thing until that evening. On Sundays, they used the same family-sized coffee maker the MPLs used each morning. Judging by its size, the urn was certainly a relic of the good old days when St. Jacks-across-the-tracks boomed. Calvin worried that the ladies were expecting an unrealistic turnout, judging by their unearthing of the urn, at least.

His worries were unfounded. Over the course of the next hour, more people arrived than Calvin had met in his four months in town put together. By the end of the evening, the goods on the table near the door had overflowed onto not one, but two more tables. Bags of flour and sugar; canisters of baking powder and salt; boxes of cereal, oatmeal, and baking soda; rice, peanut butter, cooking oil, broth, pasta, and more weighed down the three tables. Someone had even brought a set of spices, many of which Calvin had never seen, let alone tasted before.

The parish hall overflowed, as well. Conversations broke out in the kitchen and hallway. Calvin wandered from one knot of people to the next, shaking hands and introducing himself, though he knew he couldn't hope to retain the names of his new acquaintances. Every few minutes, he also spotted a familiar face.

"Nice to the see the place so full," said Harold the golfer. Calvin still didn't know his last name, not to mention those of Phil and Phil, who flanked Harold like an honor guard. They hurried out of the early service every Sunday, so Calvin had not had a chance to chat with them.

"Indeed it is," said Calvin. "Where's your fourth?"

"Carl is reveling in another successful reelection campaign," Harold said. "But he said he might stop by."

Calvin moved on, saying, "welcome" and "glad you could come" and "nice to see you" to everyone he met. Then he spotted the Stewarts and, in need of a breather, he took the seat next to Rebecca.

"She could come any day now," she said, stroking the pregnancy bump in her lap.

"We're starting month number nine," said Brad, as he returned with a plate of cookies for his wife.

"Can't wait," said Calvin. "You call me soon after. I want to come and bless that baby. You call your parents, your sister, your grandmother, your best friend, and then me, got it?"

"You bet," said Brad.

Calvin moved on again until he saw Josie Temple-Jones holding court near the coffee urn. "Do you see this lovely, lovely, lovely urn," she was telling a group of onlookers. "My mother, Marion Temple, gave this urn to St. John's when I was just a little girl. I used to hide in it—oh, not when there was coffee inside, of course. But isn't it simply gorgeous. Yes, there are mother's initials etched at the bottom. Just there. 'M. P. T.' My husband, God rest his soul, used to joke that those letters meant that the urn was *empty*. What a wit Mr. Jones had, God love him."

"Josie, let me guess," said Calvin. "You brought that set of spices."

"You bet your cute little . . . " She stopped and considered her word choice. "Tush," she apparently decided was an appropriate word for church.

Calvin blushed.

"So" said Josie, circling Calvin like a drill sergeant. "I hear through the grapevine that you still haven't been to see a certain young dentist. A certain young, pretty, very pretty dentist."

Calvin blushed harder.

"This simply won't do," concluded Josie.

"Don't worry. My appointment is for tomorrow morning."

"And you intend to keep this appointment." It wasn't a question.

"Yes, ma'am."

"Good." And then she overwhelmed him with one of her hurricane-like hugs.

"Josie," he said, extracting himself from her embrace, "you have talked to her, right?"

"Of course, I've talked to her. Monica is a darling. Quite the conversationalist."

And with that, Josie Temple-Jones whipped around and engulfed an unsuspecting Avis Noon with a Category Four hug.

Calvin melted away from Josie before she could spin and crush his ribs again and found himself face to face with Ruby, who had once again witnessed their exchange. And once again, she was rubbing tears of laughter from her eyes. "You'll do fine, dear," she said. "Just remember that you are out there looking for the girl who is going to make your toes curl."

"My toes curl?" he repeated.

"Don't settle for anything less."

"I don't even know what that means."

"You will when it happens. Although, if you're anything like me, it might not happen right away. Just be patient."

"Took a while for Whit to curl your toes?"

"A while. I'll tell you about it sometime."

"Where is he tonight, by the way?"

"Oh, he's just a bit under the weather, but he should be right as rain tomorrow."

Calvin was about to ask what was wrong, but as he opened his mouth, a voice boomed over the din of the gathering.

"Excuse me, I'm sorry so to interrupt, but I just wanted to thank you all for coming to this wonderful event. The folks at Bethany House will be so pleased with this outpouring of support from our church family."

Applause filled the room as Calvin turned around to see Carl Sinclair, the newly reelected mayor of Victory, standing on a chair near the door. "And thank you for your votes yesterday. Without you, there would have be no victory for Victory."

Calvin had heard the slogan on Carl Sinclair's local TV spots. *I guess it's never too early to start campaigning for the next election,* he thought.

The crowd apparently thought the mayor's pronouncement signaled the end of the event because the hall emptied soon after, leaving Calvin and the MPLs with a formidable clean-up looming.

Esther Rose sat in her accustomed seat near the small coffee maker not saying a word to anyone. Calvin knew that she was fuming about Carl's speech and nursing her personal vendetta against him, so Calvin kept his distance. But Mary voiced a kinder version of the thought that was surely running through Esther Rose's mind: "What was that old politician doing, taking the credit for our event? I mean, honestly, the nerve."

"I suppose he can't enter a room full of people without making a speech," said Avis. "But he could have at least given credit where credit is due."

"Oh, who needs credit when we have all this food," said Ruby as she gestured to the three tables loaded with bags of groceries. "Say, why don't we wait until next week to take these bags to Bethany House. I have an idea."

Everyone stopped to listen. Even Esther Rose looked up from the table in the corner.

"Tonight we bring all the food into the church. Everyone can see how much was brought in to give to the folks at the food pantry. Perhaps seeing it all will spur folks to keep donating over the long run. And Calvin can bless this food on Sunday morning."

"And I can give thanks to the four of you for organizing this event, which was wonderful, by the way," said Calvin.

Avis and Mary agreed, and they began hauling the staples into the sanctuary. As they went back for the last trip, Esther Rose joined them, no longer scowling, but not exactly smiling, and helped move the final items. There were so many goods that they ringed the windowsills in the nave and filled all the floor space in front of the altar. Calvin had much to bless the following Sunday.

But first, Thursday loomed.

⸺⸺

"All done," said Dr. Monica Dennis. She took off her mask and handed Calvin water in a small paper cup. "You've got a small cavity on your second premolar." She smiled and pointed to one of her own teeth. "Right here."

"Okay," said Calvin, but he wasn't really listening to the diagnosis because of the dazzling smile aimed at him. This woman is definitely the daughter of a dentist, he thought.

"It's not serious, but let's nab it now before it gets out of hand. We're going to have to schedule you another appointment to take care of it."

Second date, thought Calvin. Who needs a motorcycle when you've got cavities?

He decided on the spot to go for it. "How about tomorrow at the end of the day, then dinner, and perhaps a movie afterward?"

At least, that's what he wanted to say. But what he really said was, "How about that cavity for dinner, then a filling, I mean movie afterward?"

Thankfully, there had been a problem with the suction machine, and the hygienist had put a piece of gauze in each of Calvin's cheeks and under his tongue to soak up spit. So what came out was: "Haw bout catty or dinnah, ten illin, ah een hooey ahterars?"

"What was that?" she said, as she dug out the gauze.

Calvin gave himself time to reorder the sentence by swishing the water around his mouth and spitting into the little sink attached to the dentist's chair. "I said, 'How about tomorrow at the end of the day, then dinner, and perhaps a movie afterward?'"

He flashed her three years of orthodontia. His teeth weren't dazzling like hers, but they were straight and pleasantly symmetrical.

"Can't do that, I'm afraid," she said.

His smile fell. "It's 'cause I'm a patient, right? Or 'cause I'm a priest? Or my breath? Or . . . "

"No, no," she said, cutting him off with a hand on his shoulder. "It's because the filling will need to set, so we should probably do the movie first."

"So what can you tell me about Monica Dennis?" said Calvin as he sliced a golf ball into the netting along the side of the range. He stooped down to retrieve his tee, saw that it was broken, and fished a new one from his bag.

"Monica?" asked Brad Stewart. Her name hung in the air through Brad's backswing. Then he grunted and sent the ball straight down the fairway where it landed just in front of the 300-yard marker. It was Calvin's day off, and Brad had invited him to the driving range. His date with Monica Dennis was less than three hours away and doubt was settling in for the ride. It didn't help that he was a terrible golfer.

"We went to high school together, though she was a couple years behind me. Pretty girl, cheerleader, nice smile, great . . . "

But what was great about Monica was lost in another grunt as Brad deposited a second ball in front of the 300-yard marker.

"We're going out to a movie and then dinner tonight. Josie Temple-Jones sort of pushed us together. But I've never been good at the first date thing."

"Don't know what to tell you, man. I've only ever been on one first date myself. Rebecca and I have been together since tenth grade."

Calvin hit another ball, and this one skidded along the ground for about a hundred yards, but at least it went straight. "Tenth grade. Wow."

"When you know, you know, and I knew."

"That's what people keep telling me. Ruby Redding told me my toes would curl when I was with the right person."

"I don't know about that," said Brad as he selected an iron from his bag. "But I do know that when you're with the right person, everything is just a little bit easier. It's not easy . . . " Another grunt. This time Brad drew the ball from right to left and landed it near the pin on one of the target greens. "Just a bit easier."

"I imagine the baby will complicate matters."

"She might. I'm not looking forward to the diaper thing for one."

"Never changed one myself."

"And you wouldn't believe the amount of new stuff that's in my house. Rebecca had the baby shower last week, and the whole place is suddenly pastel." Brad arched a ball high into the air and watched it bounce once on the green, catch, and spin back to land within the shadow of the pin.

"How do you do that?" said Calvin, who had just sent a second ball into the side-netting.

"Years of practice. I started playing about the time Rebecca and I got together. In fact, one of my first rounds was with T.J. about a month after she and I started dating. He told me he wanted to get the measure of me."

"It wasn't to have an excuse to threaten you with metal sticks?" Calvin hefted his seven iron like a baseball bat.

"That too," said Brad. "When my daughter starts dating, I'll take her boyfriend golfing too. And hey, maybe T.J. will come along." He tested the weight of the club in his hand. "Talk about intimidating."

"It's a good thing I'm a terrible golfer then," said Calvin. "Doctor Dennis won't be taking me for a round."

"Hey man, don't get ahead of yourself."

"Thanks for the vote of confidence. Got any advice in there to go with it?"

"You want some?" Brad launched another ball toward the target pin.

"Couldn't hurt."

"You're opening up the clubface too much. That's why you're slicing."

"I meant about Monica."

"Right. Okay. Just be honest with her. If it works out, it works out; if it doesn't, it doesn't. No use lying just to get another date. Plus, the truth is easier to remember."

"Got it. At least that's one thing I have going for me. I'm not good at lying. Not even bluffing."

"Then we should play poker sometime."

"You'd clean me out."

"Exactly."

Calvin got a hold of a ball and sent it straight down the fairway. "Finally," he said, admiring the flight of the ball. He pushed the club back into his bag and turned to Brad. "Really, I'm a pretty trustworthy guy. I don't think my boss would be very happy with me otherwise."

"Who, the bishop?"

"No." Calvin pointed to the sky.

"Oh, right," said Brad.

—◦◦◦—

Calvin didn't even think about trying to hold Monica Dennis's hand during the movie. It's not that he wouldn't have wanted to. Rather, he spent the whole film massaging his jaw because he had kept it open during the entire procedure beforehand. He had passed the time while she drilled away the cavity trying to refine his description of the color of her eyes, but glacier blue won again. So he moved on to her hair, which a person with a less expansive vocabulary than Calvin's would call blonde. Calvin passed through many descriptions in his mind, most having something to do with the harvest. But by the time Monica had finished filling the cavity, he had settled on salted butter blonde. Since he didn't voice this description to her, she never had the opportunity to ask him if there was a difference between salted and unsalted butter blondes. If she had, Calvin would have told her it was a personality thing.

The movie finished with a kiss and a declaration of undying love between the two people who seemed unlikely at the beginning of the film to get together. Calvin wished he had vetoed the romantic comedy because now he felt some pressure to live up to it. But he hadn't, so he and Monica made their way to dinner talking about the funnier parts of the movie. Calvin was glad the filling needed to set because the movie gave them something to discuss.

Josie was right. Monica was quite the conversationalist. Calvin could hardly get a word in edgewise, but that suited him fine because his jaw didn't feel much like forming them. By the time they sat down at Year of the Dragon, Monica had told him about the antics of several drunk dental students who got their hands on an x-ray machine, though she would neither confirm nor deny if she had been one of them; about a spur-of-the-moment drive to Mexico during her sophomore year of college, in which she and her friends were stopped by the police and suspected of being drug mules, even though they just wanted to say they had been to Mexico; and about her roommate's cat, who hated her.

Calvin chuckled, gasped, and raised his eyebrows in all the appropriate places. He asked clarifying questions to demonstrate that he was engaged in her stories. But when Monica paused her narrative to peruse the menu, Calvin realized that he was employing his seminary training in the conversation. He was, after all, a trained listener. During his time as a hospital chaplain intern, he had to remember and later write down the dialogue of conversations he had with patients. This taught him to shut off his inner monologue and stay present and aware of the other person when he or she was talking. He never thought he would use this skill on a date. Monica was not a member of his church or a patient in the hospital. So why did his training kick in?

A small voice responded inside him: *Because you're not really interested in what she has to say.*

Calvin kept the menu in front of his face even though he had decided on sweet and sour chicken before they sat down. *No, I am*, protested a louder voice.

The small voice grew in strength: *You're annoyed that she hasn't asked anything about you yet.*

Well, I have kept the conversation focused on her, said the louder voice, but now Calvin couldn't distinguish between the two.

So try to talk about yourself and see what happens. Both voices said this together.

Calvin dropped the menu to the table and announced, "Sweet and sour chicken for me."

"Oh, that's so bland," said Monica. "I need something spicy."

She laughed and tossed her salted butter blonde hair, and most of Calvin didn't register that she had put down his selection of Chinese food. But the part of him that owned the small voice did.

"Okay," he said after they ordered. "Let's play a game. I'll say something like favorite kind of food or favorite television show, and then we both say our answers at the same time."

"All right," said Monica.

"Here we go. Favorite kind of music."

Monica said, "Country," at the same time Calvin said, "Indie." He noticed a passing wrinkle of her nose that he was sure she saw reflected on his face, as well.

"Your turn," he said.

"Favorite season."

He said, "Winter," and she said, "Summer."

The pattern continued throughout dinner.

Mexican. Italian.

Go out clubbing. Stay in reading.

Dogs. Cats.

By the time Calvin paid the check, he could only count three things they had in common, and none of them had come up during dinner. They were both young. They were both single. And they were both lonely.

And that wasn't enough.

Calvin saw her again six months later at his next appointment.

—⊷⊶—

April 8, 2010

Dear Rev. Calvin,

The day D.B. joined the army, I gave him the little wooden angel Mort had left on my pillow years before. I prayed that the angels, which I imagined Mort etching into the steel beams in Bethlehem, would keep the naval ships safe, so I reasoned that the wooden one would do the same for D.B. I'm not sure if I was superstitious or if I just needed something ordinary like the carving to focus my prayer to God. At sixteen, I suppose I was just superstitious. But I think God counted my superstition as prayer just the same.

D.B. went through his training in the first half of 1942, then shipped off and landed in Morocco in November. The Vichy French were there, and we Americans went in to take over North Africa. I don't know how long D.B. was in Morocco, but he used to joke that he took Ingrid Bergman out to dinner at a little bar every night after combat. Oh my! You probably don't know who she is, do you, Calvin?

After North Africa, D.B. was redeployed to Europe, and he was there for the rest of the war manning the anti-aircraft guns. They were the kind of guns that pointed up in the air, so wherever he and his team parked them, they needed to dig trenches. His unit's motto was, "Dig down, fire up." You see, when they fired the gun, it would recoil down into the trench. The gun loaded from the back, so D.B. had to stand in the trench to push new rounds in. Maybe that's why he was in combat for three years and never got a scratch on him. He was below ground! But his hearing suffered. I suppose he always tilted his head the same way to shield himself from the boom of the gun, because he never heard much through his left ear after the war.

He liked to tell a story about marching through Belgium. I must have heard it a dozen times. His unit was retreating, discouraged because they could hear the sounds of combat away in the distance, but they weren't in it. They marched for miles and miles, grumbling about going in the wrong direction. The commanding officer finally called a halt at a makeshift supply depot, and D.B. spotted a massive piece of equipment that he called a tank-mover. He never explained what it was exactly, but I suppose it was big enough to move tanks around. He went over to take a look and found a fellow soldier perched atop it eating something. He clambered up the machine, introduced himself, and this fellow up and offers him a piece of fruitcake sent from his mother in Oklahoma. How about that?

That is the kind of story D.B. told about the war. I'm sure he didn't want to remember the bad parts, which, I assume, made up much of those three years. So he stuck to the fruitcake and to fictions about Ingrid Bergman. And I never pressed him to tell me what it was like to shoot an airplane from the sky. I suppose I never wanted to know because the airplanes were just special metal tubes with wings—what D.B. was really doing was killing their pilots. I know it was war, but the thought of killing is just so foreign to me. I can't imagine how D.B. did it. Or how Whit did it on the other side of the world. I bet it's easier to kill someone who is trying to kill you—not easy, mind you, but a bit easier. Still, I can't even imagine.

So I won't, and instead I'll just tell you what I was doing when D.B. was overseas. The year that D.B. and Whit joined the army, I graduated from high school. I was only sixteen, but I was a smart cookie. And I was so antsy that I kept learning ahead of the pace my teachers set. With my brother gone to Europe and my father at the steel mills in Bethlehem, I felt it was my duty to help the war effort too. I couldn't just sit home twiddling my thumbs. So I found a red bandana with white polka dots on it and started gathering my hair in it. Now you've only ever seen me with short hair, but back then I had thick, wavy strawberry blonde hair, and I had to twist it just right to get it all under that bandana. A pair of denim jeans and a blue denim shirt later, and I was the spitting image of Rosie the Riveter, except without the muscles or makeup. I even went around Jericho telling people, "We can do it!" and singing the song: "All day long, whether rain or shine, she's part of the assembly line." Folks at church started calling me Ruby the Riveter, which I took as a great compliment. I was my own little bit of government propaganda. But I believed what I was saying too.

So I begged my mother to let me go work on an assembly line somewhere. She wasn't too keen on the idea, but she knew how much she and I were alike, so she knew I wouldn't take no for an answer. We agreed I would wait until I was seventeen, which was at the end of 1942, a month after D.B. landed in Morocco. At some point during that summer, Mort was home for a weekend, and I asked him what it was like to work at the steel mill. My father was never much of a talker, and all I got out of him were two words. "Hot and loud," he said. Then I asked him if he knew where the trains took the steel. "Don't ever ask. Don't much care," he said. Now I know Mort had a soft side because of that angel on the pillow, and he showed it again when he saw how crestfallen I was at that response. So he said, "Last time I heard, the steel was heading to Quincy, Massachusetts. Navy ships, you see."

From that moment on, I planned my trek to New England. Sure there were factories and depots and shipyards closer to Jericho. But I wanted to go where Mort's steel went. I wanted to see if I could find a beam with a little etched angel on it, if one even existed outside my imagination.

The one thing I forgot in all my planning was that I would be traveling in December. And New England is cold and snowy in December. But I was too excited to wait until spring. Anyhow, would Rosie have let a little snow get in her way? No sir. She was "making history, working for victory," as the song goes. I wanted to work for victory too. Funny how I've been living in Victory for so long now.

I took the train to Philadelphia, then switched to one bound for Boston. I had scoured Jericho for a map of Massachusetts, but couldn't find one, so I figured I'd just go to Boston and then ask for directions to Quincy. Turns out I could walk all the way there from the train station. It was a long walk, but doable in an afternoon. The swirling snow just meant I was making even more history. "Ruby the Riveter trudged ten miles through thick snow drifts to make it to the factory to help America win the war! We can do it!"

I know this sounds a bit silly, but I was young and enthusiastic. Now I'm old, but you can take it to the bank that I'm still enthusiastic. It's just that the years have a way of taking the energy out of my enthusiasm. The years, experience, grief. Melancholy has tempered my enthusiasm, but it's still there, underneath it all. Little Natalie Stewart brings it out of me. So do Avis and Mary and E.R.

Avis came to the basement choir room with me this morning after prayer. I played that beautiful grand piano, and we sang together—"The Church in the Wildwood," "In the Garden," "Mourning to Dancing," and others. Avis has a pretty voice: untrained and unsure, but when she's singing a song she knows, the sound is just lovely. "In the Garden" is Avis's favorite song, and she sings it well. I love the line, "And he tells me I am his own." I can't tell you how much comfort that brings me, and when I hear Avis singing it, it's like God is singing through her to me. And I hear the truth in those words all the more clearly. She is a gift to me right now.

I trust that you have been recovering from all your Holy Week and Easter services. Don't forget to take some time for yourself. It should be just about swan boat season. Go to the Public Garden and see!

And remember that you are God's own.

Love,

Ruby

P.S. The elevator still works just fine, you old worrywart.

6

We had nothing in common. I mean *nothing*."

"Oh, the impatience of youth. My, my, my. You just didn't dig deep enough. All that surface-level stuff . . . "

"Matters." Calvin interrupted Josie Temple-Jones. "We have opposite interests. We didn't agree on anything. We had no connection."

Josie had pestered Calvin for three Sundays following his date with Monica Dennis, and he had managed to evade the interrogations. But the next Monday she had camped out—not literally, but knowing her, Calvin wouldn't have put it past her—on the steps outside the church office and ambushed him. At least she had brought him a cup of coffee.

"You might have a connection if you had kissed her. Then you would have had aligning interests and very much agreement."

"I don't think that's true. I do know what I'm doing here." That was a lie. He had no idea what he was doing where dating was concerned. But Calvin was tired of people second guessing him and deciding that he lacked the experience to make important decisions. The last three weeks had not been his favorite ones since he started working at St. John's.

"All I'm saying is that every relationship starts somewhere," said Josie.

"Look, I appreciate everything you did for me in setting us up. But our relationship started and ended that night. I know it. Monica knows it." Exhaustion crept into Calvin's voice. "There were no fireworks. We didn't even have sparklers." But wishing not to offend Josie's matchmaking prowess, he cast around for something good to say about the date. "I guess I had a nice time, but there was nothing there."

"Oh, honey, what I wouldn't give to have a 'nice' time on a date."

Josie always hovered at the extremes of emotions, ready to laugh or cry at the drop of a hat. But Calvin could tell these words came from a deeper place, one that she hid behind her normal bravado. And for the first time, Calvin saw her for who she really was: another lonely soul seeking connection. Josie had run off by herself to Europe for six months. What was she doing there if not escaping the brutal loneliness of Victory; if not chasing adventure; if not having a fling with a gondolier in Venice or a sommelier in the south of France? Whenever she mentioned her late husband, she kissed the rock on her left hand. Calvin had thought it mere affectation, but now he reassessed and saw it as a desire to be kissing her husband, or at least someone who loved her like he had.

"It's hard dating as a priest," said Calvin. "I imagine it's harder dating at . . . " He trailed off, realizing that he was about to say . . .

"At my age?" Josie finished his sentence.

Calvin put up his hands defensively, but Josie shook her head. "You're right, of course," she said, "though I don't like to think about it. I've pretty much stopped dating now. There's really no point. The men in my dating pool—let's just say there's a reason they are single."

"Oh, really?" Calvin took the chance to turn the conversation. "So considering I'll probably still be single then, what do I have to look forward to in twenty years?"

He shot low on purpose. Josie arched her eyebrows and pointed up.

"Thirty years?"

She pointed up again.

"Forty years?"

She smiled a small smile, the kind you give yourself in the mirror when you tell yourself a secret that half of you was hiding from the other half.

"Josie, you are not in your sixties."

"Guilty," she said.

"I don't believe it."

"I'll be sixty-one in February. Just don't tell anyone. I've been thirty-nine for such a long time. Wouldn't want to give that up, now would I?" A hint of her bravado leavened her voice. "All right, so what do you have to look forward to in forty years? Or should I say, here's a list of things to avoid when you take ladies like *moi* out on dates when you're in your sixties."

And for the next half hour, Josie told Calvin horror stories of the dates she had been on since her late husband ("God rest his soul") passed away. Calvin was so engrossed that he missed Morning Prayer entirely. When Josie finished her tale, she gave Calvin a hug—a tender one, not like her normal gale force ones—and thanked him for listening.

It was the first time he felt like he had done something right since the Church Warming Party. The last three weeks had been rough. It had started at November's vestry meeting, the monthly gathering of the lay leadership of the parish.

⸺◦◦◦⸺

"Didn't they teach you in seminary that a new priest should never 'move the furniture' for at least a year after he comes to a church?" Chief Stern sat in one of the chairs in Calvin's office a half hour before the vestry meeting. He was still wearing his uniform. Every crease was perfect, every inch of his shoes shined to high gloss. Calvin's eyes traveled to the Chief's torso where his hat sat in his lap, and Calvin noticed he had left his sidearm elsewhere. Best thing for a vestry meeting.

"No, they didn't," Calvin said. "I pretty much learned how to read the Bible, preach a sermon, and not spill the wine when celebrating communion."

Calvin had just told the Chief his plan to move the piano from the basement choir room to the church proper. As Ruby predicted, the Chief had not taken to the idea with the kind of enthusiasm Calvin was hoping for.

"And when people say that a new priest shouldn't 'move the furniture' they really mean the priest shouldn't change things in general," the Chief said. "But you're talking about actually moving furniture, which gave its name to the whole can of worms in the first place."

"Wait a second. How do you know that this 'move the furniture' thing is a real deal? Maybe its one of those things that people have repeated for so long that they only think it's true—like lighting never striking twice in the same place."

"No. People have repeated this one for so long that it has become true."

"But it's a good idea."

"You're right. It is." The Chief leaned forward in his chair and pushed the tips of his fingers together. "But Calvin, when they are timed wrong, good ideas look an awful lot like bad ones."

"Okay, okay. I just want to take the vestry's temperature tonight. Nothing threatening."

The Chief sat back and scribbled something on his meeting agenda. "All right. But don't say I didn't warn you."

The vestry members began trickling by the office. Calvin and Chief Stern made their way to the parish hall, turned on the coffee machine, and moved four tables into a square.

"Hey, Chief, look what we're doing," said Calvin as they hefted the last table into place.

"Very funny," said the Chief.

It was the priest's prerogative to run the vestry meetings, but Calvin had asked Chief Stern, in his capacity as senior warden, to chair them since Calvin had arrived. With four meetings under his belt, however, Calvin decided he was ready, and he took the reins for this one. He looked around the table as they approved the minutes from the previous meeting. Eight of the nine vestry members had shown up, plus the two wardens and Calvin. The group dispensed with a few mundane issues, passed a resolution commending Ruby and the other ladies for their effort with the Church Warming, and looked over the budget for the last two months of the year. An hour and a half in, the meeting was officially boring, a good thing as far as vestry meetings went. Interesting vestry meetings almost always equaled contentious vestry meetings.

This meeting got interesting.

Calvin filed the budget papers back in his binder, thanked Emily Lincoln, who was the treasurer, for her report, and took a deep breath. Then he launched into his plan to remove four pews from the nave and move the piano from the basement into the vacated space.

When he was finished, the only sound in the room was the gurgling of the third pot of coffee.

Then Carl Sinclair (of course, he's on the vestry, thought Calvin) did something Calvin never expected. Carl Sinclair, the mayor of Victory, laughed. Then the men flanking him— Harold and one of the Phils (of course, he's got two of his cronies, I mean golfing buddies, on the vestry too, thought Calvin)—laughed as well.

Calvin looked around the room. A few others were smiling, but only with their mouths, not their eyes. Emily Lincoln bit her lower lip. Chief Stern frowned.

"I'm glad to see our young priest has a sense of humor. I haven't heard much of it from the pulpit yet," said Carl. "But come now, Calvin, is the vestry really a place to try out new material?"

"I'm being serious, Carl," said Calvin, and he was gratified to see a shadow cross the mayor's face when he called him by his first name.

"Oh, my boy, I know you are," said Carl, and with lightning speed he shifted into the voice Calvin had heard in the debate televised on local access. Here was Uncle Carl. "But I think it's easier if we just pretend you were pulling our collective leg and move on with the meeting."

"Come on, Carl, that's not fair," said Chief Stern.

"Harry, you know this is a nonstarter just as well as I do. I'm just trying not to waste our time." Carl's tone was friendly, as if he were telling Harry that his patrol car's taillight was out.

By comparison, Calvin sounded like a child with a skinned knee. "It's not like we need those pews in the first place."

And then Uncle Carl pounced—the friendliest mountain lion who ever ripped your guts out. "So now you're saying that this church has no hope of growth? That those pews are extraneous because we will never fill them? And to think the bishop sent you here for exactly that."

"You're out of line, Carl," said the Chief.

"I'm out of line, Harry? Do you hear what this pup is saying?"

Calvin took a hurried breath and was about to respond when the Chief's hand caught his knee, and Calvin noticed a nearly imperceptible shake of his head.

"Each pew in our church has a little, bronze plaque attached to the side of it," Carl went on, his friendly tone becoming more and more acidic. "Each plaque has the name of a family on it. Each family donated their pew over two hundred years ago. Two hundred years is a long time. Though maybe infants don't care much for history or tradition."

Calvin looked around the room for some defense. Harold and Phil were nodding sagely as Carl spoke. Two others had excused themselves for convenient restroom breaks. No one met Calvin's eyes except for the Chief, who gave him an "I told you this would happen" look.

"So if we are all agreed, we can table this proposal for another time," concluded Carl and he made a gaveling motion. "Good," he said before anyone could speak up.

Tears were brimming in Calvin's eyes, but he refused to let them fall. He thought he had been prepared for some resistance, but this was totally out of proportion to what he expected.

"Well, if there's no other business, I think we can adjourn this meeting. Good work everyone," said Carl with a second gaveling motion. He stood. Harold and Phil stood, as well. The others looked confused, but started to rise anyway.

"Sit down," said Chief Stern. "All of you." No one moved. Then he used his cop voice. "Sit down." Everyone but Carl Sinclair sat down.

"It's Calvin's meeting to adjourn," said the Chief. He looked at Calvin. "It's your meeting."

Calvin looked back at the Chief. "No, it's not," he said, and he got up and walked out of the parish hall. The tears didn't start falling until his back was turned, which was a small blessing.

As he passed through the double doors into the hallway, he heard Carl Sinclair call after him, "You're right. It's not."

Calvin walked into the church and sat down in the first pew. He was too many closed doors away to hear more than the muffled sounds of the tongue-lashing the police chief gave to the mayor after he left. But he didn't much care whether or not Harry Stern came to his defense. He hadn't come to his own. How many different ways had Carl Sinclair called him young and inexperienced? Young priest. My boy. Pup. Infant. Calvin put his head in his hands.

Ten minutes later, the lights came on in the nave and someone sat down next to him. "I'm sorry, Calvin," said Emily Lincoln as she put her hand on his back. "I should have spoken up. But that Carl Sinclair can be so oily that you don't realize he's manipulating you until it's too late. My mother-in-law has the measure of him all right."

They sat in silence for a few minutes. Thoughts roiled and raged across Calvin's mind, and then one crystallized and he voiced it to Emily: "I thought people were supposed to be nice at church."

"Oh, hon," she said, and her tone was so maternal, so full of clean sheets and chicken noodle soup, that Calvin started to cry again. "People are supposed to be nice period. At home, at work, at church. But they aren't always, especially when they feel threatened."

"I don't see what's so threatening about moving a piano."

"Well, let's see. People come to church for stability. Therefore, they don't want things to change as a general principle."

"But this would be a good change. That piano is beautiful, and it's rotting—literally rotting—in the basement."

"Doesn't matter. Change is change. But it's more than that. Carl Sinclair likes to be in charge, and you saw tonight what he's like when he's threatened."

"But he's not in charge. Chief Stern is the senior warden. I'm the priest."

"If only it were that simple. Next time, try to gain some support before you bring up the idea. Convince a few people. Give them time to digest your plans. Don't just spring it on them."

"I wish it weren't so political."

"Me too." Emily rose to leave. "Keep your chin up, Calvin. T.J. and I think you are doing a great job. So does Esther Rose, though she'll never say it out loud."

"Thanks, Emily."

"Oh my," She said as she noticed something and tapped the side of the pew. "One more thing, Calvin."

He knelt down and stared at the plaque affixed to the pew, one of the four he had hoped to remove from the church.

"Sinclair," it read.

The morning after his impromptu conversation with Josie Temple-Jones, Calvin sat in a pew in the side chapel. The prayer book was open on his lap, but he hadn't turned the page since Mary Williams started reading Morning Prayer. He mumbled the responses that had been ingrained in him since seminary, but his mind and heart were elsewhere. The ladies moved through the Apostles' Creed and the Lord's Prayer. Then Mary gave way to Ruby, who led the collects and prayers. She read three of the staples: a collect for the renewal of life, one for guidance, and one for mission. The third one had always stirred Calvin's heart, ever since he first heard it during college.

"Lord Jesus Christ, you stretched your arms of love on the hard wood of the cross that everyone might come within the reach of your saving embrace," Ruby prayed, but Calvin was only half paying attention now and the words failed to move him. Or perhaps, he was so bent on remaining in his self-pitying mood that he would not allow the words to move him. Ruby finished, "So clothe us in your Spirit that we, reaching forth our hands in love, may bring those who do not know you to the knowledge and love of you; for the honor of your name."

The other three ladies said, "Amen."

"And now," Ruby said, "a collect for Reverend Calvin."

Calvin looked up and met her eye. It was the first time in weeks that he really connected with any of them. Ever since the vestry meeting, he had felt unworthy to meet anyone's eye, let alone be their priest. His sermons the last three Sundays had been dry and academic, uninspired and uninspiring. He had stared fixedly at people's hands as he gave them the bread of communion, and his iterations of "The Body of Christ, the bread of heaven" had been all but inaudible.

"Dear Heavenly Father," prayed Ruby, and Calvin noticed she was reading from a creased sheet of notebook paper. "In your wonderful wisdom, you called Calvin Harper to be a priest in your church. Grant him the faith he needs to remember that you are with him in his successes and failures, grant him the courage he needs to accept help from others, and grant him the grace he needs to rediscover that you love him no matter what . . . "

Ruby paused, and Calvin could tell she had reached the end of the handwritten prayer. His eyes were swimming, and he nodded his head in grateful thanks. But Ruby wasn't quite done, for she smiled at him and ad-libbed, "And grant him the swift kick in the pants he needs to get up off the mat and stop feeling sorry for himself. In Jesus Christ's holy name we pray."

The other three ladies final "Amen" came with gusto.

Calvin surprised himself with a watery laugh that was incongruous with the tears streaming down his face.

"Buck up, sonny," said Mary. "It doesn't do to see a man blubbering like that."

He laughed again and wiped his eyes on his sleeve.

"It was just one meeting," said Avis. "No need to make it life or death."

"Oh good, are we finally allowed to talk about it?" Esther Rose said in the voice she thought was under her breath but wasn't. Then she addressed Calvin directly: "Didn't I warn you about Carl Sinclair?"

"You did," Calvin said, "I just didn't get the message."

And at that moment, Calvin's mobile phone dinged. His eyes went wide as he expected Esther Rose to berate him for having an active phone during a church service. He whipped it out of his pocket, read the text message, and interrupted Esther Rose as she let loose with both barrels.

"How could you possibly—" she began, but Calvin said her name with such force that she stopped midsentence.

"Esther Rose, get in my car."

He started for the door. Esther Rose stayed rooted to her spot.

"Let's go," he said. "That was from Brad. The baby was just born."

The coo of rejoicing that the other three ladies unleashed was almost comical. Esther Rose did not join in. Calvin had catalogued several of her expressions by now, and the one she currently wore said she had just experienced an unforgivable personal slight.

"Why didn't my *dear* grandson-in-law call to tell me before you," she said, and the other three ladies ceased their cooing.

ADAM THOMAS

Ruby turned to Esther Rose, patted her on the shoulder, and said, "Because you don't have a cellular phone, dear. Now, go meet your great-granddaughter."

And on the word "granddaughter," the cooing recommenced. Calvin waved Esther Rose to him. She came, and a new expression replaced the previous one: the unforgivable personal slight was forgiven on account of impending great-granddaughter.

Two hours later, Calvin was holding Natalie Stewart in his arms. She had a bright red mark on her forehead and impossibly small fingers.

And when he felt her newborn warmth and the pounding of her strong newborn heart, the last three weeks vanished.

—

April 12, 2010

Dear Rev. Calvin,

I think spring is here to stay in Victory. We haven't had a cold day in over a week, and the trees know it. Everywhere you go in town, the buds are greening every branch. It's that special green of early spring—leaves comes later, and they are darker, their green bolder. But the buds seem almost afraid to be green. They are timid, like baby birds that are getting up the courage to leave the nest for the first time.

Speaking of leaving the nest, I left mine on my seventeenth birthday, and I probably should have been a little more timid than I was. In my case, I didn't know any better. I had lived in Jericho my whole life, and I expected people in other places to be like the folks from my church—like folks whom you might invite to dinner on a whim. The fellow sweeping up at the train station in Boston gave me no cause to doubt my assumptions because he was as friendly as can be. He pointed me south to Quincy and even doffed his cap when I thanked him, which made me feel like a lady.

I didn't arrive at the shipyard until late in the evening, but the clangs of production were as loud as ever. It seemed there was no quitting time with the war on. A gatehouse and a swinging gate—like a tollbooth, really, but with a much heavier pole—guarded the road, and two men in uniform guarded the gatehouse. As I was walking up to them, a jeep passed me, and they levered the barrier up into the air, letting the jeep through into the shipyard. But they lowered it again when they saw me.

"Hold up right there, missy, just what do you think you're doing?" one of them said. He was the first person ever to call me "missy" and I didn't like it one bit. Maybe that's why I remember this conversation so well—it was one of those "learning the ways of the world" moments that stick with you. I've always been a bit bolder than I really need to be, so I walked right up to the guard and told him I wanted a job building the Navy boats.

"First things first," he said. "We don't build boats here, missy. We build ships. Second, we build ships, you don't."

He was so rude for no reason. He was the kind of man who makes a woman feel like less of a person so he could feel more like one, a real bully. So I said something that under the circumstances I probably should not have said, considering he was bad-tempered, cold, most likely hungry, and had a rifle slung over his shoulder. I looked him straight in the eye and said, "Sure looks like you're guarding a gate-house, not building a ship."

The guard's face turned bright red, and he looked like he was gathering in all the swear words he knew in order to spew them at me all at once. So the other guard said (not quite as rudely), "I think you better leave, miss." And he grabbed the first guard and pulled him back to the gatehouse.

I stood there in the snow. I could see and hear my destination, but I couldn't get there. So I turned around and walked away. It was at that moment that I realized I didn't have a place to stay. Tears blinded my vision as I turned onto the main road, so I nearly bowled over a gaggle of women who had stepped onto the road from a different entrance to the shipyard. They took one look at me and somehow knew exactly what had happened at the gatehouse. I learned later that I wasn't the only one turned away by the rude guards. One of the women put an arm around me and told me everything was going to be all right. The only name I can remember from that group of women is Martha so I sup-pose it was she who first showed me kindness.

Martha brought me back to their bunkhouse and made a little nest out of odd clothes and towels for me to sleep on. She told me to try again tomorrow during daylight—right after breakfast, preferably—when a different pair of guards was going to be on duty. So that's what I did.

The next day, I followed Martha and her friends back to the shipyard. It turns out that I had approached the vehicle entrance rather than the personnel one. It also turns out the military, not to mention the shipyard, had rules! Pedestrian traffic had to enter through the personnel entrance, no exceptions. The guard from the first night could have told me that, but I guess I didn't give him much of a reason to.

Martha and the rest of the women crowded past the guards at the personnel entrance, all flashing ID badges at them. But when it was my turn, I had no badge to show. At least the guards at this entrance were not as rude as the ones from the night before. They told me the proper procedure for gaining access before I officially worked there, but for the life of me I can't remember it because I never went through the process. As I was turning to leave, a fellow in a smart Navy uniform appeared at the gatehouse and said, "Don't worry, fellas. She has an appointment with me. Let her through."

The guards looked a bit dumbfounded, but they said, "Yes, Lieutenant," and let me pass. As I walked over the threshold into the shipyard, I got a good look at the officer, and I don't think I had ever seen someone so beautiful. He looked like someone who played a sailor in the pictures, not in real life. He had dark eyes and shiny black hair and his uniform adorned what must surely have been a perfect physique. He smiled when he saw me, and I all but fell over. No one in Jericho had teeth like his.

"So you're new here?" he asked. His voice was strong and carried no trace of the rudeness of the guards.

I opened my mouth to say yes, but all I could manage was a small squeak and a nod.

"Let's take you to personnel then." He walked up to me and took me by the arm. I fell in love with him the moment he opened his mouth to speak. And do you know what? He fell in love with me too. His name was Mike Lawrence, and I knew from the moment we touched that we would spend the rest of our lives together.

It's funny what you think you know when you're seventeen, right?

Wishing you all good things,

Ruby

7

King Herod would be the perfect role for him," said Calvin. "You know, deception, slaughter of the infants, causing Mary and Joseph to flee."

"Calvin, I know how you feel about Carl, but you might want to keep those feelings to yourself a little more often."

"Yeah, it does you no good to be in open hostility with him."

Emily Lincoln and Chief Stern were sitting on the old couch in Calvin's office. Calvin had wheeled his desk chair over and joined them around the coffee table that was groaning under the weight of sermon research materials. Christmas was two and a half weeks away, and Calvin needed his Christmas Eve sermon to be memorable. He wasn't sure where the need came from. Was it his desire to please the folks who had been disappointed with his performance before Thanksgiving? Was it to stick it to the folks who ran him out of the vestry meeting? Was it to try to snag people who only come to church on Christmas and Easter? Or was it for the greater glory of God? If he answered himself honestly, it would not have been the latter.

But Calvin had put his sermon research on hold for the meeting with Emily and the Chief. He had asked them to come in and discuss a brainchild that had hit him while he was cooking dinner the night before. Well, Calvin didn't really cook. He simply made food hot, or in the case of last night's pasta, hot and flexible. He was stirring the spaghetti around the pot when it formed a circle under the bubbling water that was reminiscent of a halo. Like the angel Gabriel's . . .

"Wait a moment," said Chief Stern. "Let me back up and make sure I understand. You want to have a Christmas pageant at St. Jack's even though we have next to no children in the parish. You want to have a pageant with all adults?"

"Well," said Calvin, turning to Emily, "I thought your granddaughter could play baby Jesus."

"And Brad and Rebecca could play Mary and Joseph," said Emily. "I love it."

"Hang on," said the Chief. "I'm still stuck at a Christmas pageant with all adults."

"I know it's a bit strange," said Calvin. "But I think we have some folks in the parish who would enjoy it. Esther Rose told me that when St. John's had more children, there was always a Christmas pageant on the Fourth Sunday of Advent. So why not have one and invite adults to dress the parts?"

"I don't know. When kids do it, it's cute. I think adults dressing up might look a little . . . " The Chief trailed off, unable to find an appropriate adjective.

"Come on, Harry," Emily said. "You'd make a great wise man."

"We just need to find folks who would get into the spirit of it," Calvin said. "We don't even have to call it a pageant. We can call it a living Nativity or something. That sounds more grown up, right?"

"A wise man, huh?" A smile fought for purchase on Chief Stern's granite face. "Would I get gold, frankincense, or myrrh?"

"Your choice," Emily said.

"I guess I'll take gold, then."

The Fourth Sunday of Advent came with a hard-edged chill that pounded Calvin in the center of his forehead and made him feel like he had just eaten a bowl of ice cream too fast. It was the shortest and coldest day of the year, so Calvin arrived at the church in the dark and sent up a quick prayer about functional boilers and heating ducts. The early service came and went. Only a handful of diehards braved the predawn chill, including all four golfers. But Carl, Harold, Phil, and Phil left after receiving communion rather than staying for the closing prayer, blessing, and dismissal, which were all of four minutes put together. They can't possibly be going to the golf course this morning, thought Calvin. More than likely, they just don't want to shake my hand.

Calvin pushed the thought out of his mind and turned his attention to the second service, at which the adult Christmas pageant was to take place. Calvin had reverted to calling the event a Christmas pageant despite Chief Stern's reservations because whenever he approached people to participate in the living Nativity, they asked what that was. And he explained that it was a Christmas pageant for adults. Some gracefully declined, citing family obligations or the inability to stand for long periods. Others gracefully accepted, and their excitement was palpable. Sometimes grown-ups need to be kids again, Emily had reasoned, and here was a perfect opportunity. She had even convinced her husband to be the second wise man.

T.J. Lincoln arrived at the church wearing a great overcoat, but when he shrugged it off, he was resplendent in golden fabric draped tunic-style over baggy silver pants. He had even procured a crown from the local Burger King.

"Thanks for going all in, T.J.," said Calvin as they shook hands.

123

"This is going to be fun," he said. "And anyone who says otherwise has no idea what Christmas is about."

Just then, a shivering Chief Stern stepped through the big front doors. He took one look at T.J. and let out a bark of laughter. "Your wife is a trip," he said as he hung up his coat and turned around. He was wearing silver over baggy golden pants.

"I wondered why Emily made two costumes."

"Three, actually," said Emily. She walked into the narthex with Ruby and Whit following her. Whit was decked in purple from head to toe.

"Now I don't feel quite as silly," he said when he saw T.J. and Harry, looking as if they had just stepped out of a 1980's music video in their gold and silver.

"We're kings," said the Chief. "We can be silly if we want to be." And with that, he slipped his police officer's hat on his head to complete his ensemble.

As the pageant began, Calvin looked out at the faces in the congregation. The nave seemed a bit fuller than normal to his eye, which over the months had been gaining accuracy in estimating the number of folks in the pews. Perhaps word had spread about the adult Christmas pageant. Some faces wore expectant smiles; others confused, furrowed brows. Still others just looked nonplussed, as if they had wandered into the wrong theater but decided to stay for the film anyway. But Calvin had a secret weapon, and as Emily Lincoln came to the lectern to begin her role as narrator, Calvin stole another glance at the congregation.

He need not have looked because there was an audible gasp as Josie Temple-Jones appeared from behind the altar. She, of course, had made her own costume. Her wings were fletched with real feathers and somehow she had made her halo look like it was floating above her head. Swirls of rhinestones encrusted her white robe, making it glow in the light of the altar candles. But her hair was surely what made the congregation gasp. She had straightened all those tight blonde curls, making the tips of her hair touch the small of her back. Who knew her hair was so long? The strands surrounded her like a cloak, and woven through them were flower petals, shining beads, and more feathers. Calvin could almost hear members of the congregation wondering if she were the real angel Gabriel.

Of course, when she spoke, the angel was obviously Josie Temple-Jones, master of disguise, but the spell that her costume wove held. Calvin noticed folks sit forward in their pews with excitement replacing indifference. A pageant full of kids playing little sheep and angels was cute and made for warm, fuzzy feelings, and that was all good. But there was something wonderful and majestic about seeing Josie's vision of what an angel looks like. It brought people into the mystery of God in a way that an antsy third grader could not do. Calvin allowed a bubble of hope to rise in his chest. *Perhaps, this wasn't as crazy an idea as I originally thought,* he told himself.

A few minutes later, the warm, fuzzy feelings came anyway thanks to Natalie Stewart, whose cameo as the baby Jesus, held in the arms of her own mother mild, induced a murmuring coo from all the mothers and grandmothers in the church. At one point, the month-old infant reached up out of the manger with those impossibly small fingers, and Rebecca caught her hand and kissed it. Brad stood over them, a natural Joseph, and Calvin could see on his face a look of awe at the little life that God had created out of his and Rebecca's love.

Then came the comic relief. The ripple of laughter began at the back of the church when the folks in the last pew noticed the Burger King crown and police officer's hat on the heads of two of the magi. The third, wearing all purple, had a plush camel under one arm and what looked like a hookah under the other. T.J., Whit, and the Chief made their way to the front in solemn procession, but when they spoke, the ripple of laughter expanded into a crashing wave. They had decided without telling anyone that they would rewrite the script and cast themselves not as "wise men," but as "wise guys."

"So, uh, where's this baby Jesus, for we gotta worship the kid," said T.J., doing a passable Robert deNiro. "I've got some frankincense here. Badda-bing."

"I'll make him an offer he can't refuse," said Chief Stern in his best Vito Corleone. "I'll give him all this gold and then worship him, and he can just keep on sleeping in that there manger."

They turned to Whit, who lost his composure in a fit of chortles, so T.J. took the hookah from him and handed it to Brad. "Leave the myrrh, take the cannoli," he ad-libbed.

And so the pageant began with the mystery evoked by Josie's Gabriel and ended with the comedy of the magi. Calvin was satisfied because it all seemed an appropriate retelling of the story, which really was one part mystery and one part comedy. As the participants returned to their seats, Calvin stood and said to the congregation, "I want to thank everyone who helped out with the pageant. What a splendid way to prepare for the coming of Christ. And thanks to our magi for reminding us about the humor in the situation. God did the unexpected when he sent Jesus as a baby. People were expecting a strapping warrior messiah, but they got a helpless infant, who needed his parents' love and protection. As we come closer to Christmas, I hope we all remember that in the meekness of the baby, God gave Mary and Joseph the opportunity to love and serve Jesus in a unique way, as parents. And because God gives us each different sets of gifts and talents, God also gives us the opportunity to serve Jesus in our own, unique ways."

As he finished his impromptu soliloquy, an idea popped into Calvin's head. He stepped to the first pew and whispered to Rebecca, "Let me see that baby." And, after a small moment of fear over holding the precious soul passed, his eyes lit up as he held Natalie to his chest.

He walked back up the steps, turned around, and waved Natalie's hand at the congregation. "And now may the peace of the Lord be always with you," he said.

"And also with you," came the response from the congregation. Calvin gave Natalie one of his fingers. She grabbed it, and he shook her little hand before returning her to her mother. "Thanks," he said.

"Any time," Rebecca said.

After the service, the cast of the Christmas pageant went out for a celebratory lunch at Year of the Dragon. Since T.J. and Chief Stern had worn their costumes to church, they had no choice but to remain in their finery. Whit's costume had been toga-like, so he had everyday clothes on underneath and now traveled incognito.

"Why you so shiny?" said Mrs. Chan, who owned the restaurant.

The rest of the table rang with laughter when T.J. and Harry looked each other up and down, as if they hadn't noticed the other dressed in such brilliant colors. "We are two of the three kings of Orient Are," said T.J., but Mrs. Chan had already started walking away to restock the buffet. T.J. looked at Whit and continued, "Although one of our number has abandoned his royal robes."

"It's not Orient Are, T.J.," Whit said. "They're just from the Orient, and they *are* bearing gifts and traversing afar."

"They aren't from Orient Are?"

"Nope."

"I've been singing that song for over fifty years. How did I not know that?" T.J. looked at his wife.

"I thought it was so cute I never corrected you," Emily said.

Rebecca had been tending to Natalie and just now caught the drift of the conversation. "Wait, they aren't from Orient Are?"

"Nope," chorused the table.

"They aren't necessarily kings, either," Calvin said. "Nor were there necessarily three of them."

T.J. picked up his napkin and tossed it on the table like a referee tossing a flag in a football game. "Hold it. Penalty! Are you telling me the song is just wrong?"

"Not wrong," said Calvin. "Just one interpretation of the text from Matthew's Gospel."

"I get it," said Brad. "There were three gifts, so someone decided there were three gift givers."

"You got it," said Calvin.

Mrs. Chan came back to take their order. No one disparaged Calvin's choice of sweet and sour chicken. The slight sniff from Mrs. Chan might have been a coincidence.

As they waited for their food, the conversation circled back to the success of the pageant. Everyone complimented Josie on her costume, and Josie was a picture of restrained modesty, deflecting each comment with a demure smile. But Calvin could tell she was eating it up. He watched her drink in the praise, and he realized recognition was the thing that made Josie tick. Her flamboyance was a means to an end. She just never wanted to be invisible. Calvin then looked at Ruby, who was doing the lion's share of the congratulating. Ruby would be content if someone benefited from something she had done, even if that person never knew of her involvement. She was one of God's secret agents. Calvin wondered if Ruby and Josie might be able to teach each other a thing or two. Josie could learn to let her self-worth lean less heavily on other people's approbation. And Ruby could learn to take a little more credit, if only so others could see how God was moving in her life. But, Calvin realized, they had known each other for years. If something were going to rub off, it probably would have done so by now.

Always famished after a morning at church, Calvin wolfed down his greasy Chinese food, sat back, and looked around the table at the people he was called to serve. Called to serve, he repeated in his mind. Called to serve. When the bishop sent him to Victory six months before, Calvin had gone out of a sense of duty, out of obligation to fulfill the vows he had made at his ordination. Not out of a sense of call from God to a ghost town not exactly in the middle of nowhere, but close by. What had changed? He still didn't feel particularly called to Victory. But he did feel called to these people, these few around the table and others at St. Jacks-across-the-tracks. They had made his heart glow that morning at the pageant: Josie, whose costume was so beautifully made it could have been a real angel's clothing; the Stewarts, whose exhausted, strung out, and beautiful new parental love had brought Mary and Joseph alive; the wise guys, who had the guts to quote *The Godfather* in church; and of course, Ruby, who sat in the background, always encouraging, always nudging. Calvin didn't know how long he could stay in a place that isolated him from most every opportunity for personal connection outside of church, but as long as he had these people, he could stick it out for a time.

The prospect of going home to that big, barren townhouse after lunch threatened to sour his thoughts, but they were cut short when Chief Stern spoke up.

"Here's to a wonderful morning." He raised his glass and everyone followed suit. "Cheers."

"Cheers," echoed the rest of the table as they clinked glasses.

"How about some lines from Doctor Walter Redding on this auspicious occasion," the Chief said once the toast was done.

"Oh, I think I could dredge up a few appropriate stanzas," said Whit. "Give me a moment."

Calvin leaned over to the Chief and whispered, "You did this at the picnic in the summer too. Who's he quoting?"

"Think of his name and take a guess," said Chief Stern.

Calvin thought for a moment. "Walt Whitman?"

"Bingo."

"Yes, here we go," said Whit, and he cleared his throat as only a seasoned professor could do—a combination of preparing to speak and gathering the attention of the group.

> Ah from a little child,
> Thou knowest soul how to me all sounds became music,
> My mother's voice in lullaby or hymn,
> (The voice, O tender voices, memory's loving voices,
> Last miracle of all, O dearest mother's, sister's, voices;)
> The rain, the growing corn, the breeze among the long-
>   leav'd corn,
> The measur'd sea-surf beating on the sand,
> The twittering bird, the hawk's sharp scream,
> The wild-fowl's notes at night as flying low migrating
>   north or south,
> The psalm in the country church or mid the clustering
>   trees, the open air camp-meeting,
> The fiddler in the tavern, the glee, the long-strung
>   sailor-song,
> The lowing cattle, bleating sheep, the crowing cock at
>   dawn.

"You write that, Mr. Whit?" asked Mrs. Chan once Whit had finished. Ruby later told Calvin that years ago, Mrs. Chan had thought Whit was his last name, and no matter his attempts to correct her, the name was set in stone in her venerable mind.

"No, Mrs. Chan, that was part of a poem called 'Proud Music of the Storm' by . . . "

"Too slow, Whit," said T J., who jerked his finger back behind himself. Mrs. Chan had wandered off after asking the question to refill the buffet once again. And once again, the table lapsed into peals of laughter. Whit grinned, and for the first time Calvin noticed a small, dark spot high up on his left cheek where his smile ended.

———

April 22, 2010

Dear Rev. Calvin,

I just returned from a lovely week staying with Margaret and Cooper. I know they only live a few towns away, but it still felt like a vacation! Cooper is graduating in a few months, and then it's off to college with him. But he's not going far. In fact, he'll still be living at home, since the community college is in their town. He plans to start there and then transfer after two years to a school with a journalism program. You'll have to indulge a bit of grandmotherly bragging— it's my right, after all. I've enclosed in this letter his latest article in the school paper. It's just a small thing about the start of baseball season, but I think he has a fine style.

Speaking of Cooper, remember those boxes he pulled from the attic for me? They have been gathering dust under the dining room table for a month now. Well, when I got home yesterday afternoon, I called Avis, and she came over and helped me go through one. That was all I had the energy for. But we found some wonderful old things, including my red and white polka dotted bandana. I had no idea I still owned it. It was tied in a pouch containing a few small things that I'm sure I treasured way back when. Most of them have no meaning to me now, but one does: the little carved angel that Mort gave to me when I was a kid. I let D.B. borrow it during the war, and he must have given it back when he came home. I put the angel on my nightstand next to a picture of Whit and me from our wedding. Oh, our wedding—I'll have to tell you about that, but some other time, because if memory serves, the last thing I told you about was meeting Mike Lawrence.

Until I wrote that letter to you last week, I hadn't thought of Mike in years. I'm sure there's a picture of him in one of these boxes. If I find it, I'll make a copy and send it along. I do remember he was gorgeous, and that's not a term I would normally use for a man, but in his case it was true. The Navy must have used him as the model when they designed their uniform because it fit him to perfection. And I don't mean "fit" in the sense of the right size trousers. I mean that the uniform could have been his skin. Some people are just meant to be soldiers or sailors or marines. Mike was one of them.

We dated for six months before he was shipped off to the Pacific. During those six months and for another year after, I worked at the shipyard doing various jobs. The work was either tedious or backbreaking, and nothing like my vision of Ruby the Riveter piecing together a battleship with her bare hands. Mort's description of working at the steel mill held for the shipyard, except in the winter it was cold, rather than hot, and it was always loud. I'm not saying that I hated my time working on the ships, but the dream and the reality were far apart. However, I think most things in life are like that. The dream spurs you to action, to leap into the reality. Once you're there, you can hold onto the dream and be miserable in the reality, or you can embrace the reality and every once in a while stumble onto little pockets of the dream.

During those eighteen months, I worked harder than I ever have, before or since. Martha and the other women stayed up smoking or playing cards, but oftentimes I fell asleep at the dinner table, and they carried me to my bunk. The only nights I didn't collapse were the ones on which I met Mike when he was off duty. Other nights, I forced myself to stay awake long enough to write letters to my mother back in Jericho. Until now, I've never given it much thought, but I'm sure my mother was terribly lonely, what with D.B. in Europe, Mort in Bethlehem, and me in Massachusetts. But her letters never spoke of loneliness or anxiety— she was always so strong, to a fault really, never wanting to be a burden on anyone, but willing to carry the burdens of anyone who asked her to.

Of course, in all my time at the shipyard, I never saw a steel beam etched with an angel— that was just part of the dream I had constructed in my mind. I suppose Mike was also. He would whisk me off to Boston for cocktails or a show. We saw *Casablanca* on the weekend it premiered, and from then on, Mike called me "kid," like Humphrey Bogart. Whenever we said goodnight, he would always say, "Here's looking at you, kid." Have you seen *Casablanca*, Calvin? I can't imagine you haven't, but if not, find it somewhere and watch it—and make sure it's the black and white version.

I remember one story having to do with Mike, but it had nothing to do with his model good looks or Humphrey Bogart impressions. From the day I arrived in Boston, I wanted to go dancing. I had very little experience dancing because my church in Jericho frowned on that sort of thing. I don't think it was ever expressly banned; rather, I think people just knew you weren't supposed to do it, so the elders never felt a need to address it. So until I moved to New England, the most dancing I had ever done was a brief waltzing lesson from my mother back when I was still small enough to stand on her feet. But I remember thinking of it as spinning, not dancing.

But by the time I was in my Ruby the Riveter days, I had a bit of pent up rebellion in me, so I chose dancing as my modest mutiny from the strictures of my upbringing. Now, men like Mike—confident, attractive, sweep you off your feet kind of men—don't enjoy activities that display their weaknesses. Well, I suppose no one does, but men like Mike, especially. They would rather impress you with their prowess at such and such and wait for you to clap or smile in adoration. They need that kind of attention and affirmation.

Mike looked wonderful walking or running or standing still. But as a dancer? No rhythm, and all flailing limbs. And he knew it, so he preferred to stand against the wall, posing like the model he could have been. At least, that's what he did most of the night the one time I convinced him to take me dancing. I had a grand time. Mike sulked in the corner. I tried to tell him that dancing isn't about how you look doing it, but about how you feel. He didn't buy it.

So there I was, dancing away while a live Big Band played. I didn't know any of the steps. Maybe I was just spinning in place, but it didn't matter. Couples whirled and stepped around me, hooting and hollering, calling out for their favorite tunes. I danced by myself, trying to have a good enough time for both of us because Mike was propping up the wall. Then, a sailor came up to me, bowed, and held out his hand. By the insignia on his jacket, I could tell he was a lieutenant like Mike, but his uniform didn't fit nearly as well as Mike's did. Anyway, I was so taken aback by his stately air that I put my hand in his without question. And we danced. He was horrible (I probably was too), but he was having such a good time that his ungainly steps and lack of beat made no difference.

When the song ended, the sailor said, "Thank you, milady." No one had ever called me "milady" before, so of course I asked him to dance another song. As our fourth song in a row ended, I noticed the look on his face go from excitement to alarm. I turned around and saw Mike stalking toward us.

"Just wait a minute and let me explain," he said as Mike reached us on the dance floor.

"There's nothing to explain," said Mike. "You're trying to steal my girl."

I probably would have reacting poorly to being referred to as property, but there was no time because Mike reared back and socked the sailor in the jaw. The sailor crumpled to the floor, and Mike stepped toward him. I was about to protest that we were just dancing, but there was still no time because the sailor sprang from the floor and tackled Mike around the waist. They went down in a heap and rolled around the dance floor, throwing punches. (It was the most dancing Mike did all night.)

Finally, a couple of MPs in army greens pulled them apart. They stood up, looked at each other—and grinned. They had been pulling all of their punches. I expected a couple of black and blue faces, but it was all faked! Then they shook hands and came over to me, arms around each other's backs. "Hey, kid," said Mike, "I'd like to introduce you to my best friend, Walter Redding."

My future husband finished Mike's sentence: "But everyone calls me Whit."

I was trying to keep that a surprise, Calvin. Did I succeed? I hope so! Perhaps, the seed was planted that night at the dance hall, with Whit's terrible, carefree dancing. He didn't need to be good at it to enjoy himself. That was the difference between him and Mike. Whit didn't have quite the looks or the confidence, but he would dance with me. That should have been a clue. At the time, however, I was head over heels for Lieutenant Lawrence, and their friendship just made Mike look better in my eyes.

They grew up together on Long Island, New York. Mike was the athlete, Whit the brains, but they got along famously, as only fellows can who knew each other from as far back as either could remember. Mike's the person who gave Whit his nickname because he always carried around a battered old copy of *Leaves of Grass*. They joined the Navy together on the same day that D.B. joined the army. They stayed in the same unit, but I hadn't seen Whit around the shipyard because I only had eyes for Mike. And Whit wasn't really the kind of man who called attention to himself—another thing I loved about him later on. Whit's also the one who acquainted me with the swan boats. Have you gone yet, Calvin? I'm sure they're open by now!

After Mike introduced us, the three of us met up often, usually with another woman in tow that Mike would have procured for Whit. Never the same one, and they all seemed more interested in Mike, so it was like Mike was on a date with two women and Whit was along for the ride. But Whit was a genuinely nice guy, so we had good chats when the other women were fawning over Mike.

Those first six months at the shipyard were wonderful. I was pretty hysterical the day Mike and Whit shipped off for the Pacific.

I hope you are getting these letters, Calvin. Let me know how things are going with you in Boston.

Yours,

Ruby

8

Christmas came and went in Victory. St. John's was packed on Christmas Eve with all the people of Victory who had both a vague connection to the church and some sort of sense of duty or tradition to attend on the big holidays. See you all at Easter, Calvin thought at the end of the service. On Christmas afternoon, Calvin drove home to his parents' house and spent the week between Christmas and New Year's not thinking too much about St. John's. It was his first vacation since he started there in June and long overdue. Needless to say, there was not a parish picnic two days after Christmas on the feast of St. John the Evangelist.

Calvin returned to Victory at the beginning of January, but he might as well have stayed on vacation since he spent the month sleepwalking through his duties. He was just so unprepared for the exhaustion that Christmas levied on him, a deep physical and spiritual exhaustion that left him empty of the nourishment he needed in order to nourish others. He was not gun shy like he had been in November after the horrible vestry meeting; rather, he was just absent even when he was present. And because he was simply going through the motions, he never delved prayerfully inside to see the bare pantry within him.

That is, until the last Wednesday in January when God forced him to open the cupboard and see that it was bare. The noon service of Holy Communion was progressing as normal. There were the readings, a short off-the-cuff homily, the prayers, and a round of handshakes at the Peace. The service took place in the chapel were the ladies read Morning Prayer, and the cast of characters was similar, if expanded, at the Wednesday Eucharist. Three of the four ladies were there (with Avis out because she was visiting her daughter in Florida) along with a few people who worked in downtown Victory in the small number of businesses that still had "Come in, we're open" signs in the windows.

Calvin shook each hand at the Peace, and then turned to the altar to set the table with the bread and wine. The altar in the chapel rested against the wall, so Calvin had his back to the people as he went through the motions of lining up the chalice and paten. Calvin placed the bread on the paten, turned, and said, "The Lord be with you."

"And also with you," chorused the small congregation.

"Lift up your hearts," said Calvin.

"We lift them up to the Lord," came the response.

"Let us give thanks to the Lord our God." This was Calvin's favorite part of the dialogue because in it, he asked the congregation for their permission to pray for and with them. And whether he himself was empty or full, they always finished the exchange with affirmation.

"It is right to give him thanks and praise."

Calvin turned back to the altar and continued with some special words for the season of Epiphany, which falls between Christmas and Lent. He held his arms out with palms up in the ancient prayer posture known as the *orans* position. He worked his way through the prayer of consecration, thanking God for sending Jesus Christ, who, on the night before he died sat down at table with his friends. Calvin touched the bread and recited the words Jesus said to his disciples in the upper room: "Take, eat: This is my Body, which is given for you."

Then Calvin reached for the chalice and froze. It was empty. He had forgotten to fill it when he set the table. Calvin stared in horror at his own face staring in horror back at him from the shiny silver vessel, distorted by the concave depths of the cup. His heartbeat quickened—the first time it had done so since Christmas. He took two shuffling steps to the right and retrieved the two small cruets, which held the wine and water. He shuffled back to the center and poured the belated wine into the chalice with a trembling hand. After adding a few drops of water, he set the cruets down, and continued: "After supper he took the cup of wine . . . "

"No yellow sheets of legal paper this time, Esther Rose, please. I know what I did wrong," said Calvin after the service.

"Do you?" she said in a voice, which suggested that Calvin did not, in fact, know.

"I forgot to put the wine in the chalice."

"Well, yes, there is that." Esther Rose sniffed. "In all my years attending the Episcopal Church I've never seen quite that mistake before. Congratulations for being the first."

"Um . . . thank you?" Calvin didn't know where this conversation was headed, but he felt sure there would be forced self-improvement in his immediate future.

"No," Esther Rose continued. She held her gloves in one hand and slapped them into the other. "Your error in this service was that you were not actually there. The wine mishap was but a byproduct. I expect my priest to attend the services himself and not just show up as a mouth with legs."

Calvin opened his mouth to protest, then closed it again. He looked at Ruby and Mary, who were clearing the altar of the Eucharistic dishes. Ruby said, "I may have put it a bit differently, but Esther Rose is right, dear."

"You're tired, sonny," Mary said. "Everyone can see it."

Calvin sat down in the back pew, tilted his head back, and rested it on the wall. They were right, of course. Esther Rose was coarse but accurate. Her ability to diagnose a problem was second to none.

A long moment passed. Ruby and Mary returned to the chapel from their trip to the sacristy to drop off the vessels and linens. Ruby sat down next to Calvin. Esther Rose stood her ground, awaiting a response to her critique. Mary busied herself straightening and smoothing the already straight and smooth fair linen that covered the top of the altar.

Calvin took a deep breath and exhaled slowly. When the breath was almost finished, he used the last of it to say, "I'm empty."

"Empty of what, dear?" said Ruby.

"I don't know. Whatever it was, it's gone: my energy, my enthusiasm, my initiative, my drive, my faith. Take your pick." He put his head in his hands and ran his fingers through his hair. "I got back from vacation after New Year's and left it all somewhere." He looked up at the altar, at the dark wooden cross that stood out against the blonde wood of the reredos. "And I can't find it." The last words came out as an accusation, but whether he was indicting himself or God, he didn't know.

"Listen to yourself," said Ruby. " 'My energy. My faith. I can't find it.' My, my, my. I, I, I." She squeezed his shoulder. "You're trying to water the yard with the hose turned off."

"I'm what?"

142

"The boy can be thick sometimes, can't he," said Esther Rose in her not-quite-under-her breath tone of voice. "Come on, Mary, let's get some coffee."

The fair linen on the altar was as straight and smooth as it was going to be, so Mary took Esther Rose up on the offer. "Get some sleep, sonny, and have a bowl of soup," was her parting advice.

Ruby and Calvin stayed seated in the back pew. "I'm what?" Calvin asked again.

"You're trying to water the yard with the hose turned off," repeated Ruby. "It means that you're attempting a task, but you've cut yourself off from the source you need to accomplish the task."

"I'm just empty. I've got nothing left in me. Ever since Christmas."

"But this isn't about you. It's about God. What about God's energy, God's enthusiasm, God's faith?"

"What about them?"

"Well, they're certainly not gone, right? They haven't been spent, right?"

Calvin put his head back on the wall and closed his eyes. "I suppose not." He let out a long sigh, another exhalation that concluded with, "But they aren't in me anymore."

"I think you're wrong. I'm pretty sure God is everywhere, and that includes you."

"But I'm nowhere."

Calvin opened his eyes in time to see Ruby wince at his melodrama. Then she shook her head. "Wrong again. You are sitting in the beautiful chapel of St. John's Episcopal Church. And you will soon get that garden hose turned back on." She winked. "I guarantee it."

Calvin smiled in spite of himself. Ruby's enthusiasm was infectious. So why wasn't God's, Calvin wondered. Why wasn't God providing the energy and enthusiasm he needed? Then a new thought occurred to him. Maybe God was providing—in the form of a little old lady who could always get him to smile.

"Come with me, Calvin," Ruby said.

"Where are we going?"

"You'll see."

They stood up and exited the chapel. "Tell me, Calvin: why did you become a priest?"

"Because I wanted to help people. I wanted to be there for people in the big moments of their lives. I wanted to be like the priest at my church growing up. I wanted to baptize people, support their faith, offer them communion."

"What a lovely answer," said Ruby. They reached the elevator, and she opened the grate. "Oh, get in. One ride won't kill you."

"Want to bet?" But he got in just the same. The elevator screeched downward, and they exited into the choir room.

"A lovely answer," repeated Ruby. "But you answered a different question than the one I asked. You answered the question 'Why did you *want* to be a priest?' And it was a lovely answer," she said a third time. "But I asked, 'Why did *you* become a priest?' "

"I'm not sure I follow you."

Ruby sat down at the piano and waited. Calvin shot her a plaintive look, but he knew he was on his own now. After all, Ruby had been a teacher for forty years, so she knew how far to guide people before insisting they go the rest of the way to discovery alone. Calvin drummed his fingers on the top of the piano, wracking his brain. Then a small piece of a thought occurred to him, and he chased it all the way to its source, deep down in his guts where thoughts have yet to be put into words.

"Because God called me to be one," he said at last.

"Yes," said Ruby. "And the church affirmed that call, which is why you're here in this choir room with me right now." She played a chord, and the deep resonance of the Steinway filled the cinderblock-walled room. "You're not nowhere."

"Because God called me," said Calvin again, this time under his breath.

"I want to play you a song that my mother taught me," said Ruby. "I think you'll like it."

Calvin sat down next to Ruby on the piano bench. "Fire away," he said.

Ruby played a short introduction and then started singing. She could not draw much breath at one time, making her voice quaver. But no matter how many times it faltered, Calvin could hear in her voice all her years crystallizing into the notes of the song: all the tragedies, all the joys, all the small moments of whispering love, all the snow angels and slow dances, all the barefoot hikes and skipping stones, all the casseroles and darned socks, all the poetry of a simple life stitched together by God's subtle presence.

I cried unto you, O God, and you heard me;
My foes who had lured me to death have all fled.
I cried unto you, O God, and you healed me,
Saved me and sealed me lest the grave be my bed.
You've turned my mourning to dancing,
Taken my sack-cloth and clothed me with joy.
Yes, Lord, your grace is entrancing;
Waken my singing, my praises employ.

I sing unto you, O God, and I thank you;
Angelical ranks do all join in my song.
And yet I am tired, O God, of my weeping,

So when I'm through sleeping let joy come along.
You've turned my mourning to dancing,
Taken my sack-cloth and clothed me with joy.
Yes, Lord, your grace is entrancing;
Waken my singing, my praises employ.

I cried unto you, O God, you were hidden,
And trouble unbidden unfurled in my way.
Have mercy on me, O Lord, be my Savior
And help me not waver in trusting today.
You've turned my mourning to dancing,
Taken my sack-cloth and clothed me with joy.
Yes, Lord, your grace is entrancing;
Waken my singing, my praises employ.

Ruby's voice clung to the last note as the final chord soaked into the walls. She kept her fingers pressing down on the keys long after the sound died away, savoring the moment of silence that always follows a piece of beautiful music. Before the applause or exclamations of gratitude, there is always a moment of silence. It's part of the music really.

"That was wonderful," said Calvin.

Ruby beamed at him. "I can teach it to you," she said.

"You know I'm not much of a singer."

"I know nothing of the sort. You have a fine voice. It just needs a shot of confidence, that's all."

"You seem to be well-stocked with shots like that." He put his fingers on the upper keys, mimicking her last chord, and played the sonority in a higher register. "Thank you."

"You are entirely welcome. When I get home, I'll dig out the old hymnal the song is from, and we can make a copy of the music."

"Some of it seemed so familiar, but I don't think I've ever heard it before."

"It's called 'Mourning to Dancing.' It's got some lines from a psalm in it—thirty or thirty-one, I can't remember."

Calvin thought for a moment, and then he stood up and looked around the room. Spotting a red prayer book on the organist's desk, he retrieved it and flipped open to the Psalter. He found Psalm 30 and read, "You have turned my wailing into dancing. You have put off my sack-cloth and clothed me with joy."

"Yes, that's it," said Ruby. "The song says 'mourning into dancing.' Must be a different translation."

"Probably the King James."

"You know, I learned to read from that book. My mother taught me. For years, my vocabulary included words like 'beseech' and 'verily.' "

"Really? You'll have to tell me about that some time."

"Oh, dear. I'm just pulling your leg. I had a primer like everyone else. But the King James was the Bible we had in our house."

"Well, it was the Bible back then."

"Still is for a lot of people." Ruby shifted on the bench, and Calvin jumped to his feet to help her up. "Oh, Calvin, I can manage. I'm not immobile yet."

"Yes, ma'am."

"And what did I tell you about that 'ma'am' business."

"Sorry. It just slipped out."

"That's all right. Come on, let's head back upstairs. I need to take Whit to the doctor this afternoon."

"Ruby." Calvin stopped in front of the elevator grate and turned to face her. "Whit is sick, isn't he?"

"Come now. No need to talk like that just yet."

"If you don't let me know when something's wrong, how will I know to pray for you?"

"No use making a fuss until there's something to make a fuss about." Ruby pushed past Calvin and opened the grate. "You prefer the stairs anyway," she said as she pushed the button.

Calvin watched her ascend into the ceiling. Then he turned and raced up the stairs. He was waiting for her as Ruby stepped off the elevator.

"It's can—" he started to say, but she cut him off.

"Don't say it."

"Ruby, you help me all the time. You are always encouraging me, making me smile." Tenderness crept into Calvin's voice. He put his hand on her shoulder. "Now let me help you."

Tears brimmed in Ruby's eyes. Then one spilled over and traveled sideways down her cheek, caught in the channel of one her wrinkles. Then another and another followed. Soon she was crying.

Mary and Esther Rose swung open the doors from the parish hall to see what was wrong. Without hesitation, they swarmed Ruby, enfolding her in a double embrace. The three of them spun slowly on the spot.

Ruby's sobs echoed up and down the cinderblock hallway. After a while they grew weaker. Finally, they dissolved into sniffles and coughs. Through it all, the embrace of the three ladies continued. Calvin stood sentinel, remembering a similar scene last summer with Avis at its center. It was the morning he met the four of them, and he had felt so inadequate in the face of her pain. Now, as he watched the scene unfold again, his inadequacy returned. But in its wake came the words Ruby had spoken to him earlier: "But this isn't about you. It's about God. What about God's energy, God's enthusiasm, God's faith?" God's faith—something Calvin couldn't control or understand. But that faith existed inside him. He knew God because God knew him.

"It's cancer, isn't it?" he said, the tenderness still leavening his voice.

Ruby looked him in the eye. He met her gaze and tried to radiate to her all the love that he felt for her and her husband.

"We'll find out this afternoon," she said.

And the three ladies pulled him into their embrace.

"The good news is that Doctor Maroney said it is highly treatable. She didn't catch it as early as she would have liked, but it's still early enough, I suppose." The four Morning Prayer ladies and Calvin sat in the parish hall sipping coffee. Ruby had just told them about Whit's appointment, and she concluded, "All in all, I feel a bit silly for having broken down the way I did yesterday in the hallway."

"Nonsense," said Esther Rose. "Whit still has cancer, treatable or not. You were more than entitled to that breakdown."

"Did the doctor really say that it was 'the good kind of cancer'?" asked Calvin.

"No, no. That was Whit's line. Finding the silver lining, I suppose. Usually that's my job," said Ruby.

Avis had returned to Victory late the night before, but she still managed to arrive on time for Morning Prayer. She said, "Didn't Whit see the dermatologist back in, what, October?"

"September, actually," said Ruby.

"And there was no sign of skin cancer then?"

"Apparently not. Or else she just missed it, which is unlikely given that it's on his cheek. And she didn't use the term skin cancer. She had one of those long unpronounceable medicalese names for the particular condition, but I can't remember it."

"Basal cell carcinoma?" asked Calvin.

"That's it. How did you know that?"

"My father had one removed from his forearm a few years ago. And he's been fine ever since."

"Well, that is good news," said Ruby. "But just the same, Doctor Maroney is watching a few other spots that might be more threatening, doing tests, trying to rule out melanoma, which is much worse than what he has. And she referred Whit to an oncologist just to make sure she didn't miss anything under the surface. We haven't made that appointment yet. I think Whit is a little disappointed. He's a bit sweet on Doctor Maroney."

The four ladies chuckled, and then sipped their coffee for a while in silence. Ruby rose to refill the coffee mugs. For Christmas, Calvin had ordered them personalized mugs with a picture of St. John's and their names printed on them. Three of the ladies had taken to them right away. But a month later, Esther Rose hadn't touched hers. It remained upside down next to the coffee maker. She preferred disposable paper cups, she had said back in December. Calvin had smiled and agreed that disposable cups had their merits, though he was glad she never made him name any.

Ruby returned to the table with the refills, and they recommenced their morning ritual. Three sips in, Calvin noticed Ruby smiling. Then Avis began to chuckle, and Mary followed suit. He glanced at Esther Rose, who drank away from her personalized mug. He was about to comment, but Ruby put her finger to her lips. Then she returned to their previous subject. "Well, Doctor Maroney is quite a beauty. I don't blame Whit for his little crush."

"And she's single," said Mary. "My Arthur sees her as well. I think he's a bit sweet on her too."

"She can't be more than thirty-five or forty," said Ruby.

"Maybe we should set her up with our young priest here," said Avis.

Calvin had been watching Esther Rose drink from the mug. She still hadn't noticed that Ruby switched her cup. But Avis's suggestion pulled him into the conversation. "Wait. What? I'm only twenty-five. I think that's a bit of an age difference."

"Alexander was twelve years older than I," said Avis. "It worked out for us."

"Yeah, but it's different when the woman is the older one."

"Is it?" said Ruby and Mary at the same time.

"Either way, please don't set me up. I've had enough of that from Josie Temple-Jones."

"Ah well," said Ruby. "Sooner or later, you'll meet the woman who will make your toes curl. We won't force the issue." She winked at the other women.

"Seriously," said Calvin, "I can find my own dates."

"Have you been on any besides the one with Monica Dennis?" asked Avis.

"No."

"Must not be looking too hard. You're a handsome young man, sonny," said Mary.

"The population of single women in their twenties in Victory is severely limited," said Calvin. "I'm pretty sure I've already dated it."

"I'm sure there are more out there," said Ruby. "I could ask my grandson Cooper if he knows anyone."

"Cooper's still in high school!" said Calvin.

"Too young, too old. There's no pleasing him," said Esther Rose.

The rest of them stared at her and then, as one, turned their gaze to her coffee mug.

"Oh, I suppose it'll do," she said.

———∞∞∞———

May 1, 2010

Dear Rev. Calvin,

I was so happy to receive your letter that I just had to write back immediately. Hearing that you are thriving up there in Boston does my heart more good than you can know. I'm surprised that your parents never showed you *Casablanca*, but I suppose they weren't alive yet when it was around, so maybe they didn't grow up with it either. Perhaps they just aren't movie people.

As far as your "mysterious news" is concerned, I think I've cracked your code. After all, you never would have gone to ride the swan boats by yourself. (I'm glad you had a good time—they are idyllic, are they not?) I won't ask who she is. I understand if you want to wait to tell me about her until you are more serious. But if I'm right about this news, then you make sure she's the one who makes your toes curl. I don't want you to tell me about anyone else, do you hear me? I know I told you about Mike Lawrence before telling you about Whit, but that was because I wouldn't have met Whit without Mike. I tried to surprise you in my last letter, but I suppose you figured out who the mysterious sailor was right away, didn't you.

After they shipped off, I was beside myself. The man I loved and his best friend had gone to certain death in the Pacific, so I wore black clothes that whole summer to demonstrate my grief. Black jumpsuit, black bandana—I even tied a black armband to my black sleeve. Looking back on that summer of 1943, it all seems a bit silly. I concocted all this drama with my attire and my attitude, but none of it assuaged the real pain and fear I felt for those two sailors. I suppose I shouldn't be too hard on my seventeen-year-old self. She fell hard for Mike Lawrence, and Whit Redding was just too nice to die fighting over some remote Pacific island.

From the second day of my time in Quincy, I had defined myself by my fling with Mike. When I was working on the line, I was counting the minutes until I got to see him. When he said, "Goodnight, kid," I was already counting the minutes until I saw him again. Those first six months, I wasn't really in Massachusetts. I was in Lawrence-land. I suppose it's always that way with first loves. They occupy all the space that your eyes can see. Your whole world orbits theirs, for good or for ill. But there comes a time when those first loves stop being planets and become people. They lose their atmospheres and gravity, so to speak, and you find yourself breathing normal air and walking on solid ground again. For Mike and me, this happened on the day I received my first letter from the Pacific. The letter wasn't from Mike, but from Whit.

And you'll never guess! Avis and I went through another box yesterday and found an old cigar box containing a stack of letters from Whit. What treasures! I haven't read them all yet because I am savoring each one. They are simply wonderful. Even at age twenty or twenty-one, he could craft his words—must have been all that poetry he read. Avis and I sorted them by postmark, and I found the first letter dated September 1943. I'll copy out a bit for you. Here's Whit talking about the voyage to the Pacific.

While steaming through the Panama Canal, I nearly forgot we were at war. This lazy, man-made river cut through the heart of the jungle and skirted the Aztec mounds and opened onto a great lake with trees clinging all along the shore. Birdsong and the chatter of wildlife who know nothing of war filled the air and offered an accusing counterpoint to the hum of the ship's engines. What I wouldn't have given to dive over the side and make my way into that jungle and live as a hermit. But duty calls louder than birdsong. The canal was so beautiful I nearly forgot we were at war; that is, until we reached the locks approaching the Pacific side, where the ship was at its most vulnerable. There the shore swarmed not with clinging trees but with soldiers with their guns. There the trees were gone so the enemy would have nowhere to hide. There the birds fell silent, and all I could hear were the engines and the dirty water swelling into the lock. And I realized I missed my chance. I realized beauty was behind me, and

war was ahead. And war rips the beauty from
this world.

Simply wonderful, isn't it? I'm so glad Avis
and I found these letters. I'll have to find more
pieces to share with you, Calvin. In this one,
I think Whit was expressing in words what
I was expressing with my dramatic attire. I
wore black to signify what the war had already
done—take them away from me—and what it
could do—take them away from me forever.

But with Mike and Whit gone, I had to pull
myself together. After a summer in all black
(which, I am now chiding my younger self,
is a rather silly time to wear it), I returned to
my normal clothes. Perhaps, paradoxically,
that first letter from Whit helped me reclaim
my own identity. He told me about his experiences, which meant that I had to have my own.

I stayed in Quincy another year. The women
of the shipyard threw me an eighteenth birthday party that I wish I could remember. It's
the only time in my life I have had alcohol to
the point of amnesia. I do remember the next
day when I couldn't stand the noise of tools on
steel. That birthday was the two-year anniversary of the attack on Pearl Harbor. We were
helping to replace the ships lost on that fate-
ful day, though we never really knew where the
ships went after they launched.

We built aircraft carriers and cruisers. The
speed with which those ships went from skeletal to seaworthy was breathtaking. The cruisers
were over two hundred yards long and the carriers nearly three hundred, yet I helped build
nine cruisers and four carriers in just my year

and a half in Quincy. Every time I wrote home to my mother, I told her about the ships we were working on. The Navy named them after cities mostly, but I had my own names for them. The carriers were my steel flowers. I called them the USS *Daisy,* the USS *Tulip,* the USS *Lilac,* and the USS *Peony.* The cruisers were my steel pollinators because I imagined them buzzing around the carriers out in the water. I remember naming the USS *Butterfly*, the USS *Honeybee*, and the USS *Yellow Jacket.* Then, wouldn't you know it—the Navy went and named one of the carriers the USS *Wasp*, and my whole system got turned upside down!

The women of the shipyards used the language of giving birth when the ships where launched. "We were in labor a long time with that one," Martha would say. Or, "Hate to see my baby go." Those ships were ours because we built them. Then the men would sail them away to be destroyed. Because I named each one secretly, I never knew what became of them once they left the womb. That is, except one. The Navy called my USS *Honeybee* the USS *Pittsburgh*, which is in my home state, as you know. A couple years after it launched, I heard all about it. But you already heard that story, as far as I know.

On Monday, I'll give everyone the hugs you sent with your letter, and I'll make sure to check whether or not Esther Rose has reverted to her paper cup. I honestly haven't noticed. Make sure you rent *Casablanca.* You can watch it with your "mysterious news." And while you're at it, rent *To Have and Have Not,* as well. It's nearly the same film—Humphrey Bogart in a bar during the war—but Lauren Bacall really shines. You'll love it, I promise.

Until I reread Whit's first wartime letter today, I had forgotten how he ended them. His farewells were simple but endearing. I'll imitate him this time.

Missing you.

Your friend,

Ruby

9

At the beginning of February, fog tumbled down the mountains and clung to Victory for weeks on end. On the days when the fog was thinnest, rain or light snow fell, but the fog always returned, a drizzle suspended in time and space. Calvin Harper didn't mind being cold, but cold and wet was another story. On a morning in mid-February, he jumped out of his car, wrapped his raincoat around himself, and hurried for the side door to the St. John's offices. As he mounted the steps, he caught blue and red flashes of light out of the corner of his eyes. The water vapor in the fog caught the light from the police cruiser and expanded it so that all Calvin could see was a diffuse glow flickering between blue and red. The car itself was lost in the mist. Calvin wondered if the cruiser was speeding to a prescription drug heist, with the criminal, no doubt, looking for some pills to dull the depression caused by lack of sunlight. I could use some too, thought Calvin, who was now drenched with tiny particles of water because he had stayed on the steps too long, mesmerized by the light show.

He took the rest of the steps in one go and entered the austere hallway of St. John's. He heard shuffling sounds coming from the church, and he knew the ladies would be getting ready for Morning Prayer. All except Ruby. She had taken Whit to the hospital for a procedure that morning, and Calvin knew she would miss the service. In all his months at St. John's, he couldn't remember her being absent from a single Morning Prayer. Until today. Until the angry spot on Whit's left cheek needed to be dealt with. Calvin shook the suspended drizzle off his jacket, and, remembering the police car hurtling down Washington Street, a lump caught in his throat. What if the accident had been Ruby and Whit? The fog made driving difficult for anyone. Calvin himself had driven to the church with his emergency flashers blinking.

But, no. Couldn't be. His anxiety over Whit's procedure was just playing tricks on him. The danger for Whit was not the fog. It was a patch of purple-black skin reaching its spiky tendrils across his cheek. Maybe the doctor will be able to scrape it all away today, thought Calvin. And in a moment of spontaneous devotion, triggered somewhere in Calvin's uncharted depths, a prayer rose to his mouth, a simple prayer that continued to rise throughout that morning. "Hold them in the palm of your hand, Lord. Just be with them. Be present." He whispered the prayer to himself and to God. And then he walked into the church for Morning Prayer.

"Fine weather we're having today, isn't it, sonny," said Mary Williams as Calvin took his seat in the chapel.

"Good Irish weather, Mary," said Calvin.

"That it is."

"Well, for us West Virginians, it's horrid," said Avis. "I expect that Esther Rose might have a sheet of yellow legal paper to give to God one of these days."

"Don't think I wouldn't," said Esther Rose.

Avis mimed writing on a pad while she spoke under her breath: "Number One. No sun for two weeks. Number Two. Clouds aren't supposed to be this low. Number Three."

"Yes, very clever," said Esther Rose. She tapped her wrist. "But it is 8:16. I think we better start."

"How do you know it's 8:16 if you haven't got a watch?" asked Mary.

"I just know," said Esther Rose.

Mary raised her eyebrows. "No, really."

Esther Rose drew a boxy mobile phone from her purse. "T.J. made me join the information age. If I fall again, it will be good for me to have a phone nearby. At least, that's what he said. But honestly, all I can do with it so far is tell the time."

"I'll program it for you, if you like," said Calvin.

Esther Rose gave him an appraising look. "I'm not just some old granny who can't learn to use a telephone, you know."

"No, ma'am."

"I've got the manual. I can figure this out on my own."

"Yes, ma'am."

Esther Rose sighed and lapsed into the voice she might have used if she had been one of the minor English nobility talking to the butler of her country manor. "But since these old fingers would find it quite tiresome to push all those buttons, perhaps I will take you up on your offer."

Calvin grinned. "You've got yourself a deal."

"But first, it is now 8:18," said Esther Rose, as she dropped the phone into her purse after glancing at the time once again.

"Whit's procedure starts in twelve minutes," said Avis.

"Then we better get to praying," said Mary.

"I will give you as a light to the nations, that my salvation may reach to the end of the earth," began Calvin, and they settled into the familiar rhythm of Morning Prayer.

———

When they were finished, Esther Rose and Mary took up residence at their usual table in the parish hall while Avis and Calvin donned their rain jackets for a trip to the hospital.

"We wouldn't want to overwhelm her," Mary said, after Calvin asked if the three of them would like to accompany him to sit with Ruby during the rest of Whit's procedure.

"And I spend enough time at that blasted place my own self," said Esther Rose. "But when you return, Calvin, you can work on this device for me." She waved the boxy mobile phone in the air like a white flag of surrender.

"No problem," said Calvin. "Any message for Ruby?"

"Just tell her we love her," said Mary.

"And that it's okay to grill the doctors with every question she can think of. I highly encourage it," said Esther Rose.

Avis and Calvin swam through the fog to Calvin's car and limped along to the hospital with the emergency flashers going. The hospital complex sprawled out from the base of the western mountain, which abutted the valley that was home to Victory. As they drove, Avis pointed out various buildings, saying, "The population of the town was aging, so more and more buildings kept springing up around the hospital: clinics, radiology labs, fitness centers, specialists' offices, restaurants. This hospital complex is so big now it's a town within the town."

Calvin navigated the car up the shallow rise to the hospital proper. When they finally parked—after a half hour of white-knuckled driving for a trip that usually took ten minutes—they both exhaled a sigh of relief.

Calvin and Avis entered the main atrium of the hospital through a double set of automatic sliding doors. Whenever he visited the hospital, Calvin had to get his bearings. The surgery suites were down one hallway, the Emergency Department down the other. The elevators were down the left hand corridor, and they reached the patients rooms on the floors above. As Calvin looked at the signs above each hallway, he spotted Chief Stern, hat in hand, striding toward him from the hallway that led to the Emergency Department.

"Reverend Calvin," said the Chief. "You got here quick. I just phoned the church a few minutes ago."

Alarm bells began ringing in Calvin's head, his instinctive pastoral senses shifting into high gear. "Avis and I came to sit with Ruby during Whit's procedure. What happened, Chief?"

"It's not good. The slick roads. The fog. His car went off the side of the road and rolled several times down a hill." There was an edge of panic in the Chief's voice that Calvin had never heard before.

"Whose car?"

"Phil Erickson's. I assume he was on his way to the office. Call came in about 8 a.m."

"I saw a cruiser speeding down Washington Street when I was going into the church."

"That was probably mine. Paramedics and the fire department responded, as well."

"Is he going to be okay?"

"I don't know. The engine block collapsed toward the cab, and both of his legs were crushed under the steering wheel housing. I don't know the damage. Several abrasions from broken glass. Nasty bloody cut on his scalp. Concussion. Broken arm. Don't know about internal bleeding. But he was breathing when he went into the ambulance." The panicked note in the Chief's voice began to subside as he reported to Calvin.

Calvin turned to Avis. "See if you can find Ruby. Tell her what happened. Tell her I'll be along if I can."

163

"I know this hospital like the back of my hand," said Avis. She squeezed Calvin's arm and headed down the surgery wing.

"God, Chief," said Calvin. "I hate to ask this. But which one is Phil Erickson? I've only ever called them Phil and Phil because they are always together with Carl Sinclair."

For a moment, Chief Stern gave Calvin a hard look. Then he said, "Phil Erickson is not the Phil who is on the vestry. He's the other one."

Calvin mentally scanned last week's 7:30 service and found Phil Erickson in the back with the other golfers. He had never spoken much to Calvin, and Calvin had only ever seen him as one of the mayor's entourage.

"I've barely ever talked to him," said Calvin.

"Now's your chance," said Chief Stern. "Come on." He led Calvin down the hall. "It's a good thing you're wearing your clerics today." The Chief gestured to Calvin's black shirt and collar.

"I knew I was coming to the hospital."

"Didn't think you were coming for this, though."

"No, sir."

They checked in at the nurse's station. The nurse on duty waved them down the hall, and they stopped by the sliding glass door to Phil's room. "The docs have stabilized him as best they can for now. The loss of blood was the real problem, so they're fixing that now." The Chief pointed to a bag hanging from a hook above Phil's bed. "You probably won't be able to recognize him too well. He's pretty banged up."

Calvin took a deep breath and put his hand on the door.

"Oh, and Calvin," said Chief Stern. "I don't know if you know, but Phil's got . . . " He swallowed hard, and the panic resurfaced in the Chief's voice. "He's got a wife and two kids—Sam and Kelly. They're eight and ten."

164

"What?" Calvin was stunned. Phil Erickson was one of the golfers—he easily could have been retired. He had elementary school-aged children?

"He had a divorce about a dozen years ago, and then remarried a much younger woman, Christie. She worked for him in his office. But that story doesn't matter now. What matters is that he's got a young family. He also has a couple of adult children, and some grandkids, but they all live in other states, not sure where."

"I had no idea," said Calvin, and he really didn't. In his mind, Phil Erickson was just another pew sitter, who took off early to shoot eighteen holes.

"I think Christie is Roman Catholic, so she takes the kids to her church. But Phil's been a fixture at St. John's for years, so they split up on Sunday mornings."

"God," said Calvin. The word was half exclamation and half prayer. "He's got two little kids."

"We just got his wife on the phone before I saw you in the atrium, so she should be here any minute."

Calvin took a deep breath, then another. "Okay. Thanks, Chief, for catching me up to speed."

"That's what I do," said Chief Stern. He pointed to Phil and then pressed his hands together in a gesture of prayer. "And this is what you do. Remember that. You bring the Big Man into that room."

"Yes, sir," said Calvin, sounding more confident than he felt. The Chief donned his hat and strode back out of the Emergency Department. Calvin took another deep breath and slid open the door. The beeps of a half-dozen machines spilled into the hallway. Calvin took in Phil's heart rate, oxygen level, and blood pressure, though he only vaguely knew what was good or bad. Calvin slid the door closed and tiptoed to the bed. Phil was covered in gauze and tape. Thin cords snaked out from his hospital gown and from the IV in the crook of his elbow.

Calvin placed a hand gingerly on the shoulder attached to Phil's unbroken arm and whispered, "Phil, it's Calvin Harper from St. John's. Harry Stern called me, asked me to come see you."

Phil opened his eyes halfway. They were glassy. Painkillers, thought Calvin. Phil reached his hand a few inches off the bed, where it hovered for a moment before dropping back down. Calvin took this as a sign that Phil wanted his hand held. Calvin slid his hand under Phil's and held it there. They stayed frozen hand in hand for an indefinite moment marked only by the beeps of the machines, Phil's shallow breaths, and Calvin's guilty thoughts. Why did I never get to know you before now? Why did it take a car accident to put you on my radar? Who else have I ignored at church?

"I'm sorry," Calvin whispered. It was both an apology and a statement of empathy. Unbidden, a single tear spilled down each of Calvin's cheeks. He could feel in his own bones the pain emanating from the broken man on the bed. He looked at the foot of the bed and imagined the crushed legs beneath the covers. As he did, he caught movement at the door. He just had time to wipe the wetness from his eyes when a woman came tearing into the room. In the moment between her entering the room and reaching the bedside, a small, detached part of Calvin's mind noted that she was stunningly beautiful, even in the midst of distress. She collapsed to her knees on the other side of the bed, never giving Calvin a look. He let go of Phil's hand and melted into the corner of the room in order to allow Christie Erickson the space she needed in the initial minutes of seeing her husband so seriously injured.

Ten minutes later, Calvin stepped forward and said in his softest voice, "Mrs. Erickson?"

She looked up. Her mascara had run in wandering rivulets down her cheeks. Her eyes narrowed. "He's not dying," she said. "He doesn't need a priest!"

"Mrs. Erickson." Calvin's softest voice became even softer. "I just came to sit with him, not to give him last rites."

She stared at him, mascara tears still streaming down her face. "Oh." She sniffled.

Calvin grabbed a box of tissues from the nurse's computer console and offered it to her. She took one and blew her nose.

"I'm Phil's priest from St. John's. My name is Calvin Harper."

"You're so young."

So are you, he thought. But he said, "Yes, I am." He moved a chair from the corner to the side of the bed he had been occupying when she entered the room. "Why don't you sit here? He didn't hurt this arm too much. You can even hold his hand."

Christie Erickson took the chair. "Thank you, Father."

"Please, you can call me Calvin."

She smiled a small smile as she took hold of Phil's undamaged hand. "Our anniversary is next week. Eleven years. Neither of us wanted a winter wedding, but I was . . . " Her voice trailed off, and Calvin did not ask her to clarify. With a ten-year-old daughter, he could guess.

They sat in silence for a while. A nurse came and went. People in lab coats and raincoats wandered by down the hall on the other side of the glass door. Calvin gazed at Phil. Fragments of prayer stole into his mind, and he lifted them to God in silence. Christie's mascara continued to slide down her cheeks with each wave of tears. The machines beeped a steady rhythm in time with Phil's heart. At last, Christie broke the silence. "Father Calvin, I know you're not Catholic, but do you know the rosary?"

Calvin looked at her. He hadn't expected her to be particularly spiritual, but he had no real reason for thinking so. "I used to pray it in college," he said.

She produced a string of pink beads from her purse. "Will you pray it with me?"

"Of course."

They bowed their heads and said together, "In the name of the Father, Son, and Holy Spirit. Amen."

They moved to the Apostles' Creed and the Lord's Prayer, each whispering under their breath, each focused in prayer with the half-conscious Phil between them. They said the Hail Mary three times and the Gloria. And over the next half hour they surrounded Phil with prayer. The machines didn't matter. The people in the hallway didn't matter. The drip-drip of the IV didn't matter. Only God and the injured man and the young mother and the young priest and the prayer mattered.

They were on the final Hail Mary when it happened. "Hail Mary, full of grace, the Lord is with thee. Blessed art thou amongst women, and blessed is the fruit of thy womb, Jesus. Holy Mary, Mother of God, pray for us sinners now and at the hour of our . . . "

As they said the word "death," Phil convulsed, and a cacophony of new sounds filled the room. The door flew open. "He's coding," someone yelled down the hall. "Get the crash cart."

Before they knew it, Calvin and Christie were on the other side of the sliding door, their faces pressed against the glass, their hands holding each other's with the rosary beads dangling to the floor, the crucifix resting on the shining linoleum.

An hour later, a doctor said something about a blood clot from his leg and something else about not being able to do anything and a third something about being really sorry.

And Calvin held Christie Erickson in his arms in the hall on the wrong side of the glass as she wept anew.

May 7, 2010

Dear Rev. Calvin,

I gave everyone the hugs you sent, but Avis made me stand on a chair because you're so much taller than I am. Imagine me trying to clamber up onto a chair. Well, I made it in the end, and she got her hug. And then I needed help down! So far, May in Victory has been beautiful. April showers really do bring May flowers. I used to teach that little rhyme to my kids in school, and they would always finish it by asking what May flowers bring. Pilgrims, of course.

Avis and I have been working through that cigar box of Whit's wartime letters. They are so precious that I've asked Cooper to type them up and save them on the computer just in case these old pieces of paper start disintegrating on me. They've lasted all these years, but you never know when things are going to turn to dust. I'm working on another letter to you that is a compilation of pieces of many of Whit's letters from the war. I'll let the young version of him tell you firsthand about some of those experiences. One frustrating thing is that he was always so vague in his letters—perhaps he wasn't allowed to be specific in communication. I don't know. But they are wonderful letters nonetheless. Be on the lookout for that letter soon. We are almost done with the cigar box.

I only have a few minutes to write today, so I'll keep this brief. I think last time I was telling

169

you about building all those carriers and cruisers. I worked on the ships for all of 1943 into 1944. Then one day in early summer I received a telegram, my first ever, from my mother. All it said was: "Mort. Accident. Come home." I walked right into the foreman's office, told him I was leaving, and walked out again before he had time to say anything. I probably lost my last paycheck over that, but I didn't care. I packed up my belongings, which still fit into just one bag, and stopped long enough to dash off a quick note for Martha. I left it on her pillow. It contained my address in Jericho and a thank you for all her kindness. The ladies were all on the line when I left, so I never got to say goodbye. I walked back to Boston, boarded the first train for Philadelphia, and arrived home less than a day after my mother sent the message.

Mort was in bad shape. Burns that just didn't look like burns. Mother said they were made by chemicals, not by fire. The hospital sent him home because there weren't enough doctors to go around. He was either going to get better or get worse on his own, and they didn't want him taking up a bed. My mother had the pot going again, and she fed him soup whenever he looked hungry. And I fed her soup whenever she looked hungry. She took care of him. And I took care of her. She never asked me to, but I knew what to do without needing to be told.

All day long, Mort lay in bed, his knife in one hand and a stick in the other. But he didn't have the strength to carve. He hadn't said a word because the chemicals had hurt his throat and lungs. But his eyes followed me whenever I sat with him. I told him all about my time in Quincy, the ladies, the ships. I didn't tell him about the men because I didn't know if he would approve, and I didn't want to upset him. Whenever I spoke of launching a ship, his eyes smiled, but the rest of his face was too ravaged to move. His eyes smiled because I used the steel that he made. I got to see the finished product floating away—thousands of tons of metal floating, against all odds. Imagine that!

Ten days after I arrived back in Jericho, Mort's lungs gave out. He died in his own bed at home with his wife and daughter by his side, though his son was thousands of miles away fighting the war in Europe. He died surrounded by the love that he himself had so much difficulty showing. He died with his knife and stick in his hands. We buried him in the family plot in the churchyard at the end of July. Oh my, does it all come back to you. Writing this to you, Calvin, makes it feels like yesterday.

After Mort died, I decided not to return to the shipyard. I decided to enroll in teacher training school. I matriculated in September of 1944. It was my own little D-Day, my own promise that there would be a future after the horrific war was over. But that will have to wait because Avis is picking me up for the movies in a few minutes, and I want to drop this letter at the post office.

Missing you.

Your friend,

Ruby

10

As his car crept along in the wake of the hearse toward Victory Place Cemetery, Calvin reflected on the last three days.

On the afternoon of Phil Erickson's death, Calvin had found himself in a well-appointed living room on the good side of the tracks. He had sat on a plush ottoman facing a couch with four little legs dangling off it. The legs were too short to touch the floor. They belonged to Sam and Kelly Erickson, who stared at Calvin, waiting for him to speak. Sam kicked the front of the couch with the heels of his feet. Kelly held a throw pillow across her chest like a shield.

"Sam, Kelly," said Calvin, with Christie standing behind him. "Your mother asked me to talk to you about something. She would tell you herself, but she hurts too much in her heart to talk about it right now, so she asked me."

"Where's Daddy?" asked Sam. He looked at his mother. "Mommy, where's Daddy?"

Christie's tears seemed inexhaustible. They began again. "Oh, baby," she cried, and she squeezed between her children on the couch. Kelly remained silent.

"Your Daddy had an accident this morning," said Calvin. Oh God, he thought, how do I say this? He paused, pressed his hands together, inhaled. "It was very foggy outside and his car went off the road. An ambulance took him to the hospital, but something went wrong there, and he . . . and he . . . and he . . . "

"And he's paralyzed?" Sam asked. The same small, detached part of Calvin's mind that had noticed Christie's beauty wondered where an eight-year-old learned that word. "If he can't walk anymore, I can push him around," Sam continued. "I can feed him too."

Christie's tears moistened her son's hair, and she reached down and kissed him fiercely atop his head. "My love," she cried. "Of course you would." Kelly remained silent.

"Sam, you father isn't paralyzed," said Calvin. "Something went wrong at the hospital and your Daddy . . . " A deep breath. Something inside Calvin that wasn't him pushed the words out. "He died."

"But he's coming back, right?" asked Sam. "In my video games, when I die, I always come back. He's coming back, right?"

Calvin looked at Christie. Something in her son's plea galvanized her to action. She gathered him to her. "It's just me, you, and Kelly now," she whispered. Kelly remained silent, but Calvin saw great bulbous tears drip from the corners of her eyes, and he heard a deafening noise as each hit the pillow she clutched to her chest.

Now, as he relived the scene in the living room, Calvin's own tears mirrored hers, and he was glad no one had ridden with him to the cemetery. No one to see the outward reflections of the remembering.

The day after Phil's death, Calvin's office had filled with people. Too many people. In the two high-backed chairs across from his desk sat Christie Erickson and Helen Erickson Fletcher, Phil's eldest daughter by his first wife, Doris. Christie and Helen couldn't have been more than a year or two apart in age. On the couch against the wall sat Phil Junior, who introduced himself as Chip, and Jennifer, the youngest of Phil's adult children. Calvin did some quick mental math and judged that Jennifer and Chip had been in college when their parents divorced. Bet that was horrible, thought Calvin. Helen's husband Doug stood next to the couch with his back against the wall. Mercifully, Doris had stayed at the hotel with Doug and Helen's two children.

Unmercifully, the final person in the room, the one sitting in Calvin's own chair, which he had rolled around to complete the semicircle, was Carl Sinclair. With no more seats available, Calvin perched on the edge of his desk facing the offspring, the wife, and the mayor.

"We are not having any music," said Helen for the third time. "Dad went to the early service for a reason—because there are no songs at it. It's quick and simple, and so should be his funeral."

"My husband went to the early service because he played golf afterward, not because he didn't like music," said Christie. She addressed Calvin when she said this, as if he were a referee. An hour into the meeting, Calvin had yet to see the Christie who had taken on the challenge of comforting her children in the midst of her own grief, the Christie he had seen the day before. Today she was nothing but combative. She was, however, outnumbered four to one.

"Here we go again," said Jennifer, who clutched a throw pillow to her chest, making her look an awful lot like a grown-up version of Kelly.

"So we have a few songs," said Chip. "Big deal."

"Sure, Chip, side with *her*," said Helen. Apparently, based on the way she spit the word out, *her* was an expletive in Helen's vocabulary.

"I'm not siding with anyone, Helen." Chip sounded exhausted. Tiring work, being the peacemaker when neither side wanted peace.

A long, tense minute passed. No one looked at anyone else. Finally, Calvin tried a new tactic. "Helen," he ventured, "I wonder if there's a way to honor your father's desire for a simple service but still provide some music, say during communion perhaps?"

Christie answered first. "Whoever said Phil wanted a simple service? He never told me that. We never talked about it. He played golf, simple as that. That's why he went to 7:30 church. Tell them, Carl."

But before the mayor could open his mouth, Helen went on the attack again, though she still didn't look at Christie. "He and Mom talked about it when she was sick. But you wouldn't know that, would you?"

"I knew she was sick."

"Didn't stop you, though, did it."

"What's that supposed to mean?"

"How long after she got home from the hospital was it?" Helen's voice rose, and she spoke each word as if they were the stabbing points of knives.

"I don't know what you're talking about." Christie's voice lowered as Helen's rose, more blunt weapon than knife's edge.

"Ladies, please," said Calvin, but no one was listening to him. Chip and Jennifer were sitting on the edge of couch. Doug moved to stand behind Helen's chair.

"Don't play dumb with me," said Helen.

"Your mom's cancer devastated him," said Christie.

"Oh, so what, you were there to comfort him."

"Yes."

"I bet those were a lot of comfort." Helen turned to Christie and pointed a finger at Christie's chest.

"It didn't start out like that."

"But it ended like that. How else could it have gone? Wife comes home from the hospital after a double mastectomy, while the secretary's are spilling out of her sweater."

Calvin tried again. "Ladies, please."

Helen ignored him. "I'll ask again. How long after Mom came home did it take for him to grab a hold of those?"

Christie's lips quivered, but she said nothing.

"How long?" pressed Helen.

The first tears Calvin had seen Christie cry since he left her house yesterday began running down her cheeks.

"How long?" said Helen a third time, and her voice was a shrill ring that filled the office and the hallway and spilled into the parish hall where the ladies were still nursing their coffee.

"Okay!" shouted Christie, and then she said in a lower voice, "Okay. I guess you can't hate me any more than you already do."

"Want to bet," said Helen, her voice more even now, but still cutting.

Christie looked her square in the face. "It wasn't after she came home. It was the night your mom went *into* the hospital." She said it like a confession, and then she slumped forward, head in hands.

Chip and Jennifer sat back on the couch simultaneously, as if Christie's words had shoved them. Doug gripped the back of the chair with his fingernails.

"You wh . . . " said Helen.

"That's enough," said Calvin, and he found that his voice had some force behind it. "After tomorrow, you two can ignore each other for the rest of your lives, but for the rest of today and tomorrow, I will not have the sins of the past destroy Phil's funeral."

He stood up and walked behind his desk. "Now I want everyone to take five minutes. Get a drink, use the restroom, walk around, do whatever you want. But when you come back into this office, you will be civil, you will compromise, and we will all find a way to honor Phil tomorrow. Go."

The five of them looked stunned, but without another word they all got up and left the room. All but Carl.

"Calvin, I just want to say . . . " Carl began, but Calvin wasn't done.

"As for you, Mr. Mayor, you can help me or you can leave, but if you decide to stay, you will give me back my chair."

His commanding tone faltered on the word "chair," but he held his gaze and stared Carl down. And Carl Sinclair, the mayor of Victory, laughed. But it was a different kind of laugh than the one Calvin had heard at the November vestry meeting.

"Calvin, I was just going to say . . . " He took a breath, as if the next words were going to cost him. "Good job. I didn't think you had it in you to corral these people, but you do."

The memory faded as Calvin pulled into the cemetery behind the hearse. His tears stopped, and a small smile creased his face. The mayor's grudging vote of confidence had given him the courage Calvin needed to work with Christie and Helen, and they had put together the service. No one was happy exactly, but when the alternative is all out war, not exactly happy is pretty good.

As he walked to the gravesite, his white surplice blowing in the wind, he thought back to the events of that morning. So far the ceasefire had continued, and even the weather joined in. It was the first and only sunny day of the month of February, and the sunlight on Calvin's face teased him with the thought of spring, which wouldn't arrive for another month. He prayed Morning Prayer with the ladies, who then bustled off to prepare the parish hall for the reception following the funeral. The Mary Magdalene Guild was famous for their luncheons and receptions. They always churned out a dozen of the fluffiest quiches, crackers and cheese, vegetable trays, cookies, brownies, tea, and coffee. Calvin expected today to be no exception. After all, the food would have to be good to keep the détente going.

Calvin had put Christie Erickson, Kelly, and Sam in his office before the service and led the others to the library. Doris, Phil's first wife, had joined them, but "only to support my children," she made sure to tell Calvin. The service began with Phil's first family in the front row on one side and his second on the other. The carpeted center aisle was the only thing that separated them. The carpeted center aisle and a dozen years of broken trust and painful memories.

Where's the reconciliation, the redemption, Calvin thought? Isaac and Ishmael came together to bury Abraham. Could that happen today? Not likely, but he added the dream to his prayer to God.

Ten minutes later it happened. Not much. Just a peek. Just a sliver of how the world of those two families could be if they allowed God to unleash the power of forgiveness. Helen and Christie had decided that ten-year-old Kelly would read one of the lessons. She was an innocent in the war, after all. She could not help that she was the product of betrayal. Calvin was nervous because he had no firsthand knowledge that Kelly could even form words, let alone speak in front of a church full of people. The psalm concluded, and Kelly marched to the lectern. For a moment she stood there, silently staring at the crowd. Another moment passed, but just as Calvin was about to help her, she began to speak.

"A reading from the Revelation to John." Her voice was a child's voice, but the conviction she possessed far surpassed her years. Or perhaps, thought Calvin, conviction begins high and just ebbs away over time. Kelly read about the peoples from every language and nation praising God before God's heavenly throne. All those people crying out in one voice, their differences not forgotten or purged, but coalescing into the music of heaven. Could that happen in this broken family, thought Calvin?

Kelly continued, her voice growing stronger, the unfettered belief of the child spilling into each word. "Then he said to me, 'These are they who have come out of the great ordeal; they have washed their robes and made them white in the blood of the Lamb. For this reason they are before the throne of God, and worship him day and night within his temple, and the one who is seated on the throne will shelter them. They will hunger no more, and thirst no more; the sun will not strike them, nor any scorching heat; for the Lamb at the center of the throne will be their shepherd, and he will guide them to springs of the water of life, and God will wipe away every tear from their eyes.'"

She paused, looked up, and said, "The Word of the Lord."

The congregation responded, "Thanks be to God."

Kelly marched back to her seat, but as she entered the aisle between pews, Helen stood, moved into the aisle, and took Kelly into her arms. Christie looked on, disbelief written on her face. Helen embraced Kelly for a full minute in the center of the aisle of St. John's Church.

Now at the graveside with no aisle separating them, Calvin could hardly tell who belonged to which part of Phil's family. They all stood together, the war momentarily forgotten. Would forgiveness and new beginnings come out of death? Would resurrection? Calvin hoped with every fiber of his being that they would.

But he never found out. After the reception, Phil's adult children went back to their lives, and Christie and her children continued at the Roman Catholic church. For less than one week, these people had been the focal point of Calvin's ministry. They had consumed his thought, surfaced in every prayer. He had barely known Phil in life, and now he knew Phil's entire family—his entire beautiful, broken family.

But now they too were gone. Only Carl remained of those who met in Calvin's office. In the months after the funeral, Calvin noticed Carl's manner toward him soften. The hard edge of calculated disrespect was gone, and the glimmer of approval would flash across his face from time to time. Calvin would never know if the two halves of the Erickson family would come together, but for Calvin and Carl, Phil's death was a new beginning.

The following Monday, Calvin slumped into his seat at Morning Prayer. The intense ministry of the last week had caught up with him over the weekend, and only the last crumb of his conviction dragged him out of bed in time for the 8:15 prayer service. Well, almost in time.

"8:17." Esther Rose held up her mobile phone and then let it fall into the jaws of her open purse.

"I'm sorry," said Calvin through a yawn. "I could swear I flew to Japan and back this weekend. I feel jetlagged."

"You look jetlagged, sonny," said Mary in a sympathetic tone. And he did. His sweater was wrinkled, and he didn't have time to shave that morning. And then there were the bags under his eyes.

"Good thing there's quiche left over from the reception," said Avis. "We'll get some in you after prayer."

"8:18," intoned Esther Rose.

"It's good to see you," whispered Ruby, and she patted Calvin on the knee. They had shared the pew ever since Calvin's second day in Victory.

"You too," said Calvin.

But in his mind, he was kicking himself. Whit's surgery was last Wednesday. Calvin had gone to the hospital with Avis to sit with Ruby, but then everything had happened. The accident, Christie weeping, telling the kids, the fight in the office, the funeral, the exhaustion. Calvin had not spoken to Ruby since before Whit went into the hospital. He had been so consumed with the emergency that he had been derelict in his other duties. Throughout Morning Prayer, shame, then guilt, then sorrow welled up within Calvin. Then after sorrow, the old self-pity returned. People having surgery, others dying in car crashes, plus all the normal day to day stuff of running the church, plus Sunday services, preaching, leading classes—no wonder he felt so worn out. How could he possibly be expected to deal with everything?

Morning Prayer ended, and Ruby looked up at him. "You are awfully withdrawn this morning."

"I've got a lot on my mind."

And as she so often did, Ruby read him perfectly and even turned the page before he did. "Let me guess. You feel guilty that you never saw Whit and me after the procedure. You feel overwhelmed because you just dealt with a horrible tragedy and now you're trying to sort everything out." She paused for a moment. Calvin wondered if she might pull out a crystal ball. But, of course, she didn't need to resort to showy antics. And she wasn't really a mind reader. She was a heart reader. "You are also feeling sorry for yourself because you feel so beset."

"Um," said Calvin.

"Well, let me tell you something, my dear." Ruby creaked to her feet and beckoned Calvin to join her as she ambled to the parish hall. "Avis brought your prayers with her. You don't need to be physically present to have an impact. You were where God needed you most." She stopped outside the door to the hall. "And God is where you need him most." She steadied herself on his shoulder and pulled his ear close to her mouth, as if her next words were a secret. "Don't think for a moment you got through the last week alone."

"But you and Whit. I wanted to be with you."

"Don't think for a moment that we got through last week alone either. God was present. The doctor is confident that Whit's . . . " She hesitated. " . . . that Whit's problem is under control."

"That's wonderful news. When can I see him?"

"He's a little weak, but he hopes to be up for Ash Wednesday service in a couple of days."

"Oh no."

"What is it?"

"I completely forgot that this Wednesday is the start of Lent. I was going to get everything ready last week, and then . . . " Calvin started counting on his fingers. "I need to make sure the altar guild is ready to change colors. I need to ask if St. John's traditionally does anything different during Lent— wooden candlesticks instead of brass and the like. I need to put together the Ash Wednesday service. I need to write a sermon. And I need to make the ashes. I don't even know how to make the ashes."

Ruby cocked her head to one side and frowned. "There you go again. I, I, I." She dragged him into the parish hall. "Our young priest needs help," she told the rest of the group. "I hope you will all say yes to what he is going to ask us to do."

The rain lashed the windows of St. John's, and the constant drone of water on glass accompanied the dozen voices sharing the middle of an ancient and lengthy psalm.

> As far as the east is from the west,
>   so far he removes our transgressions from us.
> As a father has compassion for his children,
>   so the LORD has compassion for those who fear him.
> For he knows how we were made;
>   he remembers that we are dust.
> As for mortals, their days are like grass;
>   they flourish like a flower of the field;
> for the wind passes over it, and it is gone,
>   and its place knows it no more.

As the psalm concluded with several verses of blessing, Calvin looked up and surveyed the hearty souls who had ventured forth into the flood for Ash Wednesday. Esther Rose sat with T.J. and Emily, who had baby Natalie asleep on one arm. Brad and Rebecca were observing Ash Wednesday by going on a date, Emily had told Calvin before the service. She, of course, was more than happy to take the baby. Avis and Mary sat with Ruby and Whit. Josie Temple-Jones sat by herself in the front row, while Carl Sinclair occupied the back. Chief Stern, wearing an acolyte's white robe, sat to Calvin's right.

They moved through the second reading, Gospel, and homily. Calvin read the traditional invitation to the observance of a holy Lent and then invited the small congregation to the altar rail. He picked up a silver dish that fit in the palm of his hand. In it were ashes made from dried palms from the previous year's Palm Sunday service. The ashes were black as coal and gritty. Calvin didn't know by what mysterious alchemical process Avis Noon had distilled such perfect specimens, but he was thankful nonetheless.

Calvin turned and looked at the eleven unadorned faces, soon to have two lines of ash scraped onto their foreheads. Two lines of ash forming a cross, a reminder of life's transience, of the need for repentance, of Christ's sacrifice, and of God's love for even the most fleeting of God's creation. The Chief was first. Harry Stern looked up at Calvin. Calvin ground his right thumb into the ashes and scraped it across the Chief's forehead, a forehead usually hidden beneath a police officer's hat, the mark of a protector, a servant of the people, which Harry Stern was. "Remember that you are dust, and to dust you shall return," said Calvin.

He moved a step to his right. Carl Sinclair had squeezed in between the Chief and Emily Lincoln. The bald mayor's forehead stretched all the way to the back of his neck, and for half a second, Calvin thought about taking up all that real estate with the ashy cross. But he played by the rules instead. "Remember that you are dust, and to dust you shall return."

He moved another step to his right. Emily, still clutching little Natalie, radiated the fresh love of a new grandmother. "Remember that you are dust, and to dust you shall return."

Again, Calvin shuffled to the right. T.J. Lincoln had one hand on his wife's back and the other on his mother's. "Remember that you are dust, and to dust you shall return."

Esther Rose was next, but she stopped Calvin and gestured back. Of course, he had missed someone. He knelt across from Emily and with the tiniest amount of ash and the tiniest amount of pressure, he dabbed a tiny cross on baby Natalie's tiny forehead. "Remember that you are dust, and to dust you shall return."

He returned to Natalie's great-grandmother and placed a cross on her venerable wrinkled forehead. How much longer did she have, wondered Calvin? "Remember that you are dust, and to dust you shall return."

Josie Temple-Jones knelt to Esther Rose's left. Her ringlets spilled in all directions, so Calvin lifted a lock of her hair to reach her forehead. "Remember that you are dust, and to dust you shall return."

Avis Noon came next. Three widows in a row, thought Calvin. They all know about the dust. Avis smiled proudly at her handiwork, the black ashes clinging to Calvin's thumb. "Remember that you are dust, and to dust you shall return."

Mary Williams remained standing because her knees weren't up to the task. "Thank you, sonny," she whispered after Calvin had said, "Remember that you are dust, and to dust you shall return."

Ruby and her husband came last. Calvin scraped a cross on Ruby's forehead, said the words, and made to move on. But she caught his arm, and pulled him to his knees. Then she put her thumb in the ashes and scraped them on Calvin's unadorned forehead. "Remember that you are dust, and to dust you shall return," she said.

Finally, Calvin came to Whit. His face was bandaged, sagging. He looked tired, but knowledge and fire still burned behind his old eyes. As Calvin placed first the vertical and then the horizontal lines of the cross on Whit's forehead, he wondered if there were still any cancer cells eating away at Whit's flesh, if there were any that had escaped the doctor's knife, if there were any hidden away under the surface, invisible but for the tests that would surely come. "Remember that you are dust, and to dust you shall return."

May 10, 2010

Dear Rev. Calvin,

This old cigar box is a treasure chest. I'm surprised I never made a map with a big X pointing to the attic. I haven't read these letters in probably forty or fifty years, but as I look through them, I find thoughts and sentences that burrowed into my mind or my heart and never left. Now I know where they came from! Whit wrote them to me before we ever became a couple, back when he was my boyfriend's best friend. But considering he was the one writing me letters and not Mike, I should have realized the truth. Whit was in my future, and Mike was in my past. But I didn't know that at the time.

I am so very excited to share some of these letters with you, Calvin. I could have told you about Whit's war years, but with the discovery of our buried treasure, you can read about it for yourself—and in the words of a young version of my dear husband. Looking at these envelopes, I can tell the letters went through hell and high water to get to me. But they got to me, indeed. I have Martha from the shipyard to thank for that. All of Whit's letters were delivered to the bunkhouse in Quincy, but after I left, Martha forwarded them to me in Jericho. What a sweetheart. I wonder what ever happened to her? We lost touch after the war.

Anyway, without further ado, here are selected scenes from Whit's wartime letters. It almost feels like an exhibit at a history museum. Except there's only writing, and it's vague in places—I think Whit wanted to tell me about the hellish details of war and spare me at the same time. I'll try to pick out the best parts. Here's Whit in late autumn 1943:

> Our ship, the USS *Bunker Hill,* towers over the water. Out on deck, you can forget that you're not on dry land because all you see is flat runway, and you swear that you're at an airfield that just happens to be near the ocean. Except the planes are all pushed together like sardines, and their wings are all folded up, so you know that something is amiss. And then you feel the ground roll ever so slightly under your feet, and you remember that you're on a flight deck and that you're in the Navy and that you have responsibilities other than ruminating on the size of the ship. Mike likes to call it a "boat" just to aggravate the other officers. I call it a floating steel island, a little piece of America built in Massachusetts and steaming out in the Pacific, halfway around the world. I guess Mike and I were lucky to be stationed together on the same ship. Well, us and 2,598 of our closest friends. 2,600 fellows aboard a steel island. I don't think I've met that many people in my whole life, and yet here we are, thrown together for good or ill.

I spent a good deal of time on the decks of aircraft carriers myself when I was building them in Quincy, but I never went aboard one once it was launched. And I never saw one with all those sardine planes out on the deck. I suppose it was a sight. Here's Whit again in the spring of 1944:

We do quite a bit of waiting here on the *Bunker Hill*. Mike can't stand it. I keep some poems in my pocket to while away the dull hours. The Navy doesn't train you how to wait: it only trains you how to act. So you have to get good at waiting. You can't lose focus. You can't daydream. You can't take forty winks because you never know when you'll have to jump to action. And yet, we wait more than we act. The senior officers have taken to scheduling drills at all hours so we don't become listless. I can understand why. Being aboard this ship is so very isolating. I can look out across the water and see other ships in our fleet, but I'm confined to this steel island. I envy our pilots. At least they get to fly away from here for a time. Of course, they are speeding into danger while I hang back getting the deck ready for their return, but a part of me would relish a little danger. Sometimes I wonder if I'll ever see the enemy face-to-face rather than just launch planes at them from a distance. I know I sound disillusioned, but I think that's a good thing. Getting rid of my illusions makes me a better officer, if a less happy one. But there is one thing that fills my heart with joy. Every evening, I walk to the bow of this manmade island, and I watch the sunset. My friend, you have never seen anything so beautiful in all your life. There's just you and the water and the sun. The steel island ceases to exist, and there's just you walking on glistening liquid fire and never getting burned. The sun has never been so close. You feel like you can reach out, take the red disc between your fingers, and hand it back to God for safekeeping.

This is one of those images that has always stuck with me—handing the tiny sun back to God. Being in West Virginia for as long as I have, I can hardly imagine all that water. It must have been frightening to know there was no escape from the "boat," as Mike called it.

The first letter that was delivered to me back in Jericho via Quincy (and who knows where else) came a few weeks after my father's death. It was just what I needed at the time: a communication from the other side of the world to remind me that life was bigger than my tiny home.

Finally some real action. The sky was full of fighter contrails—lines of smoke spelling all kinds of strange spiraling shapes as the Hellcats engaged the Zeroes above us. Nine dive-bombers broke away from the dogfight and came right for us, but our anti-aircraft gunners were up to the task. We took some casualties when one bomb exploded a little too close, but we kept on fighting. After two days of solid action, I was out on deck directing aircraft to land when one of our boys misjudged his line. It was nighttime, which makes landing on the carrier much more difficult, but he was off by more than a bit. I feel horrible saying this, but I'm glad he missed the mark so widely because if he had missed closer, he could have crashed on the deck or into the hull, which are nightmare scenarios. As it was, he went into the drink about fifty yards short of the carrier. I never knew his name.

This was the last I heard from Whit for nearly six months. In that time, I alternated between being worried that something had happened to him and Mike and focusing on my new schooling. I started college in the fall of 1944, so I didn't receive the next letter until I returned home for Christmas.

We've heard tell of a new tactic the enemy are using, and it's horrible. They've made planes that are built for no other purpose than to crash into our ships. Can lives be so expendable that they would stuff them inside bombs? Has it really come to this? Has the hunger of the beast of war started demanding such willing sacrifices? They call them *kamikazes*. It means "divine wind." I can't think of a more incongruous name. But whatever they call them, I don't mind telling you, Ruby, they terrify me.

Later in the same letter, Whit told me of his transfer.

Mike is still aboard the *Bunker Hill*. Right now it's steaming for Washington for refit, so Mike's out of it for a little while at least. I'm still in the thick. The day the *Bunker Hill* received her new orders, I received mine. I'm now aboard an LST—it's a landing ship that delivers tanks and heavy equipment to beachfronts. I wished to see the enemy face-to-face. Be careful what you wish for.

I headed back to school in January of 1945 following the Christmas holidays. I was nineteen years old, I was training to be a teacher, and I loved every minute of every day at my college. I was safe and sound. I was learning all sorts of new things. And all the while my boys, who were barely two years older than I, were risking their lives to take over tiny specks of land no one had ever heard of and living all the while under the specter of death by pilot-guided missile. It wasn't fair. Part of me wanted to be suffering with them on the beaches and at sea. The other part wanted them to be studying with me in the library.

Sometime in late spring, my mother forwarded a letter from Whit that was written in March of 1945.

The fighting lasted for over a month, and still I cannot get the first day out of my mind. It was February 19th. My LST was waiting its turn just off the island, and I watched the first wave of Marines take the beach. They started creeping up the strand as more and more of them emptied from the landing craft. But they struggled to keep their footing in the dark volcanic sand. There's something eerie about sand that isn't the right color. And I knew the tanks my ship was carrying would have trouble in it. More and more Marines poured onto the beach. Oh God, Ruby, it was so deathly silent. There was neither shot nor yell from the enemy's position. At first we thought the bombardment had devastated them. But no. They were simply waiting. The silence. The dark sand. It was all wrong. The Marines on the front line continued creeping up the beach, and a few at the front even swaggered a little, and my heart screamed a warning in my chest. Soon the beach was full of our boys. No, it wasn't full, it was packed—they were cattle in a pen. The silence was the first casualty. The crack of machine guns, the thud of artillery, the cries of agony—I could hear them from the safety of my ship. I could see line after line of Marines cut down. And I could do nothing for them except watch and fight the bile rising in my throat. In the first few minutes after the silence died, the sand turned darker and ever more wrong. And that was just the first day. I write this to you more than a month later, and I have seen more death than sanity can bear.

He ended that letter—the only one that really hinted at the horror he witnessed—differently than the others. It simply ends: "Pray for our souls. Whit." This is the only time he ever related to me his experience at Iwo Jima.

The next time I received letters from Whit was during my summer holidays after my first year of college. It was the summer of 1945. Victory in Europe had been declared in spring, but the war with Japan dragged on. Now I remember, Calvin. I received three letters from Whit all at the same time, and they came the same day that D.B. arrived home. D.B. must have run into the postman on his way up our street, because he had the mail under one arm and his great big green military-issue bag over the opposite shoulder. So much excitement and so much despair in one afternoon.

The first letter spoke of another horrific battle, this one on the island of Okinawa. Whit's landing ship was damaged pretty heavily, so it was taken out of the fighting. In the second letter, dated May 1st he told me he was reassigned again, this time to the USS *Pittsburgh*, a cruiser that I had helped to build! It was the USS *Honeybee* in my mind, but Whit didn't know that. Mike was still on the carrier, the USS *Bunker Hill*, as he had been during their whole deployment. They hadn't seen each other in several months. I remember opening the third letter like it was yesterday. It was just one of those moments, a fixed point in my life. I'm still so glad that D.B. and my mother were there to hold me, to keep me afloat. Whit's third letter was dated May 15, 1945. Here's what it said:

Dear Ruby,

I do not know how else to start this letter, and any preparation I try to give you will not work, so I will just say it. Mike is dead. Four days ago, two kamikazes crashed into the *Bunker Hill*. There was a huge fire that I could see from miles and miles away. I think that Mike was out on the flight deck when the first plane hit the parked aircraft. All that fuel and ammunition just went up in a second. I don't think he suffered. At least, that is the one hope left to me. My other hopes are gone because they all revolved around Mike and me going home together, helping each other court our wives, having each other's kids call us "uncle." I wish we were still stationed together. I wish I had been there with him. Perhaps I would have died too, but if not, perhaps I would have been able to give him some comfort, a little remembrance of Long Island, New York, so that he wouldn't feel so far from home. I hate this war, Ruby. I want to come home.

Your lost friend,

Whit

That was the entirety of the third letter. I don't think Whit could bear to write any more. And that was good because I don't think I could have read any more. I remember collapsing into change to D.B.'s arms. My brother had returned safe and sound, but Mike would never return. And my friend was still out there—alone and waiting to die.

And he very nearly did, but that will have to wait because if I don't stop writing I won't fit all these pieces of paper into my envelope. I think I may add an extra stamp just in case.

Your friend,

Ruby

11

Winter surrendered to spring without much of a fight. By St. Patrick's Day, the trees had enough green on them to keep from being pinched, and the floral vanguard defied any final frosts from winter's death throes. Calvin drove to St. John's with the windows down, and the roars of recently dormant lawnmowers alternated with new birdsong as he covered the familiar route to downtown.

"Oh, sonny," said Mary Williams when Calvin arrived for Morning Prayer.

"What?" said Calvin. "What's wrong?"

She looked him up and down, and he did the same to her. Mary wore a lime green sweater, a khaki knee-length skirt, and lime green pumps. And she had dangling shamrocks adorning her ears.

"Oh no," said Calvin. He was wearing his standard black clergy shirt, black pants, and black shoes. The only green on him were his eyes.

"I'm afraid so," said Mary, and she moved in, fingers seeking his cheek for a good Irish pinch.

"Not so fast," said Ruby, who had wandered into the sanctuary and witnessed their exchange. She pinched Calvin on the arm, then took the green bowler hat from her own head, reached up, and planted it firmly on Calvin's.

"Shucks," said Mary.

"Ow," said Calvin.

"Just a little reminder not to forget to wear green here at St. Jack's on St. Patrick's Day," said Ruby. "Now you keep that hat on or you'll be all black and blue by the end of lunch."

And so he did. He wore the bowler during Morning Prayer (for which he received a yellow piece of paper from Esther Rose that read, "No hats in church!"). He wore it during his planning meeting with the organist. He wore it to his Tuesday group with other local ministers. And he wore it to the St. Patrick's Day luncheon, which was the real pinching danger zone.

The Mary Magdalene Guild put on several luncheons a year for the seniors of the parish, which was, of course, most of the population of St. John's. But the St. Patrick's Day one outshone the rest. Avis Noon could barely lift the gelatin mold that she had managed to keep intact all the way from her house. It was as green as Calvin's bowler, and Avis had managed to suspend miniature marshmallows throughout that spelled, "Happy St. Pat's Day." Calvin thought the marshmallows looked like teeth, and for a moment he had a vision of the gelatin mutating into a B-movie blob and destroying downtown Victory.

Rows of tables covered in green tablecloths ran the length of the parish hall. Little plastic pots filled with gold-wrapped chocolate coins sat next to rainbow-printed napkins at each place setting. And the buffet table groaned under the weight of corned beef and cabbage, soda bread, stew, and, of course, the mutant gelatin.

The guests started arriving, and Calvin noticed, much to his own chagrin, that not a one of them had forgotten to wear green. Even Chief Stern, who was in uniform, wore a green soccer scarf draped over his shoulders.

"On duty, Chief?" asked Calvin after extracting himself from the Chief's mighty handshake.

"Yes, but I can't resist Mary's corned beef." He winked at Calvin. "So I told my dispatcher that I was coming to St. John's to follow up on intelligence that this luncheon might be harboring known fugitives."

"Never hurts to be thorough," said Calvin.

"I think I'll start by questioning the buffet table."

Calvin grinned as the Chief swaggered over to the food, took a plate, and started his interrogation. He turned back to the hallway and his grin widened. Ruby and Whit were strolling arm in arm up the hall. Whit wore green trousers and a striped green and white vest over a green tie. Ruby matched him with the same stripes on her skirt and a green blouse.

"Ruby, did you make those?" said Calvin pointing to the skirt and vest.

"Why, yes she did," answered Whit. "And don't we look fine." Whit spun a slow circle with his arms out so Calvin could see the whole ensemble. "Still fits after all these years."

Ruby smiled at her husband, then took Calvin's arm and whispered to him, "Don't tell him, but I've made that vest four times since 1965."

"What are you two giggling about," said Whit.

"Nothing, darling," said Ruby.

They made their way to a table, Calvin said grace, and the luncheon began. For a few minutes, the only sound in the hall was the clink of silverware as the gathering tucked in. "The mark of good cooking is silence at the dinner table," said Avis. "Well done, Mary."

Mary tilted her head in acknowledgement, her mouth being too full of stew to respond. As plates began to empty, conversation bubbled up around the hall. Several people chuckled at Calvin's bowler, but he had decided he liked it, so he wore it with pride. It was a gift from Ruby, after all—another thing to add to his debt to her, he thought.

Calvin's musings were cut short when someone tapped him on the shoulder. He turned to find Carl Sinclair—in a tweed jacket over a green golf shirt—standing behind him. Ever since Phil's death, he and the mayor had been moving from dislike of each other toward tolerance, so Calvin decided to try some gentle joking. "Working from the links today, Mr. Mayor?"

"I do more work on the golf course than in my office at city hall, that's for sure," said Carl. "One must keep up one's game if one is to attract investment to our fair town."

"I expect you have to be just a tiny bit worse at golf than the investor."

"That's the idea. But with all the new medical facilities in Victory, I have to practice more and more. Doctors are very good golfers."

"Priests aren't."

"That's because you work on Sundays. Best day to golf in my opinion."

"Speaking of, have you found a fourth to golf with you on Sundays in Phil's memory?"

"Funny you should mention that." The mayor turned and put his hand on the shoulder of a man who had been waiting in silence. "Reverend Calvin Harper, I'd like you to meet Doctor Donald Pennyworth." Calvin stood up, and they shook hands. The mayor continued, "Doctor Pennyworth just moved to Victory to head up the new cancer clinic that is opening this summer."

"I'm one of the golfers that Carl here is slightly worse than," Dr. Pennyworth said with a smile. "And a lifelong Episcopalian. Any chance I could get a pledge card after lunch?"

"Absolutely," Calvin spluttered. "Of course. Yes, sir. You bet." No one ever *asked* for a pledge card—especially not doctors in their mid-sixties who could be counted on to put a couple extra zeros on their checks.

"Calvin," said the mayor. "You can stop shaking Doctor Pennyworth's hand now."

"Absolutely. Of course. Yes, sir. You bet," repeated Calvin, who let go and tried to contain his spluttering.

Thankfully, at that moment, a leprechaun burst into the parish hall—a tall, blonde leprechaun with a yarn beard and buckles on her shoes. Josie Temple-Jones wore a tight knee-length green skirt over green and white striped leggings. The skirt frilled out just an inch or two at the bottom, giving her the appearance of having just stopped spinning. She wore green suspenders over a green and white polka dotted blouse. She had a pipe in her teeth and round red circles on her cheeks. "Ach, me lads 'n' lasses, who e'er can catch the leprechaun gets me pot o' gold," she shouted as she bounded around the room.

"What is that," said Avis. "Scottish?"

"It isn't Irish, that's for sure," said Mary.

"None of us is agile enough to catch you, Josie," said Ruby. "Come and have a bite to eat."

"Ach, me pretty," said Josie as she skipped toward Ruby, "There's plenty o' sense in that. But someone still has tae catch me to get me . . . "

She trailed off when she reached the table and laid eyes on Dr. Pennyworth.

". . . Pot of gold," she finished, pulling off the yarn beard and flashing her most radiant smile. "And who, may I ask, are you?"

"Donald Pennyworth. I'm an oncologist with the new Cancer Research Center."

"Josie Temple-Pennyworth," said Josie. "Oops. Silly me. Josie Temple-Jones." She tilted her head back, shook her mane of blonde ringlets, and chuckled off-handedly. Calvin and Ruby smirked at each other. Well played, Josie, thought Calvin.

"Yes, well, quite," said Carl Sinclair. "Donald, shall we get some food?"

"Donald will be with you in a moment, Carl," said Josie, not taking her eyes off her quarry. "So, Donald, how is your wife adjusting to life in Victory?" asked Josie, her fake Irish brogue long forgotten.

"My wife passed away some years ago, actually," said Dr. Pennyworth.

"Oh no, I'm so sorry to hear that. So did mine. My husband, I mean, not my wife." She chuckled off-handedly a second time. "Any children?"

"Two. And three grandchildren."

"Oh, simply lovely," said Josie. "I never wanted to have children, but always wanted grandchildren. Never thought it was possible," she concluded under her breath.

"I'm sorry?"

"Oh, never mind. Donald, be a gentleman and escort me to the buffet table. We have so much to discuss." Josie put her arm in his, and they walked off, leaving Carl standing with Calvin.

"That woman," said Carl, and he stalked off after them. But Calvin couldn't tell if it was irritation or admiration coloring the mayor's voice.

"I'm confused," said Calvin once he had sat again. "Did they just get engaged?"

"Near enough," said Avis. "Josie's already planned the wedding anyway."

"Who knows," said Ruby. "Maybe God is at work. Maybe they've both reached the end of their rainbows. Wouldn't that be just lovely?"

Everyone sitting at the table assented—everyone except Whit. "What do you think, darling?" asked Ruby.

"I think I'm not feeling so well," said Whit.

Ruby put the back of her hand on his forehead. "Oh my, you are clammy, dear."

"Have some more stew, Whit," said Mary. "That will make you right as rain."

Whit gave Mary a weak smile. His face was ashen, and beads of sweat dotted his brow. "Maybe a little water," he said. "I'm parched."

"I'll get it," said Calvin. He stood up and walked to the kitchen. He had the glass under the tap when he heard the crash.

"Doctor Pennyworth!" he heard someone shout.

<hr />

Calvin followed the ambulance to the hospital, while the events of the last half hour flashed though his mind. He had raced back into the hall to find Whit sprawled on the linoleum floor, his sizeable belly poking out from under his vest and shirt. He looked for all the world like a beached whale, Calvin thought, a green-striped beached whale. Doctor Pennyworth raced over from the buffet table at the sound of his name and reached Whit just as Calvin was coming out of the kitchen. "Sir, sir!" called the doctor over and over again, as he checked Whit's breathing and pulse. Of course, Dr. Pennyworth didn't know Whit's name yet. He will after today.

On the doctor's orders, Calvin ran to the office to call an ambulance. By the time it arrived, Whit was starting to

203

come around, but Dr. Pennyworth thought Whit might have a concussion or worse, so the paramedics loaded Whit into the back of the van. Calvin had no idea how she did it, but Ruby climbed in next to Whit unassisted. Love and adrenaline trump arthritis every time.

The ambulance turned off the main road leading to the hospital to approach the Emergency Department from the rear. Calvin parked in the last row of the lot, which sprawled out like a concrete lake around the island of the hospital complex, and jogged to the front entrance. Once through the double set of sliding doors, Calvin took the right fork and headed to the Emergency Department as fast as he could walk without being accused of running in the hospital.

"You'll have to wait here," said the receptionist after Calvin told her the situation.

"But I'm his—" Calvin was going to say "priest," but the receptionist cut him off.

"I'm aware of that," she said looking him up and down and up again. Calvin wondered why she was fighting to keep a smile off her face. Whit was hurt—the most she could do was take him seriously. "But the doctors need some more time to examine him. I'll let you know the minute you can go back."

"Thank you." Calvin tried to put some sting into the words, but found it difficult to show his frustration with that particular phrase. He wandered to the rows of chairs and chose one as far from the blaring television as he could get. The TVs in the hospital were always set to twenty-four-hour cable news. Calvin looked around the waiting area. It was relatively empty, especially for a time of year when something was always going around. It was the stomach flu this year in that area of West Virginia. Ruby had told him that her grandson Cooper had recently missed a whole week of school and so did half his classmates and some of the teachers. Calvin was glad that the stomach bug hadn't hit St. John's yet. He glanced down at his hands resting on the arms of the chair and made a mental note to wash thoroughly.

He whiled away his wait trying to ignore the TV, which only made him listen more intently. Thankfully he couldn't see it from where he was sitting because the little news and stock tickers that sped by on the bottom of the screen always made him queasy. After the better part of an hour, Calvin felt a tap on his shoulder. "Father," said the receptionist.

He turned and looked up. She still seemed to be fighting to hide a smile. But her "Father" had sounded genuine, so she definitely wasn't poking fun at him. "You can go back now. Room fourteen."

That caught Calvin up short. It was the same room that Phil Erickson had died in. As he walked down the ward, Calvin tried to push away the memory of the doctors and nurses trying in vain to resuscitate Phil. But he could still hear the heavy thud of the defibrillator. He could still see the flat green line no longer pulsing on the monitor. He could still feel Christie Erickson's nails digging into his hand, hanging on to him as if she were gripping a plank of wood and trying to stay afloat after a shipwreck.

Calvin's breath came faster as he approached room fourteen. In what state would he find Whit? Would a nurse rush by with the crash cart as he arrived at the room? Would Whit already have a sheet draped over his face? Would Ruby be watering the floor with her tears? Calvin paused a moment between rooms twelve and thirteen and put his hand on the wall to steady himself. He was okay when he went into the ambulance, Calvin told himself. A little banged up, but okay.

As he stood there, hand on the wall, eyes closed, he felt a hand on his back. "Is something the matter, dear?"

It was Ruby. She had a paper cup of water in her other hand and concern was written on her face. Calvin straightened up. "No," he lied. "Nothing's the matter."

Ruby cocked her head to one side and glared at him. The look told Calvin that she was on to him.

"Geez," he said. "How do you do that? All right. The room Whit is in is the one Phil . . . "

"Phil Erickson died in," Ruby finished for him. "Oh, Calvin, what an awful memory to relive. Don't worry. No one's dying today."

She took his hand, looked him up and down and up again, and smiled. She didn't try to hide it like the receptionist had. They stepped to the door of room fourteen, slid it open, and went in.

And Whit Redding, looking worn down but quite alive, burst out laughing. His ashen face split into a grin. He tried to stifle the laughter, but that just made him hoot all the more. Ruby patted Calvin's hand and gestured to the mirror in an alcove above the sink. He looked himself up and down and up again, blushed scarlet, and removed the green bowler hat from his head.

He set the hat down on a chair, looked at it, and joined in the laughter. The last time he was in this room there had been nothing but heartbreak. The laughter somehow redeemed the space, made it a place of healing rather than a place of dying. As Calvin looked around, he could still see and hear and feel Phil's death, but it no longer threatened to overwhelm him. He put his hand on Ruby's shoulder and smiled at her.

And she pinched him.

"Ow," he said. "What did you do that for?"

"You're not wearing green anymore, dear. You're fair game."

"My vest is in that bag over there," said Whit, gesturing to a clear plastic bag that held his clothes. "But it's probably a bit too big for you."

"I think I'll stick with the bowler, but thanks," said Calvin. "So what did the doctor say?"

"I'm having a bit of a case of sudden onset pneumonia," said Whit, and he slumped back into the bed. All that laughter seemed to wear him out.

"Is there such a thing?"

"Well, they said I have pneumonia. I call it sudden onset because I fainted at church and had to come to the hospital by ambulance."

"Anything else?"

"They're running all their usual tests now. No concussion, but I have a great big bruise on my right hip. Never had one so large before."

"You've never fallen like that, darling," said Ruby. "It was like slow motion in a movie."

"I guess I'm like an old piece of fruit now," said Whit. "I bruise easily."

They sat in silence for a while, and Whit dozed off. Ruby held his hand, and she and Calvin began chatting about small things.

"Any dates for you recently?" she asked.

"Afraid not," said Calvin. "I've only had one since moving to Victory."

"Ah, yes, the dentist. Are you still in touch?"

"I have an appointment in May."

"That's not what I meant."

"I know." He sighed. "I can't help but think that maybe God is holding the right person for me, and sometime somewhere we'll meet and everything will fall into place. Is that crazy?"

"Not at all, dear. In fact, I have faith that will happen some-day," said Ruby. "You'll meet the woman who makes your toes curl. And you'll be sure to let me know."

"It's a deal," said Calvin.

"Whit and I met at a dance," said Ruby, as she reached up and smoothed down Whit's thin hair.

"And did your toes curl?"

"Not immediately. Took a long while. But there was the war on after all. It was easy to fall in love, but hard to see that love having a future."

"How'd you first know, then, if your toes didn't curl?"

"He wrote me letters."

And for a moment Calvin thought he could see the love flowing between the two other people in the room. The space between them shone like liquid gold light, and room fourteen was no longer a bay in the Emergency Department but a cathedral of God's presence. Tears brimmed in Calvin's eyes as he noticed thin tendrils of the same liquid gold reaching from both Ruby and Whit to himself.

The moment faded with the sound of the glass door sliding open. "Mr. and Mrs. Redding," said a man in a white lab coat.

Ruby squeezed Whit's hand, and he blinked his eyes open. Calvin stood and faced the doctor.

"I'm afraid that the preliminary blood work shows that our efforts last month were not as successful as we would have liked." The doctor paused, took a deep breath, and continued. "We removed the affected skin cells, but it seems that there was cancer in other . . . "

The doctor kept talking, but at the word cancer, Calvin's ears began to ring. He could see the doctor's lips moving, but his words were muffled, indistinct, as if a bomb had gone off nearby and blown Calvin's eardrums. All Calvin could do was look at Ruby and Whit and see their faces fall. Calvin blinked away his tears, and when he reopened his eyes, he thought he could see the remnants of the tendrils of liquid gold light binding their two dear hearts together.

But what good was love when Whit's own body was eating him away?

—∞—

May 14, 2010

Dear Rev. Calvin,

Avis and I finally finished going through all the boxes under the dining room table. And in the bottom of the last one, we found an envelope stuffed to bursting with pictures. I was overjoyed, let me tell you. It was like opening a briefcase that had a million dollars inside, only better because money doesn't have Whit's picture on it. Right after finding them, Avis loaded me into the car and we went to the store to buy a pair of those frames with the special mattes that have spaces to hold a dozen pictures each, plus a few tabletop frames because I've started to put pictures atop the piano. Then we stopped by the church so I could make some copies of my favorites for you, Calvin. I'm sending them in a bigger envelope so I don't have to fold them. I hope you like them. I've been in heaven walking down memory lane all these days as I've gone through the boxes. Now I'm sad again because the boxes are empty. So I suppose it's a good thing that I haven't finished telling you the story yet.

I was beside myself after reading Whit's letter about Mike's death. D.B.'s safe return was some comfort, but I was determined to be the picture of grief. It never registered at the time that Mike might not have been thinking too much about me out there in the Pacific. He never sent me a letter, after all. But my dramatic side reasserted itself upon receipt of Whit's letter, and I imagined all sorts of scenarios in which Mike died. And in each one, he died while breathing my name with his final breath. Once again, I wore my black clothes, and once again it was summer, so that wasn't the smartest idea. But whenever people saw me in town, they didn't have to ask about what had happened—they silently passed me their condolences with sympathetic looks or pats on the arm. I quite literally wore my adolescent grief on my sleeve. Since our love was supposed to be the stuff of legend, I grieved with the same hysterical ardor that makes the damsels of literature flee to nunneries upon the deaths of their beloveds.

Of course, I've never been much of a damsel. So in the dead of night during those weeks of grief, I would lie awake trying to ward off the truth that my love for Mike wasn't anything more than a schoolgirl's infatuation. And as the days wore on, I found myself playing the part so that I could garner sympathy, not because I really felt the depths of grief over the loss of a soul mate. My soul wasn't ready for a mate yet, so how could I have lost one at nineteen?

Looking back, I think I spent all of my grief for Mike in that first day of hysteria—collapsing into D.B.'s arms, yelling and screaming, and telling my mother that I wanted to die so that I could be with Mike. The grief was real that first day, but I channeled it through my theatrics. I felt like Juliet, and I wanted a happy dagger of my own. But from then on, I showed grief for Mike because I wanted our love to be the stuff of legend, not because it actually was. And I received a lot of attention from the neighbors, which I relished at the time.

But I don't chide my young self. At nineteen, I was still figuring out how the world works, and how I fit in it. I'm eighty-four now, and I'm still figuring it out. So no, I don't fault my young self. She was a person of intense emotion, who showed it with a flair all her own. I suppose I'm still that person, but I like to think that my flair has softened and deepened over the years.

I stored my black mourning garb on the day I returned to school. I had threatened all summer that I was going to a convent in the fall, but my mother never took the threat too seriously. I think she saw through my drama and got a look at the real pain underneath—the pain that began as grief over Mike and evolved into the pain of not having the legendary love that I had imagined we had. The grief went in the drawer with the black clothes, and, instead of the novitiate, I continued my training to be a teacher.

I think it's funny that if you had lived in the right town when you were in third grade, Calvin, you might have had me as a teacher. I bet you were a precocious one. I bet you could never sit still and always had your hand up to ask questions. There were always one or two in every class. But as I write this, I'm realizing that I might have been retired by the time you were in third grade. What a thought! I always forget that you are only in your mid-twenties. Perhaps when you lived here in Victory, your soul wasn't ready for a mate yet either. Speaking of, any more details about your "mysterious news" that you told me about in your letter?

I didn't have much "mysterious news" during that semester back at school. It was an all-women teacher's college, so we didn't have much contact with gentlemen callers. Or, at least, I didn't. I had friends who invaded the all-male college across town, but that wasn't my cup of tea. I studied, and I took long walks in the woods. The college was close enough to home that the forest in the area was the same kind that D.B. and I used to traipse around behind our backyard.

D.B. visited me over Thanksgiving that semester and told me all about his time in Europe and Africa. That was the first time he told me his tall tales about meeting Ingrid Bergman for dinner every evening in Morocco. And that made me think of Mike, who had taken me to see *Casablanca* two years before. I remember D.B. tensing when I mentioned Mike. He was expecting me to dissolve into my hysterics. But by Thanksgiving, thinking of Mike just made me wistful, not desolate.

That's how grief works I suppose. It's like the scab that covers an open wound. The scab means the wound is healing, even if the scab is ugly and unsightly. You can pick away at your grief and let the wound bleed afresh, but eventually, the skin will heal over. Maybe you'll even have a scar as a reminder.

But there is also grief that never seems to stops bleeding.

Oh, Calvin, I get myself all worked up. Maybe I am still that nineteen-year-old girl threatening to head to the convent. Let me see if I can find a happier topic.

I came home to Jericho for Christmas in 1945. D.B. was home for the holidays for the first time since before Pearl Harbor. It was the second Christmas without Mort, and the scab of that grief was healing into a fine scar of remembrance. I had just turned twenty, which seemed positively old and wise compared to the teenager I had been. We went to church on Christmas Eve—my mother, D.B., and I. I remember nothing of the service itself until what happened afterward. We put on our coats, turned to leave, and that's when I saw him—standing at the back of the church with a hymnal in his hand.

He wore his service uniform and the biggest grin I've ever seen. I raced down the center aisle and flung myself into his arms, and Whit spun me around and around in the back of the church. The next day, my mother invited him for Christmas dinner. She was always so perceptive. She knew before I did that my soul and Whit's were a matched set.

You be sure to look at those pictures I sent you in the other letter. There's even one from that Christmas dinner. I suppose even with the boxes empty, I can stay on memory lane for a while longer.

Missing you.

Your friend,

Ruby

12

The organ crashed to life on a grand opening chord a beat after the congregation finished their final "Alleluia." The meticulously crafted, soaring music of Johann Sebastian Bach filled the nave of St. John's. So did the scent of dozens of lilies and the buzz of conversation from the two hundred souls who had squeezed into the pews and emergency folding chairs that Easter morning. With the exceptions of Christmas Eve and Phil Erickson's funeral, Calvin had never seen the church so full. But the place seemed even fuller today. Must be all the colorful clothes. On Christmas Eve, people wore rich, dark colors. At the funeral, people wore black and gray. But today, on Easter Sunday, all the women were dressed like flowers and all the men wore light suits and pastel ties. This is how we celebrate the Resurrection—with a riot of color, thought Calvin.

He shook hand after hand as their owners exited the church, and Calvin recognized about one person in five. See you all next Christmas, he said to himself, and then he remembered thinking the same thing about Easter. There are some things you can just count on. Calvin collapsed on the back pew after shaking the final hand and exhaled a long sigh. "Finished," he said aloud to no one in particular.

From his seated position, Calvin surveyed the church. It really was a beautiful space. He so rarely looked at it from the perspective of a person coming to church on Sunday. So this is what they see, those people who love the back pew. He could understand its appeal. He could see all the stained glass windows, and the bright midmorning sun shining through them allowed him to see the images clearly, despite their grime-encrusted protective outer glass. They depicted Jesus' encounters with various people from the Gospel—the first disciples, the Samaritan woman, Bartimaeus, the rich young ruler, Zacchaeus, Martha, and Mary. Calvin remembered the picnic last June when he had learned about the conflict about which John the church was named for. Most people had settled on John the Baptist because they liked having their parish picnic in the summer. He tried to discern a pattern in the glass that told him the right answer, but the windows didn't hold one. The windows were about Jesus, and that was as it should be, he thought.

He continued to look around the church and remember his first weeks in it. That first day sitting up in the choir loft—the slave's balcony, really—feeling sorry for himself, almost getting arrested. Meeting Avis, Mary, Esther Rose, and Ruby. Thinking that the police had caught up to him when Chief Stern came to the picnic. Calvin exhaled another long sigh. He had never felt called to come to Victory, West Virginia. He had come out of a sense of duty to his bishop, to the vows he had made. But as he sat in the back pew and watched the ladies cleaning the sanctuary, he knew that there were people to whom God had called him. Maybe not this town. Maybe not this particular ministry in the long term. But to certain people to whom he had grown close. To people like Ruby and

Whit who were moving toward the end of life. To people like Brad and Rebecca and little Natalie, who were right at the start. Calvin didn't know how much longer he could stand the suffocating isolation of going home to a dark, empty, friendless house every night, but he tried to push that thought out of his mind and relish the satisfaction of having completed the gauntlet of Holy Week and Easter. Just one more thing to do, he thought, and then I can rest.

Calvin walked to his office, removed his vestments, locked the church, and ambled to his car. T.J. and Emily Lincoln's home was across the tracks about halfway up the slope of one of the squat mountains that bordered Victory. They had invited him for Easter dinner, and his longing to rest lost to his desire for a mother-cooked meal. He had warned them that he might fall asleep at the table, and they had said he could take a few minutes of shut-eye on the couch if needs be. What generous people.

His arrival was met with handshakes from T.J. and Brad, and then Rebecca greeted Calvin by depositing baby Natalie in his arms.

"But she's squirmier now than she was at Christmas. I can't . . ." protested Calvin.

But Rebecca cut him off. "You two have to get comfortable with each other if you are going to baptize her in June."

Brad took one look at Calvin's petrified face and laughed. "It's okay, Calvin. She's not as breakable as you think. I like to hold her like this. See."

Brad took Natalie and held her lengthwise, supporting her head with his hand and letting her body rest on his forearm. He struck the Heisman pose: free arm fending off an imaginary defender, one leg in the air, knee bent. Rebecca gave him an "our daughter is not a football" look. Natalie just giggled and gurgled.

ADAM THOMAS

"See, she likes it," said Brad.

Calvin joined in on the baby's laughter. He enjoyed Brad's easy demeanor and sense of humor. During his first months in Victory, they had gotten together several times to watch football games and drive golf balls. But that had ceased when Natalie was born. Too many diapers, I suppose, thought Calvin.

"Maybe I'll try again later," he said. "My experience with baby-holding is very close to none. I like them when they're brand new and they don't move around too much. Plus, I'm so tired after nine services this week that I don't think I have the energy to hold her."

"Okay," said Rebecca. "But fair warning—you are holding her every time we see you between now and the end of June."

"I have been warned," said Calvin.

He wandered into the kitchen to greet Emily, who was cooking about eight things at once. All the wonderful smells of Easter dinner hit him together, and Calvin thought he could die happy after a meal like the one he was about to enjoy. "Thanks for inviting me over today," he said.

"Think nothing of it," said Emily.

"Mom," came a voice from upstairs. "I can't find my sandals. Do you know where I left them?"

"Your father picked up four pairs of your shoes this morning and dumped them in your closet," Emily called back. She turned and said to Calvin. "Honestly, she's home for a long weekend, brings half her shoes with her, and then leaves them everywhere."

"Carrie's home?" said Calvin. "I knew you had another daughter but . . . "

"You two have never met?" said Emily as she handed Calvin a zigzagging metal utensil and pointed him to a bowl.

"No," said Calvin, who started mashing potatoes with gusto. "Wasn't she studying abroad last semester?"

218

"Of course! That's why you've never met her. And she didn't come home until after New Year's. Then it was right back to school." With one fluid motion, Emily opened the oven, slid in a pie, and closed it again.

"I remember you saying that Carrie and Calvin would make a cute couple," said Brad who was leaning against the doorframe.

"Oh, wouldn't they just," said Emily.

Calvin felt himself blush violently.

At that moment, Carrie Lincoln entered the kitchen. She wore a yellow and white seersucker sundress and white sandals with miniature sunflowers atop them. Her hair was done in twin braids, which lay on her shoulders. "Who wouldn't just what?" she asked.

"Oh, nothing, dear," said Emily, who turned and winked at Calvin. "Carrie, this is Calvin Harper, the young priest from church."

"Hello," said Carrie. She gave Calvin a small wave from the other side of the room, which about started his stomach somersaulting.

"Hi," Calvin stammered, and he waved back. Of course, he thought. Just my luck. I'm about to have dinner with a beautiful girl, but I'm not on a date. Calvin mentally checked off all the reasons why he would never be able to ask out Carrie Lincoln: she doesn't really live in Victory because she's in college, she's the daughter of parishioners, and she probably already has a boyfriend back at school. So close yet so far. Calvin glanced at Carrie again and let out a wistful sigh. So why'd she have to be wearing a sundress?

"Keep mashing, Calvin," said Emily, shaking him out of a daydream, in which he and Carrie were on a picnic and she was wearing that dress.

"Yes, ma'am," he said, feeling guilty about where the day-dream would have gone if Carrie's mother hadn't made it vanish into thin air. Calvin wiped the idyllic scene from his mind and finished mashing the potatoes.

At one o'clock on the nose, the doorbell rang, and, a moment later, Esther Rose swept into the dining room with a flourish. She took one look around and let out a sniff of disapproval. She turned to Emily. "It gets better each year," was her attempt at generosity after she surveyed the array of dishes and their presentation on the sideboard.

Emily forced out a "Thank you."

The four generations of Lincolns and Calvin sat down to dinner. It was as marvelous as Calvin had hoped.

Two hours and two pieces of pie later, Calvin said his goodbyes and drove home. He unlocked the front door to his townhouse and swung it open. He flicked on the lights to reveal a living room with an old couch opposite the TV stand. No other furniture cluttered the room. He wandered into his kitchen, which still contained a patio set for his dining room table and chairs. He opened the refrigerator to deposit the left-overs that Emily had gathered for him, and he found the fridge to be empty save for a bottle of ketchup and half a case of beer. Walking upstairs, he went to the bedroom to change his clothes. His closet wasn't even close to half full; it could easily have stored a second person's entire wardrobe. Even though it was barely four in the afternoon, he changed into pajamas, returned to the kitchen, popped open a beer, and sat in one of the plastic chairs.

"Home, sweet home," he said to the silence.

The shrill sound of the phone ringing woke Calvin from his nap at the kitchen table. With one hand he cast around for his glasses and with the other for his mobile phone. Instead, he came in contact with not one but four beer bottles. *Did I drink all of those,* he thought absent-mindedly.

Standing up, he confirmed that, indeed, he had.

He found his glasses on the floor, and by the time he discovered his phone in between two couch cushions, the ringing had stopped. He waited for a voicemail to chirp into existence, which it did after a minute. But just as he was starting to listen, he felt a sudden, violent urge to dash to the restroom. He dropped the phone and stumbled to the toilet. Ten minutes later, he emerged after depositing the contents of his stomach in the porcelain basin. "Four beers is too many," he said to the empty bottles on the kitchen table. Wagging his finger at the evidence of his inebriation, he slumped down in the patio chair, chest still heaving with the exertion of vomiting, and lay his head back down on the table.

Once again, the shrill sound of the phone jerked Calvin from sleep. He looked around and found that the sun had set while he rested his eyes. He counted the bottles again. Still four. Good. He stood up. His head felt clearer, but his insides roiled and his mouth tasted like he had swallowed a pack of cigarettes dipped in motor oil. Again, he was too late to answer the call. So while waiting for the second chirp of the voicemail, he listened to the first message, forgotten in his race to the toilet.

"Calvin, it's Ruby. I'm so sorry to bother you on Easter. I know you are beyond tired. But I thought you should know that Whit went back to the hospital this evening. We are here now."

Hearing Ruby's voice on the phone snapped Calvin to full attention. *It's just like her to be thinking of me when she should* be thinking only of herself and her husband. He checked the time of the message. 6:10 p.m. That's when I vomited up four beers, he thought. But what time is it now? The phone read 9:30. I slept for three hours? He checked the second message.

"Whit has an infection. The doctor thinks he picked it up here at the hospital when he was in for pneumonia and all those cancer screenings over the last few weeks. Please come if you can."

Calvin took the stairs three at a times, threw on his black shirt and trousers, gave his teeth a furious brushing, and headed to his car. But before getting in, he reviewed his evening. I drank four beers between 4 p.m. and 6 p.m. At 6:10, anything that I hadn't already absorbed left my system. Then I slept for three hours. All this on a very full stomach from dinner with the Lincolns. He said the alphabet backward to himself. He walked a straight line in the parking lot. Satisfied, he drove to the hospital and arrived without incident.

Whit was once again in a bed in the Emergency Department. Calvin entered the room to find Ruby in a chair by the door rather than at the bedside. "We aren't allowed to touch him," she whispered to Calvin. "The nurse said that they don't know how contagious he is."

"But they let us in the same room?" said Calvin.

"They know it's not an airborne thing—they are calling it MRSA for now, and he's already on antibiotics."

Calvin looked over at Whit. He was fast asleep, but his face looked even more worn than it had the last time Calvin saw him. Because of the busyness of the last seven days, Calvin hadn't visited Whit in well over a week, and the intervening time had taken its toll. How much more abuse can his body take, Calvin wondered. Cancer, pneumonia, now . . .

"MRSA," Calvin repeated, sounding out the letters so the diagnosis came out "Mersa."

"It's difficult to treat because it resists a lot of common antibiotics," said Ruby. "At least, that's what the doctor said. He also said that sometimes it's mild and sometimes it's really dangerous."

Calvin nodded and took the seat next to Ruby, who continued, "But at Whit's age, everything is really dangerous." She lifted her hand off the arm of the chair as if to reach out and touch her husband, but, of course, she was too far away. "Do you know that Whit has never broken a bone in his body? Since his medical discharge from the Navy, I don't remember him ever coming to the hospital before this year for anything besides routine screenings. Then, all of a sudden . . ."

Her voice trailed off, and Calvin supplied the rest of the sentence.

"His body stopped working properly."

"To put it mildly."

Whit grunted in his sleep, and Ruby's hand stretched a little farther toward him. But he was still a good seven or eight feet away. Might as well have been a thousand miles. Calvin scooted his chair closer to Ruby's and put his hand on the arm of his chair palm up. Slowly, she brought her arm down and rested her hand in his, a proxy for the hand she wanted to hold. They sat there in silence, connected through the warmth of their hands.

After a long while, Ruby said, "God is in this room right now." It wasn't a question. It was a statement, and one that is truest when spoken aloud.

"What made you say that?"

"Oh, I was just telling the old bad thoughts to take a hike."

"What do you mean?"

"Call it the devil or a demon or just old-fashioned negative thinking—but sometimes, I get in these ruts where my thoughts spiral downward and the farther down I go the farther away the light is. My mother used to call them her 'lean times.' So before I go too far down, I tell that pit devil that God is in the room, so he—the devil I mean—better skedaddle."

Calvin smiled at his elderly friend's faith, so unencumbered by showy piety, yet so integrated into her being that he saw it every time he looked at her. "Does that work?" he asked.

"I suppose so. I've never sunk so deep that God wasn't able to pull me back up again."

"That's a good way to look at it."

"You know what they say," said Ruby. "The difference between God and the devil is that the devil is most effective when you don't notice him."

"And God is most effective when you do notice God," Calvin finished. "Who says that?"

"I think it was in one of your sermons."

Calvin grinned. "Oh, that sounds a bit too wise for me."

"Then maybe I said it, and you quoted me," Ruby teased. "Anyway, knowing God is in this room, in the warmth of your hand, in Whit's breath, in our bond so long in the making . . . it keeps the darkness at bay."

"The bad thoughts," said Calvin.

"The lean times," said Ruby.

"God is in this room," said Calvin. But what about in a big, empty townhouse? He didn't want to go back there to the emptiness.

He looked up at Ruby and noticed tears gathering in her eyes. "God being here in this room doesn't mean I shouldn't cry, though," she said, and she gestured to the box of tissues on the wall next to the nurse's computer.

But the moment Calvin stood up, his body decided to protest several things at once. In no particular order, these included his having been running on fumes for days, his having had nothing to eat in seven hours, his drinking and then throwing up four beers, and his having drunk nothing since his bowel inversion.

His head spun, and all the breath seemed to leave him. He felt his knees cave, just before the room went dark.

⁂

A steady beeping sound and the low murmur of voices were the first things Calvin's conscious mind processed when he came to. The next was the harsh fluorescence of the light shining on the other side of his eyelids. He tried an experimental squint and found himself in a bed in the hallway of the Emergency Department. He closed his eyes, squeezed them shut to dispel the cobwebs from his mind, and opened them again. The first thing he saw was a thin tube protruding from the back of his hand. He followed the tube with his eyes as it rose to meet a bag of clear liquid, which was suspended from a metal rod attached to his bed. The second thing he saw was Ruby sitting guard duty nearby.

"Calvin," she said. "You're awake."

"I am?" Apparently there were more cobwebs than he realized.

"You fainted in Whit's room. You scared me half to death."

"I don't remember."

"The good news is that you fell rather gracefully and didn't bang your head on anything. You just . . . well . . . folded up right there in the middle of the room."

"How's Whit?"

"The same. He's still asleep."

"What time is it?"

Ruby craned her neck to look at the big analog clock on the wall. "Three in the morning."

"Well, at least I got some rest," said Calvin, trying to inject some humor into the situation. But his smile turned into a grimace. "I feel awful."

"You were dehydrated," said a new voice, and Calvin squinted up and saw an angel with a clipboard.

"This is a saline drip," said the angel. "It's your second bag."

He squeezed his eyes shut a second time, reopened them, and the last of the cobwebs finally dissolved. And with them went the angel's wings, which became a white lab coat. And the angel herself became a young woman, who could have had a lucrative career as a runway model if the whole doctor thing didn't pan out, thought Calvin. His eyes automatically went to her left hand. A massive diamond glinted in the harsh fluorescence. Of course.

"We've been forcing the fluids into you up till now," she continued. "We'll do one more bag and just let gravity do its thing, okay?"

"Okay," said Calvin, but with a face like hers, Calvin probably would have said "okay" to quadruple amputation if she had suggested it. He slumped back on the inclined bed. I really need a date, he thought.

"Well, she sure is a beauty," said Ruby after the doctor had catwalked away. "And she's in medicine too. Must have some smarts in that head of hers."

"Don't remind me," said Calvin.

"You should ask for her telephone number."

"You didn't see the rock on her hand?"

"Oh, I suppose my eyes don't notice things like that anymore." She fingered her own wedding ring, a simple band of yellow gold with a small diamond adorning it, inside which her finger had adapted over the last fifty or so years. "Too bad."

"Well, I'm not really in my best first impression mode right now, anyway," said Calvin.

Ruby chuckled. "That's for certain."

"You should really go back and check on Whit."

"Oh, he'll keep."

The three words hung in the air after Ruby said them. They looked at each other, and Calvin saw the tears forming once again in the corner of Ruby's eyes. He felt sure that she would have seen tears in his eyes too if he hadn't been dehydrated. "Go to him," said Calvin in a hushed tone.

"I think I will." She rose to her feet and patted Calvin on the hand without the IV. "I'll come back and check on you soon, okay?"

"Okay." Calvin watched her plod down the hall to the spotless room that held her ill husband. *Oh, he'll keep.* The three words still hung above Calvin's head like toxic fumes or like false prophecy.

May 18, 2010

Dear Rev. Calvin,

You've probably guessed by now how much I enjoy writing letters. Even with all this new-fangled technology—electronic mail and that text messaging Cooper does—I think I'll stick with a piece of nice, thick stationery and a ballpoint pen, thank you very much. There's something so impersonal about electronic mail. Cooper made me an account, but I can't imagine reading letters from people without holding the paper or seeing their handwriting. Besides, I have too much stationery lying around the house to let it go to waste. If there are two good

227

things about you moving away, Calvin, then the first is your "mysterious news," and the second is I have someone to write letters to.

Speaking of writing letters, Whit and I corresponded for the entire time he was at Columbia. He enrolled in the winter of 1946, which put the entire state of Pennsylvania between us because I was in Pittsburgh at my school. Still, that was better than the whole continent of North America and the Pacific Ocean! I looked through all those boxes and couldn't for the life of me find any letters from when we were in college. They must have been lost in the constant moving from dormitory to home and back. Or else they just didn't seem as special as the ones he wrote me during the war. And that's too bad, because they certainly would be special now if I still had them.

I do remember that he still signed his letters "your friend." He was always so cautious. During those years, he hid his feelings for me, though they were plain to see in the devotion with which he wrote me letters. Years later, he told me that he felt it was a betrayal of Mike's memory to court me. They had been best friends, after all, for their entire lives. I can't imagine the guilt Whit felt for wanting to be with me, especially after Mike's death, which stayed with him for years and years. Every year on the anniversary of Mike's death, Whit used to go to a special place near where they grew up to remember him. He took me there many times, as well, later on. But I don't want to get ahead of myself.

If you recall in my last letter, my own grief for Mike had burned out quickly over the summer. When I looked deep down to find those intense feelings of loss, they just weren't there. Instead, I found something I didn't expect: the seed of affection for Whit. And when he surprised me on Christmas Eve in 1945, the seed took root. Now, before you start wondering, my toes weren't curling just yet—that took a while longer. But the seed was there.

Of course, there were two problems. First, Whit was in New York and I was in Pittsburgh. And second, because of Whit's loyalty to his deceased friend, he never said a thing about his feelings. So it was up to me to take the bull by the horns, so to speak. I wasn't going to let social convention or distance or Whit's timidity or his guilt stand in the way of our storybook romance.

We saw each other over the summers of 1946 and 1947, and we wrote letters in between. My mother always agreed to host Whit at our home in Jericho. That way she could keep an eye on us. But really, at that point, there was no need for a chaperone. We would walk in the woods, sit by the railroad tracks, talk late into the night—it was all very romantic, mind you—and yet he never tried to kiss me. I think he would have responded quite positively to my trying to kiss him, if I do say so myself. But then I imagine he would have fallen back into guilt. So I was the picture of patience. Well, at least until the summer of 1948.

I graduated in May of that year, and D.B. took me on a trip to England to celebrate. D.B. had done quite well for himself in the years after the war doing this and that—he was always so coy about his business ventures—and he insisted on treating me. So I said, "Why not?" I wrote to Whit to tell him that my brother was whisking me off to Europe, and he wrote back asking me to pick him up a souvenir, something he couldn't get in the States.

So I had a challenge from Whit, and I had no idea what I was going to get him. But to be honest, his souvenir fell from the top of my mind the moment we arrived. There was just so much to take in, so much to see and do. We traveled by train around the country—Cambridge, York, Whitby, up into Scotland to Edinburgh, back through the Lake District, Stratford, Oxford, London. There was still so much devastation from the war, but you could tell that England was rooted and ancient and would return again to the glory I imagined it had before the Blitz.

I remember the awe and the joy I felt traveling by train across the countryside and seeing soaring cathedrals rise out of the fields. You just don't get that on this side of the Atlantic. I dragged D.B. into every church I saw—they were so old and I could feel the history and all the years of praying that soaked into those stone walls. I became an Anglican on that trip because of those churches and the beautiful services we attended. I think after a few days, D.B. was sorry he invited me on the vacation! He didn't dislike going to church, although it was never his first choice of activity. But it rapidly became mine. I fell in love with the service of Evensong: the little boys with the little ruffled collars singing their hearts out to God, the organ music reverberating down the colossal naves, the chanting of the psalms. My current love for Morning Prayer was born then, as well, I think.

We arrived in London on the last day of our trip, and I dragged D.B. to Westminster Abbey. After the service, we took a long winding route back to our hotel. While walking through Hyde Park, I realized that I had forgotten to look for Whit's souvenir. What I really wanted to do was bring him some of the magnificent singing that I had heard. That was a bit too abstract, however. We had wandered through many a knickknack store, but nothing had jumped out to me. He didn't seem like a knickknack type of person.

But in Hyde Park, I found the perfect present. We walked up to a rose garden in full bloom and stopped to admire it. I remarked to D.B. that they just didn't grow them so lovely in Pennsylvania. At that a gardener appeared out of nowhere, doffed his cap, and handed me a rose he had just cut from one of the bushes. "Here you go, love," he said. "And thanks for the compliment."

Well, I took that rose right back to the room and hung it upside down to let it dry. When it was time to leave, I packed it ever so carefully in my luggage. And when Whit came to visit Jericho the next month, I presented him with the dried rose. "You sure can't get one of these in the States," he said.

And with both of our hands on the rose, I leaned in and kissed him gently on the mouth. And he kissed me back. I didn't plan it. I don't even remember making a conscious decision to do it. But then we were kissing and nothing had ever felt so right. As he leaned in for more kisses, my toes definitely curled.

I think that in Whit's poetic mind, the dried rose meant more than I ever thought it would. The rose was dead, but it was still beautiful. Mike had been dead for over three years, but their friendship remained strong in Whit's heart. In receiving the rose, I think Whit finally decided that Mike would want him to be happy, and I made him so. From then on, Whit signed his letters, "With tenderness" or "With affection."

Whit graduated from college in December of 1949 with an English degree. He was a poet, but he knew that wasn't going to pay the bills, so he enrolled in a graduate program to begin in the fall of 1950. We spent the first six months of that year together. I taught my kids at school, and he did odd jobs around Jericho, trying to earn a bit of tuition money. My mother gave him D.B.'s old room so that he didn't have to pay rent (and so she could continue to keep an eye on us—and now she did have a reason).

But all the plans we made in those months fell by the wayside—at least for a little while— that summer when North Korea crossed the 38th parallel. The Navy (to use Whit's term) "borrowed" him in July. He had to postpone his schooling. And we had to postpone our life together.

Whit was gone nearly a year. I continued teaching in Jericho and living with my mother. We were two peas in a pod that year. Every time we went to the grocery story, the manager asked if my mother was my older sister. I think he was a bit sweet on her. But after Mort died, my mother never had much use for romance. Because of Mort's inability to show emotion, I think my mother just didn't trust herself to pick out someone who would be able to show his love. So she went about the rest of her days as the independent woman she had always been, even when she was hitched. I loved her for that. But I also pitied her for never having what Whit and I had. I think that she was so keen on Whit and me getting together because she was able to live vicariously through me. She was nearly as devastated as I was when Whit got "borrowed."

My joy that year—well, one of my joys every year—was teaching the kids. Over the years, I taught every grade of primary school, so I can never remember which one I was teaching any given term. I taught third grade most often, and I never had a bad year in all my teaching. I don't know if I brought the best out of the kids or if they brought the best out of me. Probably both. But the year Whit was gone was special because the kids knew that my sweetheart was overseas. Since many of them were born right before their daddies shipped off for Europe or the Pacific—some never to return—they had grown up with the reality of what war can do to a family. They knew no other world. And so we comforted each other.

I received no letters from him that year, which was the hardest part. When he left he told me that was a possibility, but I hadn't wanted to believe it. When he returned he explained that he had been posted to a submarine that had to maintain radio silence a good portion of the time. He never went into much detail.

You know, Calvin, sometimes something bad happens and something good follows right in its wake. I know that to be true, though sometimes I forget. It was definitely true in March of 1951. There was an accident on Whit's submarine and somehow a chemical affected his eyesight. I wish I could tell you more, but I don't know if Whit ever even knew what happened. The chemical nearly blinded him, which led to his medical discharge. His eyesight slowly returned over time, but his glasses were always thicker than the bottoms of soda bottles.

One day in late April of 1951, he came stumbling up our lawn. I don't know how he made his way barely able to see, but I do remember what he said when we embraced on the porch of my mother's house: "Even if I were blind, I would still see you shining in front of me."

Oh, Calvin, how I miss that dear, dear man.

Your friend,

Ruby

13

Early on Easter Monday morning, Calvin left the hospital about eight or nine hours later than he meant to. On his way out, he had poked around for Whit only to find that he had been admitted as an inpatient, but Calvin had no energy left to look for him in the labyrinthine upper floors. So Calvin drove home with a bloodstream full of saline and spent the next three days on his couch recovering from his battle with dehydration.

Much too early on Thursday morning, Calvin's doorbell rang. Fumbling with his glasses, Calvin hurried down the stairs and opened the door. There, huddled on his tiny front stoop, stood the four Morning Prayer ladies.

"We are worried about you, sonny," said Mary.

"You haven't been at Morning Prayer all week," said Avis.

"I told them about your fainting, and they wanted to make sure you were okay," said Ruby.

"Are those penguins on your pajamas?" asked Esther Rose.

Calvin looked himself up and down. Indeed, those were penguins on his pajamas. They went well with his being unshowered and unshaved, he thought.

"Really I'm fine," said Calvin as he closed the door half-way and used it as a shield against his own unkemptness. "Um . . . thanks for checking up on me, though a phone call would've done just fine."

"But you can't send this through the telephone," said Avis, who stepped around Mary to reveal a casserole bursting from a rectangular baking pan. She stepped through the half open door. "I'll just pop this in the fridge, shall I?"

Without waiting for a reply, Avis walked through Calvin's living room and into the kitchen. "Avis, I can manage," said Calvin, leaving the door unguarded in order to chase her.

But she reached the refrigerator and opened it before he could stop her. It was barer than it had been Easter night: the bottle of ketchup remained, as did the empty box that had once held a dozen beer bottles. Avis slid the casserole onto the top shelf. "Oh, Calvin," she said. "This won't do."

Calvin sank into one of the patio chairs in the corner of the kitchen. Avis opened the freezer to find a tall stack of frozen pizzas and a half-gallon of vanilla ice cream. "This won't do at all," she concluded.

"What won't do?" said Esther Rose, who, along with Mary and Ruby, had invited herself in. They gathered in Calvin's kitchen, and Avis showed them the empty shelves of the refrigerator. As one, the ladies turned to Calvin, who remained seated in the corner trying desperately not to make eye contact with any of them.

"I eat out a lot," he said.

"Calvin, why wouldn't you let us throw you a house-warming party last fall?" asked Ruby. She cast her gaze around the kitchen. "Your house could use a little warmth."

"Maybe some flowers on the counter?" said Mary.

"Or some curtains?" said Avis.

"You do know that patio furniture is supposed to go outside?" asked Esther Rose.

Calvin hung his head, but something in Esther Rose's tone made him begin to flare up. "Yes, Esther Rose," he said. "Of course I know that patio furniture is supposed to go outside. But perhaps you haven't noticed that I don't have a patio. And this table and chairs cost next to nothing, and considering I make next to nothing it seemed like a good idea."

He stood up, shaking with sudden anger, and now looked each one of the ladies in the eye. "Listen," he said. "I appreciate you coming here to check on me, and I appreciate the casserole. But did it ever occur to you that this is my private space, the one spot in this town I can just be me and not have to be the priest."

He walked around them and opened the freezer. "Did it ever occur to you that I like frozen pizza and that having a freezer full of it is the result of it being on sale at the supermarket and not some sinister sign that I am unable to take care of myself?"

He stormed through the living room on his way to the front door. "Did it ever occur to you that I'm doing just fine on my own and that I don't need yours or anyone else's help?"

He opened the door and waited for them to take the hint.

Without a word, they filed through the living room. Mercifully, none of them mentioned the pile of takeout bags and fast food wrappers littering Calvin's couch cushions. Esther Rose stepped over the threshold first. She neither looked at him nor said a word, but kept on walking to the car. Mary patted Calvin on the shoulder, but he flinched away from her touch. "Oh, sonny," she said.

Avis looked wounded, but her usual jubilance could not be contained. "I suspect you're just having a rough week, Calvin," she said, casting around for a reason to explain Calvin's rudeness. "Oh, and I like your penguin pajamas."

Ruby was the last to leave. Calvin was still seething, but one look from Ruby and his anger liquefied into remorse and then into sorrow. "Perhaps we shouldn't have dropped by unannounced," she said. "I hope you are feeling better."

Calvin remained silent.

Ruby continued, "But honestly, Calvin, you may be doing just fine. Still, everyone needs help sometimes." She patted him in the same place Mary had, and this time he didn't flinch away. "It isn't a sign of weakness, dear. You just need to ask, and we'll come running."

She took the handle of the door in her hand and closed it behind her, leaving Calvin alone in his desolate home. He put his back to the door, slumped to the ground, and wept. But he didn't know whether his tears fell because he had gotten angry at people he loved, or because they had seen his style of life, for which he was, in fact, ashamed, or because he was just so lonely and didn't know how to be anything else anymore, or most likely, all three.

⸺⸙⸺

A week went by, and each day Calvin found an excuse not to attend Morning Prayer. He scheduled breakfast meetings with Chief Stern and the mayor. He brought in Brad and Rebecca Stewart to talk about baptizing Natalie, scheduled for the last Sunday in June. He even moved up his dentist appointment by a couple of weeks so as not to be in the office at 8:15 in the morning. Dr. Monica Dennis checked Calvin's teeth with nothing more than, "They look fine. Keep flossing." No recollection of their lackluster date broke through her businesslike veneer, except perhaps a bit more energy than was really necessary in scraping his teeth with her metal probe. Calvin left the office wishing he had just endured Morning Prayer rather than be reminded that he had let a beautiful single woman slip through his fingers after one date because she liked country music and dogs.

Finally, Calvin ran out of excuses and two Mondays after he was discharged from the hospital, he entered the chapel at 8:10, sat in his usual spot, closed his eyes, and pretended to be absorbed in prayer so no one would bother him. But Ruby was the first of the ladies to arrive, and she wasn't fooled. Sliding into the pew they shared, she whispered, "I've known you long enough to know that you always pray with your eyes open."

He looked at her, astonished that she could tell he was just kneeling there thinking about nothing in particular. It was as if she could tune into the prayer frequency and tell that he was on a different channel. The other ladies filed in and took their places as Ruby continued, "But if you're going to take the time to pretend to pray, you might as well just pray instead." She pulled a Book of Common Prayer out of the rack and whispered, "By the way, good morning, dear." She patted his knee. "It's good to have you back."

"Good morning, Calvin," said Avis.

"Top of the morning, sonny," said Mary.

There was a pause. The three ladies turned to Esther Rose and waited.

"Yes, all right," she grumbled. "Good morning."

Calvin had expected them to be cold. They had every right to cast him out of their circle because of his rudeness. Instead, they were being polite. And not just polite, they seemed happy to see him. Well, three out of four, he thought, but that's not a bad percentage. There was no passive aggression in their politeness either. It was genuine, if begrudging on Esther Rose's part.

Avis said, "I want to apologize for barging into your town-house. That was uncalled for and rude. I'm sorry."

Adam Thomas

"We're sorry," the other three chimed in.

Calvin wondered when they had planned this little ritual. Probably the day after the incident, and he had deprived himself of the chance for reconciliation for over a week because he was afraid to face them, afraid of what they would say. Apparently, what they would have said was, "I'm sorry." All he had succeeded in doing was delaying a chance for mutual forgiveness.

"Thanks, but . . . " Calvin stammered. "I should be the one apologizing to you. I shouldn't have blown up at you or said those things. I feel really awful about the whole thing. And Avis, the casserole was wonderful. I ate the whole thing in three days. Your pan has been in my office for a week."

"Let's all agree to share the fault and the forgiveness, shall we," said Ruby. "I can't think of a better way to start our morning than with the Confession of Sin." And with that she began Morning Prayer.

As they prayed, Calvin stole long looks at each of the ladies and listened to their individual voices blending into a fabric of pure devotion. These four women had been walking with God for decades before Calvin was even born. Their faith existed in their bedrock, not their topsoil. Their lives were woven with the glistening thread of God's movement. Their center of gravity was St. John's Church, which they inhabited day in and day out—praying, cooking food, cleaning and dressing the sanctuary. And supporting and loving me, Calvin realized. I haven't been doing any of this on my own all year. I've never been alone all this time. Except at home in that big, empty townhouse, where I feel like a ghost haunting the place.

He listened more intently to them praying and picked out each of their voices in turn as a new appreciation for their dedication to God began to leaven his own. He started with the most difficult voice. More often than not, Esther Rose spoke with a negativity that seemed at odds in someone so dedicated to her faith. During seminary Calvin had known some real sticks-in-the-mud who treated their faith as something to defend rather than as something to share, but Esther Rose had never fallen into that camp. Rather, she was more like a prophet from the Hebrew Scriptures, always bringing what sounded like messages of doom and gloom, except if you heeded the message and realized it was meant for your betterment. She spoke the truth; she just didn't always speak it in a way that made the reception of it easy. What was it Ruby had said about her? That God wasn't finished scrubbing away all her rough edges. Listening to the roughness in her voice, Calvin knew that he still loved her, despite her ability to target his deficiencies. Heaven is full of sea glass, he heard Ruby say in his mind. Looking at Esther Rose, he imagined her walking in the fullness of God's presence, polished and smooth and glinting in the light of God. And he smiled.

As they moved on to the Apostles' Creed, Calvin turned his attention to Avis Noon, who couldn't have been more of a contrast with Esther Rose. When he had first met Avis, her husband, Alexander, had recently died, and Calvin had known her only as a grieving widow, prone to bursting into tears because the loss was so raw and so near, and the hole her husband left was so ragged and tattered. Every once in a while during that period, Calvin had caught glimpses of her true nature—the irrepressible, unstoppable optimistic force. But for a long time, her sorrow had taken center stage. However, in the last few months, renewed joy had replaced sorrow as the lead character in her life. It had happened so slowly, so incrementally that it was hard to place when sorrow had given up its starring role and melted into the company. But it had. The first anniversary of Alexander Noon's death had been the week before Easter, and Avis threw what she called a "Resurrection Party" for him.

Calvin wondered what had filled the ragged hole Alexander had left, and the only thing he could conclude was that the love of God, shown especially in the three other women in the room, had poured in and overflowed and started spilling puddles of grace everywhere Avis went. Of course, since Alexander walked in God's eternal presence, Alexander's love poured in as part of God's. That's how we know resurrection is real, thought Calvin, because the love never leaves us, never dries up, never dies. He looked at the weathered, constant joy on Avis's face, and his smile widened.

The Lord's Prayer began and he shifted his gaze to Mary Williams. He could hear the lilt in her voice, the faintest trace of Irish brogue that was always more pronounced when she said the Lord's Prayer. He imagined her learning it as a small child back in Ireland before moving to the United States, and now, all those decades later, the prayer was an artifact of her ancestry, a link to her heritage that time would never erase. Calvin had met elders suffering from full-fledged dementia who could say the Lord's Prayer with such lucidity that he would never have known they were sick otherwise. If Mary's mind ever abandons her, he thought, the prayer never will. And nor will God. Calvin's imagination left the immigrant child on the shores of Ireland and turned to the elder immigrating someday soon to her new home in God's kingdom. He played the scene over in his mind, and every time he heard Mary call Jesus "sonny." That's how she signals her love, he thought—with another timeless artifact from the old country. And she uses it on me. Calvin didn't think his smile could get any wider.

As the collects began, the other three fell silent and Ruby's voice filled the chapel. She prayed in her normal speaking voice: there was no hint of performance in it, as Calvin often noticed when he prayed aloud. But as he listened to her, he realized that, after eight decades of conversing with God, Ruby no longer had a speaking voice. She simply had a praying voice that she used all the time. *That must be why I always feel better after we talk*, he thought, *because Ruby is praying even in the midst of our conversation. Christ is part of the conversation too, and whenever she talks to me, she's also talking to him.* A wisp of the Gospel danced through his mind. *Whenever two or three are gathered in my name, I am there among them.* Calvin marveled at Ruby's faith. She believed without a shadow of a doubt that Christ was there with her. And even when there was a shadow, like on Whit's x-rays, she still saw Christ in the room. Still, Calvin wondered when the breakdown was coming. *How sick did Whit have to be for Ruby to start to pull away from God? How much suffering did Whit have to endure before Ruby began railing at God rather than blessing God?* He remembered her telling him about her "bad thoughts" when they were sitting in the hospital with Whit. Calvin couldn't possibly imagine what they were because whenever he saw her, she was so full of the light of Christ that he couldn't see darkness anywhere on her. *Maybe I'm not looking hard enough*, he thought. *She isn't a spiritual superhero. She wouldn't want me to put her on a pedestal. But I have.* Calvin's smile retreated from his face.

During the final prayer, Calvin surveyed the room once more and thanked God for each of the women there. He would never have survived in Victory without them: Esther Rose's forced self-improvement, Avis's infectious joy, Mary's steadfast love, and Ruby's stalwart faith. Calvin wondered what he had brought to them besides a toddler in the faith who still needed help walking without falling down. The four of them combined had over 300 years worth of walking with God. At twenty-five, Calvin sure felt like an infant compared to that. He still had so much to learn from these women, especially the one who had been a teacher. But how much longer could he stay in Victory, drinking in their wisdom, while he slowly ghosted away in the empty townhouse?

Calvin shook the thought out of his mind as they concluded Morning Prayer. The four ladies rose and then queued up to hug Calvin in turn. "Really, I am sorry," he said after the final embrace.

"Say no more," said Ruby. "It's done. You are forgiven." She slapped the top of a pew like a judge gaveling out a session of court.

"And now, we have to show Calvin his surprise," said Avis, who grabbed Calvin by the arm and led him out of the sanctuary.

"My surprise?"

"I told them not to," said Esther Rose. "I didn't want to reinforce bad behavior, but no one listened."

"Oh hush, E.R.," said Mary. "Calvin isn't a baby."

Close enough, thought Calvin.

"Close enough," said Esther Rose.

Six months ago, that would have made Calvin bristle, but now he recognized it as the truth.

The five of them stopped at the doors to the parish hall, which were usually open, but not today. Avis put her hand on the knob and said, "We couldn't figure out how to wrap them, so we just hid them in the hall. Are you ready?"

"Ready as I'll ever be," said Calvin.

Avis opened one door, and Mary opened the other. The hall was filled as normal with folding tables and chairs, but the one closest to them looked new and out of place. It was round and made of rich, dark wood adorned with swirling patterns outlined in an even darker grain. Four matching chairs with blue and white-checkered cushions encircled the table, and atop it were a red bow and a note that read, "For Calvin, with love."

Calvin put his hands on top of his head. "Oh," was all he could think to say. He walked around the table, running his fingers along the dark grain. "Thank you. Thank you so much. But . . . "

"No buts," said Avis. "It's yours."

"So don't say we shouldn't have or that it's too much," said Ruby. "Because we should have had and it wasn't."

"But I really can't accept such a . . . "

". . . Such a what?" said Mary. "Such a gift. Sure you can. Wouldn't be a gift if you couldn't accept it."

"But the cost of something like this."

"Was zero dollars," said Avis. "Let's sit and I'll tell you all about it."

Ruby ambled over to the coffee machine and brought back the pot and a tray of mugs. Calvin slid a chair from the nearest folding table and the five of them sat around Calvin's new dining room set. "Really," he said. "This is amazing. Thank you."

"You haven't heard the best part yet," said Ruby. "Go on, Avis."

Avis clapped her hands together. "This table is from my house. Alexander built it when we were first married. He was always a dab hand at carpentry. I would have to coax him from his woodshop with sandwiches or, well . . . never mind." She blushed, and Mary let out a chuckle.

"But if your husband built it," said Calvin, "Then surely you would want to keep it?"

"Quite the contrary," said Avis. "I eat my breakfasts at the kitchen counter now, and when I entertain I use the dining room. This kitchen table hasn't seen much use for over a year now. My children are all grown with houses full of their own furniture. So I can think of nothing better than to pass it on to someone who can use it for years to come."

"Just think," said Ruby. "What would your future wife say if she saw patio furniture in your kitchen?"

"Good point," said Calvin. He ran his hand over the dark grain again. "Well, I can't express my gratitude enough. This is just wonderful. Thank you, Avis. Thank you all."

"You are entirely welcome," said Avis. "You just make sure to send me pictures when your kids are blowing out the candles of their birthday cakes sitting around this table."

"It's a deal."

———

May 25, 2010

Dear Rev. Calvin,

The last few days have been a flurry of activity here at St. John's. Perhaps you heard from someone else, but I'm going to tell you anyway, just in case you haven't. Josie Temple-Jones and Donald Pennyworth got married last Saturday! Can you believe it? They really are perfect for each other. She's so garrulous and extravagant, while he is even-keeled and temperate. They balance one another out: he reins in her excesses and she pushes him to be more adventurous. Who says you can't find love at their age?

Josie really is a woman after my own heart. Watching her court Dr. Pennyworth has been a sight these last few months. You remember how she was when he first arrived. There were a few weeks when she wasn't too subtle about her interest. Then she realized his temperament and backed off, only to begin the waiting game.

She must really like him because I've never seen Josie be so patient before. She reminds me of me back before I gave Whit that rose in 1948.

But right about the time you moved to Boston, she shifted into action. I suppose she thought that knowing each other for a year was long enough for Donald not to consider their getting together to be "hasty." However, I think in the last three months she has rubbed off on him because a one-month engagement seems to me to be about as hasty as you can be. In true Josie fashion, she popped the question. I think Donald was so taken aback that he agreed before he had time to think—which, in his case, was probably for the best. If he had thought about it too much, I'm sure he would have come up with a reason against their union. But the deed is done now, which is wonderful because they are made for each other—anyone can see that—and I wish them many years of happiness.

One-month-long engagements are most certainly hasty, but that's not to say they are a bad idea. I seem to remember one that went pretty well. Whit whisked me off to Long Island the same day he came stumbling up my lawn barely able to see. He said he had something special to show me in his hometown, so when we arrived, he took me straightaway to the hidden place that he and Mike had shared their whole lives. He told me that he wanted Mike to be a witness to what he was about to do, that it was only right for his best friend to share in the joy that he had helped bring into Whit's life, even if that friend was there only in memory.

And then Whit got down on one knee and pro-posed—in verse no less. He always was a poet. I have his proposal framed above the piano in our house. I'm sure you've seen it, though you might not have realized what it was. I'll have to share it with you, but not today because I'm writing this letter from the church, and I want to drop it in the mailbox outside.

Whit proposed at the beginning of May 1951, and we were married on the first Saturday of June. But there was no scandal in it—not like my parents' wedding. D.B. was born just five months after my parents were hitched, you remember, so anyone could do the math. But it was impossible for me to have been preg-nant when we were married, as Whit had been overseas for almost a year. Did you know our fifty-ninth anniversary would have been next week? But I can't even think about that because my hand starts shaking so. Avis is here with me, though, so I know I will make it through the day. Perhaps we will go downstairs and sing at the piano when I'm finished writing to you. We could sing Whit's song. You remember the one I sang for you that day you forgot the wine, don't you?

It's strange how thinking about the anniver-sary makes me start to cry, but thinking about our wedding day brings me joy. I suppose that's how memory works. When the present threat-ens to drown you, you can stay afloat on the thoughts of the past.

Seeing Josie's face last Saturday reminded me of my wedding day all those years ago. I didn't know it was possible for God to pour as much love into a single person as I felt that day. Every time I touched someone I could feel God's love leaping from me to him or her. When I held Whit's hand, there was a current pulsing between us, and I knew I never wanted to let go. It was just that kind of day.

We were married in the church of my childhood in Jericho, and I had never seen the simple room look so beautiful. My mother brought the ladies of the church together and tasked them with gathering all the wildflowers they could find in the days before the wedding. When they were finished decorating, you could barely see the inside of the church building at all. Every flat surface was covered with flowers, and strands of woven flowers adorned each wall. My mother had brought my beloved Pennsylvania countryside into the church, and all the colors of late spring met me when I entered on D.B.'s arm.

Now, this wouldn't be a story about a wedding if something hadn't gone wrong. I honestly can't remember how I reacted on the day of, so you'll have to excuse my recollections on this particular point. There's a good chance that I am going to come off as much more charitable than I was fifty-nine years ago.

Besides organizing the flowers, my mother made my wedding dress. She had always been a fair seamstress, having done odd jobs for people her whole life, including quite a bit of tailoring. And she used to make my clothes when I was a child. But I'm not sure she had ever tried anything as ambitious as a wedding dress before. And considering she had all of three weeks to make it, I think she did a fine job despite what happened.

The finished dress was beautiful. It was not quite white—more of a mellow ivory color because that was the fabric my mother could get on short notice. She also procured some delicate lace and about half a mile of tulle (you probably don't know what that is, Calvin—it's the stuff that makes the skirt of a dress puff out, like in animated movies with princesses). She didn't have a dress form, so I had to stand still while she pinned fabric around me. We had a fair bit of mother-daughter bonding time during those days of dress-making. (Avis is reading over my shoulder and she just laughed out loud at that sentence.)

Like I said, the finished dress was beautiful. Cinderella had nothing on me and she had a fairy godmother helping her, not just a mother. I saw that film in the theater the year before, and there's a good chance that her dress made me want mine to be all puffy. My mother insisted that the dress have sleeves because one doesn't bare one's shoulders in front of the Lord, or so she said. I didn't want them, but I wasn't in a position to argue, as she was doing all that work for me. So the dress had sleeves made out of lace, and they were quite fetching in the end. The cuffs were wide and dangled down to about my knee, so the sleeves had a dreamy quality to them. (But you probably don't care much about what my dress looked like, you being a man and all, so I'll just keep going.)

Whit and I left the church in the special Ford Model-A that every couple in Jericho borrowed on their wedding day. The reception was in the backyard of my family's home, which was all of a three-minute walk to the church. But we used the car anyway, and we drove around for a while to give everyone time to arrive at the house. When we got there, all of our guests were lined up outside ready to throw rice on us. On reflection, I don't remember why we decided to do this part upon arrival at the reception and not upon leaving. Anyway, we pulled up in front of the two lines, Whit came around to my door, opened it, and helped me out of the car. With a skirt the size of mine, I couldn't shift myself from a seated position. Then Whit shut the door behind me and we took off through the crowd as rice rained down on top of us.

And I left my right sleeve stuck in the car door. It turns out it was a little bit too long to be perfectly functional. Whit and I moved through the rice-throwing gauntlet, and it was only when we reached the front door of the house that I noticed my sleeve was gone. So before anyone else could detect the problem, I made a snap decision and told Whit to rip the other one off too. For the rest of the day, I had the dress I wanted (if a little ragged around the straps), and I didn't bare my shoulders to the Lord.

Calvin, I can't wait to hear about your wedding day, whenever that day might be. You have no concept of just how much joy you will feel on that day. It will make all those lonely days here in Victory a distant memory.

Missing you.

Your friend,

Ruby

P.S. Rev. Calvin—this is Avis Noon. I asked if I could write a postscript on Ruby's letter. She told us about your "mysterious news," which we all agree is a girlfriend. I just wanted to ask: does she like your dining room table? Much love from us to you.—Avis

14

I don't understand the procedure that Whit is scheduled for," said Calvin.

"Well, I'm not his doctor, but if you give me some general symptoms I might be able to make an educated guess," said Donald Pennyworth.

They were in the vesting room removing their white albs. Dr. Pennyworth had been at St. John's for barely a month, and he was already involved in the services as a chalice bearer. Calvin looked across the hall to the sacristy and watched Ruby cleaning the ornate silver cup, from which Dr. Pennyworth had recently been offering the Blood of Christ. There was a slight tremor in Ruby's hand that hadn't been there before, and Calvin wondered if it was a symptom of her aging or of her beginning to show her anxiety over Whit's condition. He wished he could make it all go away. He prayed for Whit, but with every passing day, an end to Whit's cancer seemed ever more remote. Or ever nearer, depending on how he looked at it.

Calvin took a deep breath and recounted what he knew about Whit's medical history. "He had what I think was a basal cell carcinoma around Christmastime. Then he had some sort of procedure in February. I'm not sure if it was chemo or radiation or surgery. I was supposed to be there, but it was the day that a man name Phil Erickson died suddenly, so I missed quite a bit of the situation. Then he developed pneumonia in March—you remember that, of course. Then he contracted MRSA at the hospital. He's been there about three weeks now. He has some sort of unrelated cancer elsewhere, but I'm not clear what kind. His surgery was scheduled for two weeks ago, but it keeps getting pushed back because he's still not free of infection. This case of MRSA just seems really nasty."

Dr. Pennyworth scratched his chin. "Getting the MRSA under control is priority number one because with it still swimming around in his bloodstream his body isn't going to be strong enough to withstand much else, let alone surgery. Especially at Whit's age. He's what? Eighty-six?"

"That's in the ballpark. I'm not exactly sure."

"Where's the carcinoma?"

"The one that I noticed was on his left cheek, but I don't know if there were other patches."

"The face is not a great region to have to fight cancer, even a relatively mild kind. There are too many important things close by. But I assume the doctors corralled the carcinoma, so there must be some underlying problem that's prompting the need for more invasive surgery. I'm not sure that Victory has the right facility or personnel for some of the more delicate surgeries that Whit could be going in for."

"I forgot—the surgery is supposed to be in Baltimore. That's what is making this whole thing so tricky. It keeps getting rescheduled, which means that new plans have to be made for the trip and all."

"Johns Hopkins is the right place in this area. He'll be in good hands there. From what I've seen in my limited interactions with Whit, the carcinoma is just the thing that we can see.

I suspect that he delayed meeting with an oncologist because the basal cell isn't too bad by itself. Not like melanoma or some other aggressive cancers. It happens all the time. Delays are never a good thing. He could be in for a tough time."

"I imagine that any form of cancer would make times tough," said Calvin.

"It sure isn't a walk in the park. And the pneumonia and the MRSA just compound the problems because the longer they wait, the less effective any kind of treatment is going to be." Dr. Pennyworth hung his vestments on the rack and turned to face Calvin. "You need to begin to prepare yourself for an unhappy outcome."

Calvin hung his head. "I was afraid you were going to say that."

"I don't mean to be Dr. Doom-and-Gloom, but at Whit's age, pretty much anything they do will buy him a few months at most if he's dealing with something worse than what's on his cheek. There comes a point when the treatments take more of a toll on the body than the disease does."

Calvin knew that, but hearing an oncologist say it made it real, and he could feel his face getting hot. "What about all the prayer I've been doing for him?" said Calvin. "Doesn't that count for something?"

"Of course it does." Dr. Pennyworth leaned against the rack where the crosses were kept and steepled his hands together. "I've been a Christian a lot longer than I've been a doctor, and I've seen some miraculous recoveries that I never thought possible. But more often than not in cases like Whit's, praying for healing is not the same as praying for curing."

Aren't they the same thing, thought Calvin. But he asked, "What do you mean?"

"Curing means being rid of disease. Healing means finding new wholeness. Sometimes healing and curing happen in conjunction with one another. Sometimes a person can be cured but not be whole. And sometimes a person finds wholeness while the disease rages on. Here I'm talking about the peace that sometimes comes when a person accepts his impending death, welcomes it even as a release and a reunion."

"Sounds like you've done a lot of thinking about this."

"I have had to. Being a man of faith in a profession that values the empirical above all has not been easy. I've had many a discussion with colleagues who have written me off as a religious nut."

"Then it sounds like they are missing an essential part of what it means to be a healer—faith."

"When you put your trust in data, then faith has trouble finding a foothold. But when you put your trust in God, then you have a new lens through which to view the data. That's how I look at it, at least."

Calvin thought about how he had been praying for Whit, about how he had been asking God to purge Whit's body of everything that was killing him. But as he and Dr. Pennyworth talked, a new prayer began to rise from deep within Calvin, a prayer for Whit to find peace, to find God's abiding presence supporting him through his affliction. And to the peace, Calvin coupled the wholeness, which the doctor had mentioned. Perhaps the wholeness would not be fully realized until Whit passed through death into new life in the fullness of God's love. And perhaps that was okay.

Heaven is full of sea glass, Ruby's voice echoed in his head. When Whit does pass away, his piece of glass will have no roughness from the cancer or anything else. He will be smooth. He will shine and reflect the light of God with his restored, radiant, renewed being.

But with such a beautiful vision in my mind's eye, thought Calvin, why do I still hurt so much?

That afternoon, Calvin boarded the elevator down the left-hand corridor of the hospital and rode it to the fourth floor. Hospitals were such busy, frantic places that a minute alone in an elevator was always a welcome relief for Calvin. Sometimes he waited in the lobby just so he could ride in a car by himself. He remembered Ruby telling him that all elevators look like the St. John's science fair project underneath their shiny exteriors, and he chuckled despite the situation.

As the elevator shuddered to a halt, he breathed in deeply, held the breath, and then blew it out again. The doors opened, and Calvin stepped into the rush of people moving this way and that. They all wore pink or green scrubs, and they held clipboards or they pushed portable testing equipment or they walked with patients at slow paces up and down the hall or they stood in little clusters discussing things. Calvin heard snatches of conversation as he strode down the hall: patients' treatments, gossip, yesterday's ballgame. The low buzz of conversation was punctuated by the various beeps and blips coming from patients' rooms.

Calvin came to a halt at the open door to Room 421. He could see the occupant's feet making a little hill under the sheets and blanket, and he knew this was Whit's room, but something always made him suspect that he was going to enter the wrong room by accident. Maybe he flipped two of the digits in the room number. Or maybe he was on the wrong floor. Or maybe the staff had moved Whit without telling anyone. Or maybe Calvin knew he had the right room and was looking for an excuse not to go in. This always happened when he was at the threshold, when he still had the option of turning back and not fulfilling his ministry, his duty to God and to the person in the room. He was always terrified to enter a patient's room, any patient's room, because he feared he would have nothing to say, nothing of consequence to offer the sick person. Calvin rested his head on the doorframe and took a couple more deep breaths.

And for the second time that day, Ruby's voice echoed in his head. *God is in this room right now.* I don't have to bring God with me. I just have to recognize that God is already here. And help Whit know it too. He took one last deep breath and crossed the threshold.

Tiptoeing around the corner that the restroom made, Calvin found Whit sitting up in the hospital bed but asleep. Again the desire to leave before being noticed hit Calvin, and again he pushed it down. One of the worst things about being a patient in the hospital, Calvin knew, is never being able to sleep soundly. There were always people coming in and waking you up to give you medicine or take your blood pressure or do physical therapy. Calvin patted the dark leather bag slung over his shoulder. Or bring you communion.

He set the bag down, pulled a small Bible from the side pocket, and sat in the chair next to Whit's bed. The chair squeaked as Calvin's weight depressed the cushion, and Whit snorted in his sleep but did not awaken. He looks so worn, thought Calvin. Even more so than on Easter Day. He thought of what Dr. Pennyworth had said and wondered just how much more abuse Whit's body could take. How many times had he wondered the same over the last few months? Calvin didn't know much about infections, but he assumed the MRSA was now under control or else he wouldn't have been allowed to sit so close. Or maybe I have no idea what I'm talking about, he thought.

Calvin let his mind wander as he watched Whit's steady breathing. For a few minutes it wandered through idle thoughts about that morning's church service, and the baseball game he had heard mentioned in the hall, and the doctor who had treated him for dehydration on Easter. And then it wandered into the silence that happens right before prayer. Snatches of petitions rose from where Calvin stored them in his heart, and he spoke them aloud to God.

"For Whit . . . for Ruby . . . be present . . . let him know your healing power . . . let her know your comfort . . . make him whole . . . make him holy . . . make him wholly new."

The silence returned, and it too was part of the prayer, just like it is part of the end of every piece of music. Calvin fingered his Bible, which was sitting on his lap. That morning on the Fourth Sunday of Easter, the readings for the day had included the most famous psalm of all time. Calvin flipped through his Bible—he had brought the King James Version with him today because he knew Whit enjoyed the poetic language. He found the words and read in a whisper, not wanting to awaken Whit but hoping the words would smuggle themselves into his consciousness.

> The LORD is my shepherd;
> I shall not want.
> He maketh me to lie down in green pastures:
> he leadeth me beside the still waters.
> He restoreth my soul:
> He leadeth me in the paths of righteousness for his name's
>   sake.
> Yea, though I walk through the valley of the shadow of
>   death, I will fear no evil:
> for thou art with me; thy rod and thy staff they comfort
>   me.
> Thou preparest a table before me in the presence of mine
>   enemies:
> Thou anointest my head with oil; my cup runneth over.

*Surely goodness and mercy shall follow me all the days
    of my life:
and I will dwell in the house of the LORD for ever.*

Calvin breathed out the last phrase. He could almost taste the words, for they nourished his soul like good food nourishes the body. No wonder this psalm is read at almost every funeral, he thought. It speaks of life here and now and life there and then. It talks of guidance, comfort, protection, abundance, goodness, mercy, and eternity.

He read it again, a little louder this time, but still Whit slept on. Calvin hoped that in his dreaming, Whit was drinking from the still waters, because in his waking, he was lying in a hospital bed, exhausted and wrung out.

Calvin fell back into silence again and let the words of the psalm dance around in his head. They spoke in poetry what Dr. Pennyworth had said about the difference between curing and healing. "He restoreth my soul . . . my cup runneth over . . . I will dwell in the house of the Lord for ever."

As he spoke phrases of the psalm softly to himself, he glanced around the room. A stack of newspapers sat on a chair in the corner. The rolling table that slid over the bed was covered with cups and used tissues. On the nightstand sat a journal open to a blank page, and next to it lay a tattered old hardback book.

Calvin picked it up and smiled with recognition. It was a copy of *Leaves of Grass* by Whit's namesake, the poet Walt Whitman. He had heard Whit quoting Whitman on occasion in the past, and now he had his hands on Whit's ammunition. Calvin thumbed through the old volume, noting that Whit had used a highlighter on nearly every page, and scrawled in the margins were illegible notes with lines attaching them to circled words and phrases. Calvin realized he was holding Whit's life's work in his hands. He was, after all, an English professor.

Calvin opened to a page that was covered in faded yellow highlights and read aloud.

> *A child said* What is the grass? *fetching it to me with full*
> *hands;*
> *How could I answer the child? I do not know what it is*
> *any more than he.*
> *I guess it must be the flag of my disposition, out of hope-*
> *ful green stuff woven.*
> *Or I guess it is the handkerchief of the Lord,*
> *A scented gift and remembrancer designedly dropt,*
> *Bearing the owner's name someway in the corners,*
> *that we may see and remark, and say* Whose?
> *Or I guess the grass is itself a child, the produced babe of*
> *the vegetation.*
> *Or I guess it is a uniform hieroglyphic,*
> *And it means, Sprouting alike in broad zones and nar-*
> *row zones,*
> *Growing among black folks as among white,*
> *Kanuck, Tuckahoe, Congressman, Cuff, I give them the*
> *same, I receive them the same.*
> *And now it seems to me the beautiful uncut hair of*
> *graves.*

"Did you know that Whitman was suffering from pneumonia when he died?"

Calvin glanced up from the poetry to find Whit looking at him through half-lidded eyes. "Whit, I'm so sorry to wake you."

"Oh, not to worry, son." Whit's smile was weak but sincere. "I could use the company. I sent Ruby home because she spends too much time in this dreadful place with me. I'm sure she'll be back soon, though. Can't keep her away." His smile strengthened. "Anyway, it's hard to get any type of real sleep in this place. I'd rather talk to you."

Calvin reflected Whit's smile. "You were saying about Whitman?"

"Oh, just that he had pneumonia. And now I've had it too, so that's another thing we have in common."

"It's a little more treatable now than back then."

"He died in 1892—a titan to some, an American hero, the voice of the nation."

"And to others?"

"A pretentious windbag, a lowborn huckster who couldn't put two sentences together."

"That's a pretty wide range."

"Genius—especially renowned genius—always brings admirers and detractors. I don't think he would have wanted it any other way."

Calvin held up Whit's copy of *Leaves of Grass*. "I take it you're one of the admirers."

"I should think so." A conspiratorial look crossed Whit's face. He glanced left and right, apparently checking for eaves-droppers. Satisfied, he whispered, "Calvin, can you keep a secret?"

Calvin leaned in, wide-eyed. "Yes, sir."

"It's a big one. I need you to swear solemnly, with your hand on your heart."

"Whit, I'm a priest. I keep people's secrets all the time."

"Swear."

"All right." Calvin put his hand on his heart. "I solemnly swear to keep the secret you are about to tell me."

Whit nodded, pulled his left arm from under the covers and tapped the book, which Calvin was holding. "I stole my very first copy from the public library."

"That's the secret?"

"That's the secret." Whit grinned as wide as his ravaged face would go. "And oh, how it has been weighing on me."

Calvin sat back in the chair. Humor is a good sign, he thought. Humor means Whit hadn't given up yet. "So, do tell," prompted Calvin.

"I was twelve or thirteen, if I recall. I read in the newspapers that a newly elected representative on the town's council was going on a book-banning crusade. It must have been the same year Roosevelt won re-election the first time, so maybe I was fourteen. Anyway, the list appeared in the newspaper before the books had been taken off the shelves, so I said to myself, 'I better get some reading done before the books are gone.' After all, any book worth banning was a book worth reading, in my mind. So I went to the library with the scrap of newspaper in my pocket. The list was fairly extensive—Lawrence, Blake, and Poe are some of the names I remember from it. The list included some of the most original thinkers of the English-speaking world, and they were going to be censored by some narrow-minded local bureaucrat. The books were going to be taken off the shelves anyway, I reasoned, so I liberated them ahead of time. At least, I liberated Blake because of the illustrations and Whitman because we shared our first name. I could only hide so much in my coat, so the others had to stay."

Calvin rotated the book in his hands and opened the back cover. "There's no library sticker on the side or checkout slip in the back." He gave Whit a sly look. "Are you making all this up?"

"Oh no. God's honest truth," said Whit, now putting his hand on his own heart. "The copy you are holding is the one I bought when I went to college. The stolen one suffered greatly during the war."

"Whatever happened to William Blake?"

"Well, his poetry was quite fine. 'Tiger, tiger burning bright' and all that. But I completely forgot about him when I opened the Whitman. And there has never been another poet for me. I like others' verse, but Whitman's was my first love. And first loves stay with you."

"How does Ruby feel about your relationship with Whitman's poetry?"

Whit opened his mouth to answer, but a voice came from the entryway. "We make it work somehow." Ruby shuffled into the room. "Hello, Calvin. I'm glad you came."

"Darling," said Whit. "I thought you were going to spend some time away from the hospital today."

"I did. I went to church, and then Avis took me to lunch. And now I'm here." She turned her attention to Calvin. "See how he tries to take care of me even though he's the one who is sick."

Bending over, she planted a soft kiss on Whit's forehead. "How are you feeling today?"

"No more tired than usual. But I'm getting sick of being here. The waiting is interminable. Calvin has been buoying my spirits, though. He read to me for a while before I was fully awake."

"That's nice," said Ruby, taking the chair Calvin had vacated for her. "It also looks like he brought communion from the service this morning. Would you like to receive?"

"I would." Whit pulled himself up into a more vertical seated position.

Calvin could see that even such a small movement taxed Whit to the point of exhaustion. Calvin breathed in a deep lungful of air, and, remembering Dr. Pennyworth's advice, breathed out a silent prayer for Whit to find wholeness in God's presence. While he prayed, he set up his travelling communion kit—a miniature chalice, into which he poured a shot of consecrated wine from a miniature cruet; and a miniature paten, on which he placed three communion wafers. He had blessed them that morning, so Whit was able to partake of the same communion as the rest of the congregation. Thus, in a way, the members of the parish were all there in the hospital room with them.

Whit, Ruby, and Calvin said the Lord's Prayer, and then Calvin put a wafer in Whit's cupped hands. "The Body of Christ, the bread of heaven," he said. He did the same for Ruby and himself, and then went in reverse with the wine, so that Whit received last, lest any residual infection somehow survive being passed through the medium of eighteen-percent alcohol.

As Calvin was saying, "The Blood of Christ, the cup of salvation," there came a knock at the door, and then Whit's doctor came around the corner. He looked from Whit to Calvin to the silver chalice and back to Calvin.

"I'm sorry for the interruption," said the doctor. "But I need to talk to Ruby and Walter."

Who's Walter? Calvin looked at Whit. Oh, of course, he thought. "We are just finishing up, doctor. Would you like to receive communion with us?"

"No, thank you. I have something important to discuss with the Reddings." His implication was clear. He had something to discuss with Ruby and Whit privately.

Ruby looked up at the doctor. "Whatever you can say in front of us you can say in front of Father Calvin."

Father Calvin. That's new, Calvin thought. She must be trying to give me more status.

"It's okay, Ruby. I need to clean this stuff up anyway. I'll be back in a few minutes." He gathered the communion kit and wandered out into the hallway looking for a public restroom. He found one near the elevator, and spent more time than was really necessary cleaning the miniature silver vessels. When he was done, he slung the kit over his shoulders and walked back to Whit's room. He arrived in time to see the doctor moving away from him down the hallway. That was a quick conversation, he thought. Then again, doctors don't tend to spend very much time with their patients. He knew the thought was uncharitable and more than likely inaccurate, but the doctor's quick exit sent a chill of foreboding into Calvin's bones.

He re-entered the room to find Ruby still sitting next to Whit. But the chair was closer to the bed now, and Ruby's head was on Whit's chest. He held her with one arm and with the opposite hand he stroked her hair. She was sobbing silently, her eyes half-closed and her body trembling. She didn't see Calvin return.

Whit stared up at Calvin, stone-faced and grim. Calvin mouthed silently, "What did the doctor say?" But he was fairly certain he knew.

"We delayed too long," said Whit simply, calmly. "It's everywhere."

"Oh, Whit, no," was all Calvin could think to say. He looked down at his hands and was surprised to see *Leaves of Grass* in them still. He must have accidentally taken it with him when he beat a hasty retreat upon the doctor's arrival. He placed the book amongst the discarded cups and tissues on the rolling table. And for the first time the words underneath the title caught his eyes.

Leaves of Grass, it read. "The death-bed edition."

June 3, 2010

Dear Rev. Calvin,

I don't know what I would do without Avis, Mary, and Esther Rose. Those three women are my life support system right now. Yesterday was hard. Talk about lean times—yesterday was the leanest of times. What's that old song? "Lean times, come again no more. For days you have lingered around my cabin door. Oh, lean times come again no more." I suppose the actual song talks about "hard" times, but I've been singing it to myself for days now with my own revision. The times they do still linger. The good news is that so do my three friends. I don't think I went anywhere yesterday without at least one, if not all three, accompanying me. Do you remember your first day with us, Calvin? We went to visit Alexander Noon's ashes in the columbarium. Well, yesterday, the ladies took me to see Whit, who is one row up and one column to the right of Alex. But you know that, don't you, Calvin? After all, you put him there last summer.

The four of us stood in the narthex beside the columbarium and told each other about our wedding days. That helped take the edge off the pain, but a blunt pain can hurt just as much as a sharp one. I've already told you about my wedding day, but did you know that Avis and Alex were married at sea? Or that Esther Rose and Ted eloped because Esther Rose's mother didn't approve? Or that on Mary and Arthur's wedding day no less than three other suitors turned up to try to convince the soon-to-be Mrs. Williams to marry them instead? Hearing their stories was a balm to me, at least for a little while. But when I was finally alone last evening as I prepared to sleep, everything washed over me. It would have been the fifty-ninth time that he read his proposal poem to me on our anniversary, but his voice is gone now. It would have been the fifty-ninth time that he surprised me with a bouquet of lilacs because he knew they were my favorites. And it would have been the fifty-ninth time that I surprised him with a single red rose. But there are no flowers on the dining room table today. By the time I finally drifted off to sleep last night, my tears had soaked through my pillow, and I had to borrow Whit's. I wish it still smelled like him.

But enough of this. You don't want to hear about this old lady's sadness. I started this letter with an aim to make good on my promise to tell you all about our time at Whit's secret spot. I mentioned in my last letter that Whit took me there for the first time right after returning from Korea. Let me see if I can describe the place. It has been so long since I've been there that my mind's eye doesn't quite feel up to the task. But I'll give it a shot anyway.

Whit's childhood home stood perilously close to the railway. I remember his mother telling me that she couldn't display her good china for fear that the trains would rattle the dishes off their stands. But by the time I came into Whit's family, the track had long since fallen into disuse. Weeds and moss and small, hardy saplings had begun to reclaim the route by the time I ever laid eyes on it. That first time, Whit could barely see, but it didn't matter because he could find his way to the spot in pitch darkness. Our short journey began by walking west down the tracks for only a couple hundred yards. Then we turned north onto a narrow path Whit and Mike had made over years of tramping along the same patch of ground. The path wound its way into the woods, took a sharp left at a rock that looked like a grizzly bear, and went over a thin stream on a pair of railroad ties they had liberated from the tracks. Once past the stream, we just had to pull back a few branches that shielded the entrance to their idyllic sanctuary.

A Japanese maple spread its branches from the center of a small clearing. I could hear the source of the stream we had just crossed—a gurgling natural spring that bubbled up to the right of the maple tree. There was a stone-lined fire pit, two stumps for chairs, and, of course, a flag. It flew from a low, gnarled branch of the tree, and it sported a red field upon which was drawn a rough sketch of an old-fashioned microphone. Whit had to explain: red field for "Redding" and microphone for "Mike," thus both of their names were represented on the flag. They must have made the flag fifteen or more years before I ever saw it, and yet it still flew. Boys will be boys.

It was the beginning of May 1951 when Whit first brought me to the spot. He sat me down on one of the stumps, pulled a crumpled sheet of paper out of his pocket, and bent down on one knee. And then he proposed, though he never looked at the paper because he had the poem memorized, which was good because he could hardly see anyway. This is what he said:

269

I never thought that war could ever bring about
A thing besides such dark despair;
For all I've seen—from ship ablaze to bloody shore
To coffins sinking in the waves—
I know that I should never wish for men to take up arms.
And yet I also know that if hostility had not returned
To nations still in mourning for the sons they lost in
        decades past,
Then you and I would ne'er have met
And ne'er have known the other's sweet embrace
That makes some sense of such a senseless world.
So while I can't forgive the beast of war that swallowed
        whole
So many sons and fathers, brothers, friends,
I find some solace, even hope, and not just hope,
But joy—so unrestrained, so full, so free—
In knowing that our love could grow
Despite the horrors of the decade past.
And as I look ahead to decades hence and see
A life where you and I redeem this ransacked world
By bringing back the love that fled when bombs and bul-
        lets came,
I sing aloud for fortune's favor—nay, for blessing from
        above,
For love will win if "yes" you say and make my joy
        complete.
My love, my life, my Ruby fair, O will you take my hand
And set a course for future bliss and leave despair behind?
My love, my life, my Ruby fair, O will you take this ring
And sing with me of love's success, O will you marry me?

He sure was a romantic. He often called me
"Ruby Fair," but never when anyone else was

around. That one was just for us. Every anniversary he read that to me again. Sometimes we were able to make it back to the spot on Long Island, but as the years passed it became increasingly difficult. But whenever he read the poem to me, I was transported back there. Writing it out for you now, Calvin, I can see in my mind the way the early morning sun hit the grass in the clearing, glinting off the drops of dew and filling the whole space with diamonds of light. The ring that Whit slid on my finger mirrored the morning dew, drinking in the sunlight and spilling out hundreds of tiny rainbows.

We returned to the spot the next spring. It was 1952. We had been married a year, and I was nearing my third trimester. Margaret had been kicking up a storm for weeks, but while we were in the clearing I never felt a thing. It was as if she realized from within the womb the peacefulness of the place to which I had carried her. Whit and I ate a picnic lunch under the maple, and we didn't have to bring beverages because the spring was close by. Then Whit read me the poem. And we embraced. We held each other for a long time, and then we began to sway back and forth. You know, Calvin, there's a moment in some embraces when they naturally and unavoidably turn into slow dances. There's no audible music, but both of you can hear it anyway. We danced and spun and laughed, and all the while the little life that would become Margaret in a few short months was right there in the midst of us.

That little life was with us the following spring. 1953 was the year of the pram. Whit and Mike obviously never thought of bringing a baby carriage to their spot, or else they wouldn't have located it down a railroad track, through the forest, and over a makeshift bridge. I ended up carrying Margaret the whole way while Whit struggled with the pram. I honestly don't know why we didn't just leave it at his parents' home. When we finally arrived, the whole family was tuckered out, so we put Margaret down for a nap and ate our picnic. Then Whit read the poem, but he also had a surprise. From under Margaret's blankets, he pulled out a new flag and hung it next to the old one on the tree. It was still red, but now it had a picture of a ruby stitched on a white circle at its center. The spot was now ours as much as it had been Whit's and Mike's. When Margaret awoke, I fed her while the three of us sat in silence listening to the birdsong and the wind.

Silence was in short supply the next year. In 1954, Margaret was nearly two years old, and everything was a mystery for her to explore. The first adventure was taking the train to Long Island. Somehow she wandered off, and I found her an hour later in the dining car looking at the funny pages and having an unintelligible chat with a plate of cookies. The second adventure was walking down the railroad tracks and through the woods. When we arrived at Bear Rock, Margaret took the left without us telling her to. Now, she only had two choices, but Whit always said that she knew instinctively where to go. Our picnic that year was not quite as peaceful as in years past, but it was ever so much more joyful. Margaret explored every inch of the clearing, named every rock, examined every branch of the maple tree. But it was the bubbling spring that amazed her most. She couldn't understand where the water was coming from. Of course, she got quite dirty in the mud surrounding the spring, but that was to be expected from my daughter, judging by my own childhood romping days. But the best part happened when Whit picked up the muddy Margaret and brought her over to the branch with the flags flying from it. He lifted her up on his shoulders and had her press her muddy handprint into our flag. From then on, the flag was for all of us; the clearing belonged to us. Or perhaps, we belonged to it.

Calvin, I'm so glad I thought to write to you today. Putting all these old memories on paper makes the lean times linger less around my cabin door, if for a little while, at least. I have a feeling that Avis will be coming around soon to check on me. She's such a sweetheart.

Remember what I said about embraces turning into slow dances. See what sort of silent music you and your "mysterious news" hear when your embraces linger. There's no better way to see if your toes curl than when an embrace turns into a dance.

Writing to you remains a bright spot in these lean times of mine. I hope that you will keep me in your prayers this month. I fear I will need them.

Missing you.

Your friend,

Ruby

15

The architect who designed the floor plan of the house on Lilac Court never meant for the master bedroom to have so many people in it. So thought Calvin Harper as he crouched at one corner of the king-sized bed with a ratchet in one hand and a wrench in the other.

"How's it coming, Calvin?" came Chief Harry Stern's voice from the far corner of the bed.

"These bolts are stubborn, Chief," Calvin called back. "I don't think they've been touched in fifty years."

"That's about right," said Whit. His voice sounded like he perpetually needed a drink of water. He sat on the chair by Ruby's vanity, his legs propped up with cushions from the couch in the living room.

"Tell me again why we're trying to take the bed apart," said Brad Stewart from another corner of the bed.

"Because this bed is made for sleeping," said Ruby. She stood behind Whit with her hands on his shoulders, as if she were worried he might fall off the chair. "Not for staying in all day long."

"The woman from hospice, Nurse Harris, suggested a hospital bed," said Josie Temple-Jones from the last corner of the bed. "And Donald Pennyworth was kind and generous and swell enough to procure one for Whit."

"You sound like you're sort of sweet on him, Josie," said Rebecca Stewart from the doorway. Baby Natalie gurgled her agreement. Mom and baby were wearing matching dresses, a gift from Emily Lincoln to celebrate Rebecca's first Mother's Day.

"Oh, you know what they say," said Josie. "An old bachelor loves his life, an old widower loves his wife, but when he makes good on his bachelorhood, the widower . . . aha . . . loosens the bolt!"

The bed shuddered as Josie pulled a bolt nearly as long as her forearm from the leg of the bed.

"I didn't know that's what they said," joked Brad.

"One down," said the Chief. "Only seven to go."

"Mine are hopeless," said Calvin.

"I'll give it a try," said Rebecca. "Here, Calvin. Switch with me."

Calvin stood up and wiped the sweat off his brow. He walked over to Rebecca, who exchanged Natalie for Calvin's tools. The baptism was in less than two months, and their rapport was still less than ideal because of Calvin's nerves. She can sense my anxiety, he thought, and she's only six months old. No wonder the women I have dated could sense it too.

"Ruby, do you have any spray-on cooking oil?" asked Rebecca.

"I'll get it," said Avis Noon, who was standing in the hallway. She couldn't quite squeeze into the bedroom with the other eight people. A minute later, she returned with a yellow can, which she handed to Rebecca.

Rebecca directed the spray at the hexagonal nuts that were holding the bolts in place. She waited a moment for the spray to work its magic and then calmly removed the now cooperative fasteners with no more effort than she would have used to turn the knobs on a radio.

"That's astounding," said Brad.

"Sometimes brute force isn't the way to go, hon," said Rebecca, as she shooed her husband away from his corner of the bed. Minutes later, the heavy oak bed frame lay deconstructed on the shag carpet.

"Take a bow, Rebecca," said Ruby. "I didn't think that thing was ever going to come apart."

Rebecca blushed but gave a slight curtsy all the same. Natalie clapped, but Calvin was fairly sure the six-month-old did so frequently and was, therefore, not necessarily cheering her mother's ingenuity.

"We'll need that brute force now," said the Chief, who was red in the face after attempting to lift one side of the broken down frame. "These things are solid. Here, Josie, help me shift this."

The two of them managed to lift the thick, oak board and navigate it out of the crowded bedroom. Calvin passed Natalie back to Rebecca, and he and Brad hefted the second long board. Straining with effort, they coaxed the wood around the corner in the hallway, walked it through the living room, and slid it atop the first board, which now lay under the dining room table.

"There's no way we're getting these things in the attic," the Chief said. "So under the table is the next best thing. I hope Ruby and Whit don't mind."

They explained as much to the Reddings when they went back for more pieces. "That'll do just fine," said Ruby. "Thank you all for helping. It means a lot to us."

Calvin watched Whit nod his agreement. Only a week had passed since he had visited Whit in the hospital the final time, but in just that short period, Whit was looking better. Sure, his voice was like gravel and he nodded off quite a bit, but his cheeks had more color and there was a bit of the old sharpness in his eye. Ruby had noticed the recovery as well and had remarked about it to Nurse Harris earlier that afternoon.

"Every so often a patient on hospice does recover from illness," said the nurse. Calvin was in awe of the way her voice dripped with compassion no matter what she said. She could have ordered a burger and fries—hold the pickles—compassionately. She purred more than spoke, making her voice nearly inaudible, but that just made Calvin want to listen harder to what she had to say.

Nurse Harris continued, "But that is quite uncommon. The more likely reason he's looking a little better is that he has gotten a couple nights of honest-to-God sleep in a row. No one sleeps soundly in the hospital. But in his own bed, he's out all night." She put her hand on Ruby's shoulder and squeezed. "Getting good sleep is still something to celebrate."

Calvin marveled at the nurse's ability to see what she had called "the little victories" in what ultimately was going to be a losing battle. Then again, he thought, the final victory has already been won. Shaking his head in confusion, Calvin picked up one of the legs of the bed and carried it to the dining room, while his mind was a couple of years away. During seminary, talk of the resurrection had been so abstract. What did the resurrected body look like? How did the disciples experience the resurrected Jesus? What are the mechanics of resurrection as elucidated by such and such a theologian? Calvin had studied resurrection for three years in New Testament and theology classes, but no one had ever told him that, in the end, resurrection wasn't something he could study. It was only something to which he could bear witness. And now, watching Whit move toward the threshold of death, Calvin had to keep reminding himself that Christ had changed the game as far as death was concerned. He looked down at the piece of wood he was carrying. Those planks under the dining room table easily could have made a cross. I believe that Jesus Christ died and rose again, Calvin told himself. But for what?

He returned to the bedroom for a final load and once again saw the cancer-ridden man dozing in his chair. And the question changed. But for whom? For Whit. He glanced up to Whit's wife, who hovered over him like a mother bird. And for Ruby. He spun a slow circle. For all of these wonderful people who gave up their Sunday afternoon to make a sick man more comfortable. His circle concluded with him face-to-face with his reflection in the vanity's mirror. And even for me. It was a truly humbling thought.

———

The sun did not retreat from Victory for the rest of the month of May, and the lilacs that grew up and down the Reddings' street erupted into bloom because of it. Calvin stepped onto Ruby's and Whit's back porch to find Whit reclining on a beach chair, drinking in the sun and the array of color that bedecked the backyard. Calvin took the wheelchair Whit had vacated and sat in silence for a moment cataloging all the different shades of purple and pink flowers that lined the fence.

"Should you really be out here in the sun, what with your . . . " Calvin's voice trailed off, and he pointed to his own cheek instead.

"Oh, son," said Whit. "The melanoma isn't what's going to get me in the end. There are plenty of other nasties inside of me that will do the job quicker. So I figure I'm going to enjoy the sunlight while I can."

"And how do Ruby and Nurse Harris feel about that decision?"

"Oh, my nurse just wants me to be comfortable, so as long as I am, she's okay."

"And Ruby?"

"Look at my face."

Calvin looked and saw a liberal amount of sun block smeared on Whit's cheeks. Ruby hadn't worried about rubbing it in. Calvin watched himself smile in the reflection from Whit's mirrored sunglasses.

"Cool shades."

"You think so? Ruby bought them for me at the store when I told her I wanted to sit outside. Part of my anti-sun protection. They remind me of the pair I wore at sea."

"At sea?"

"In the Pacific during the war. I'll tell you, at certain times of day, standing out on deck was absolutely blinding. The sun seemed to reflect off every surface, including the ocean." Whit gestured to an empty glass on the table. "Refill my lemonade and I'll tell you a story or two. And feel free to pour yourself a glass. Cabinet to the left of the oven. But you know that, don't you."

Calvin went to the kitchen, retrieved a glass for himself, poured the lemonade, and walked back outside. "What are the two empty vases on the dining room table for?" he asked.

"Old tradition. You'll see when Ruby gets home."

"So, sir," said Calvin as he and Whit clinked glasses, "story time."

"I was on three ships over the course of the war. A carrier called the USS *Bunker Hill*, an LST—that stands for 'Large Slow Target,' mind you." Whit took a long draught of lemonade and smiled at Calvin's shocked expression. "Well, not really. It stands for 'Landing Ship—Tank.' But the boat was large and slow, and the Japanese liked to use it for target practice. But, boy, was she durable. We nicknamed her the 'Holey Moley' after our first mission because she must have taken a dozen or so shells to her hull, and they barely fazed her."

"Sounds like a well built vessel."

"That's nothing compared to my last ship, which my dear wife helped build, by the way. You should ask her about working at the shipyard sometime. She calls them her 'Ruby the Riveter' days." Whit chuckled, but the chuckle turned into a cough, and the cough turned into a wheeze.

Calvin didn't know what to do. A moment ago Whit had been laughing and carrying on, but now he seemed to be struggling to breath. Calvin went down on one knee to face Whit at eye level. "How can I help?" he shouted over Whit's wheezing.

Whit shook his head and gestured for Calvin to sit back down. A minute later, the wheezing regressed into coughing, but the coughing did not regress into chuckling. Rather, Whit lay in the chair, panting and trembling. "Sometimes it sneaks up on you," he said between gasps.

They sat in silence for a while as Whit recovered. Then Whit sent Calvin to the bedroom in search of a certain prescription bottle. The tabletop of Ruby's vanity looked like a shelf in a pharmacy. Calvin looked at the labels of the containers and sounded out the names of the various unpronounceable drugs held within. Finding the one he was sent to retrieve, he headed back to the porch to find that Whit had drifted off to sleep. Calvin tiptoed back to the wheelchair, but the squeak of the wheels as he sat down woke Whit from his light doze. He took the medicine and finished off his lemonade.

"Are you ready to hear the rest of the story?" Whit asked.

"Am I ready? Are you okay to tell it?"

"Oh, a little coughing never hurt anyone."

"That wasn't a little coughing, Whit."

"I suppose you're right. So I'll just give you the abridged version, shall I?"

"It's a deal."

"My last ship of the war was a cruiser called the USS *Pittsburgh*. I was transferred there in the spring of 1945, just in time for our fleet to be caught in a typhoon. You know how the *Titanic* broke in half? Something like that happened to the *Pittsburgh*. She was tossed upward, the deck buckled, and a hundred feet of the bow broke clean off. The miraculous thing is that we didn't sink and we didn't lose a single man during the storm."

"That's the second crazy story you've told me in the last month," said Calvin.

"It's all true. We patched up as best we could and steamed for Guam. Some clever fellow nicknamed her the 'Longest Ship in the World' because we left the front of the vessel out in the middle of the Pacific, so there was quite a bit of distance between bow and stern."

"I don't know," said Calvin. "I might have to look up this USS *Pittsburgh* when I get home."

Whit chuckled at Calvin's playful unbelief, and this time the chuckle did not degenerate into wheezing. "I have an old newspaper clipping that tells the whole story. I also wrote a poem about it that someone or other turned into a song.

"The first mate said, 'We're in the drink,'
When the storm around them swirled;
But the captain said, 'She'll never sink,
Not the longest ship in the world.'

"Not my best work, for sure, and I can't remember any more, but that sure was a time. I used to joke with Ruby that her workmanship was shoddy if one little storm could break a ship in two. She always said that she considered it great crafts-manship that the *Pittsburgh* didn't sink when it broke in half—and that she only worked on the stern anyway."

"Speaking of Ruby, where is she?" asked Calvin.

"Oh, I suppose she's out seeking my anniversary present." Whit pointed to the lilacs in the yard. "I have an unfair advantage. Calvin, do me a favor: go down there and cut a few different colors for me. I would, but I fear I can't make it down the steps."

"You just sit tight, sir," said Calvin as he picked up a pair of pruning shears from a bucket nearby. A few minutes later, Calvin had a nice bouquet of lilacs in his hand. "What are these for, Whit?"

"Did Ruby not tell you? Today's our fifty-eighth wedding anniversary. I give her lilacs every year. And she gives me . . . "

"A single red rose," said Calvin.

"Yes, how'd you know?"

"Because she's standing right behind you."

"Oh, dear," said Whit. "Ruby, close your eyes for a moment, will you?" He gestured to Calvin, who handed him the bouquet. "All right, you can open them."

Ruby did so, and they exchanged flowers.

"It's time for my poem," said Ruby with a quiver in her voice.

"Indeed it is," said Whit. "Calvin, perhaps we can chat again soon?"

"Of course," said Calvin.

"Maybe I'll be able to dig up a few more verses from that song," said Whit as he held out his hand for Calvin to shake. Calvin could tell that Whit was trying to grasp his hand but his muscles just weren't cooperating.

Ruby walked Calvin to the front door, and Calvin told her about the wheezing attack.

"He's been having those about once a day in the last week or so," she said. "Nurse Harris says that his body is doing its best with limited resources, and sometimes those resources are a little low."

"He still seems in good spirits."

"He has his good days and bad days. You caught him at a good time. It's our anniversary after all." She began to say something more, stopped, and thought better of it.

"It's okay, Ruby. You can tell me what's on your mind."

She took Calvin's hand and patted it. "It's just . . . I wasn't sure we were going to make it to today."

"I'm so glad you did."

"It's another little victory to hold on to."

Calvin visited the house on Lilac Court every few days over the next couple of weeks. Sometimes Whit was asleep or Nurse Harris was giving him treatments, so Calvin sat with Ruby in the living room or listened to her play old hymns on the piano. The Sunday before Calvin's first anniversary at St. John's, he sat with Ruby on the bench in front of her old upright and listened to her sing her favorite hymn, the one she had played for him back in January. "You've turned my mourning to dancing, taken my sack-cloth and clothed me with joy," she sang, and to Calvin the lyric sounded like Ruby reminding God of a promise that God was bound to fulfill at some future time. She knew she would mourn—was, in fact, already mourning—and she had faith that she would dance again. Whether the dance would happen here on earth when she reached a new sort of normalcy or in heaven when she was reunited with Whit, Calvin didn't know. But listening to her sing of God bringing hope and love into grief and fear gave Calvin the courage he needed to keep coming to the house with the dying man inside. When Phil Erickson had died, everything had happened so quickly that all Calvin had to deal with was the aftermath. But with Whit, Calvin was along for the whole ride. And he knew the stamina he was showing by coming to Lilac Court again and again was from a wholly other source than himself. It came from God, channeled through the enduring, faithful, and now painfully sad woman at the piano.

Calvin sang the final few lines with Ruby. He knew he did not have a strong or confident singing voice, but that hardly mattered when the song was really a vehicle for prayer.

"It's a beautiful song," said Calvin when the last notes of the piano had whispered into silence. "I could listen to you play it over and over again."

"Whit said the same thing yesterday. I have been playing it over and over again, and I thought he would have been tired of it by now." She shut the lid of the piano, stood up, shuffled across the room, and collapsed into her rocking chair. "But he said it gives him comfort too, so I keep playing it."

"I can't think of anything better than filling the house with prayerful song," said Calvin while he crossed the room and took a seat on the couch.

"Whit said that he was looking forward to seeing what kind of new clothes he gets to exchange his sack-cloth for." Ruby began rocking in the chair, and the squeaking of the old wood punctuated her words. "He's looking forward to dying. Looking forward to it."

Calvin sensed that this was one of those moments when remaining quiet was the best thing he could do.

Ruby continued, "I'm just so confused. I have all these conflicting thoughts running through this old head of mine, and none of them makes sense with the others." She began ticking things off on her fingers. "I don't want Whit to die because I love him and I can't imagine my life without him in it. At the same time, I know that when he dies he'll be free of pain and he'll be with God, and then I feel horribly selfish because the reason I want him to stay is so I can be with him. I don't understand how a loving God could possibly allow something

285

like cancer to kill so many people. At the same time, I know that Jesus never promised life without suffering; he promised life with himself bearing our suffering with us. But sometimes that tradeoff just doesn't seem to be worth it because sometimes it's just so hard to remember that Christ is here with me."

Ruby paused and gave Calvin a helpless look. He opened his mouth to say something, but no words came. So instead he scooted forward on the couch cushion and took Ruby's hand in his.

"People tell me that Whit is going to a better place," she continued, her voice steadily rising in volume. "And I know that's true, but whenever I hear someone say it, I want to scream because it just doesn't sound good enough. It doesn't sound like a fair trade. It doesn't sound like a change in scenery is worth dying for." Her breath caught in her throat, and now tears were streaming down the lines of her wrinkles. The crescendo fell away, and she whispered, "Oh, Calvin, I have faith, I do. I believe . . . but God help my unbelief. If my faith tells me that Whit is going to be that smooth, shining piece of sea glass, then why do I hurt so much?"

Calvin remembered wondering the same thing weeks before. He opened his mouth to say something, but he had no idea what words would come, if any would at all. So he was surprised to hear himself say, "Because you love him."

Silence descended on the pair of them. The squeak of the rocking chair filled the room, but it too dissipated as Ruby slowed down her rocking. With the squeaking gone, they could hear Whit's faint coughs from the bedroom. "Because I love him," repeated Ruby.

"It doesn't answer any of your questions," said Calvin. "I don't think those questions even have answers—at least not ones that aren't thin platitudes. But it is the truth."

"And my love for him isn't going to go away when he dies," said Ruby through her tears.

"Not in the slightest."

"Maybe that's how we know that resurrection is real."

———oooo———

June 17, 2010

Dear Rev. Calvin,

I'm sorry I haven't written to you in a while. I haven't felt like doing much of anything really. I haven't even touched my piano. But Avis told me something yesterday that I wanted to tell you, so I got out the stationery. But first, I want to tell you a little more about my daughter.

Our Margaret was born in August of 1952, a little over a year from Whit's return from Korea and our wedding. It took us a good six months for me to get pregnant, which was unfortunate because June, July, and August are the worst months for a third trimester, let me tell you! When you have kids, Calvin, try to have them in spring or fall—that way there's less over-heating in the summer and less chance of being stuck in a blizzard on your way to the hospital in the winter.

Even though she was born during the most uncomfortable of times, Margaret was just per-fect—ten little fingers and ten piggy little toes and a set of lungs that could have filled Carnegie Hall. We tried to have more children, but I kept miscarrying, so eventually we just gave up that dream and focused on the one dream we did have. Margaret was wonderful as a little girl, and I taught young ones my whole life, and that nearly made up for not having any more children. I suppose I should count the blessings I do have, not the ones I don't, right?

There's one blessing I have now that I won't have much longer. Avis Noon is moving to Florida at the end of summer to live with her eldest daughter. She has been so wonderful this year since Whit passed away. She lost her husband just two years ago, so she has known every single thing I've been feeling over the last year, and she has been there for me, especially in these last few months since you moved to Boston. I honestly don't know what I'm going to do when she leaves, as well. Esther Rose and Mary will still be around, of course, although E.R. hasn't been looking too well recently. But it's hard to tell with her. She's been in and out of the hospital so many times with various injuries; one would think they are bound to catch up to her someday. But I think she's too stubborn to give in to any sickness. Then again, she's past ninety. And thank goodness, she's not driving anymore. Her broken wrist in March finally put an end to that. So Mary picks her up for Morning Prayer, and God forbid if she's ever late to Esther Rose's house. We would never hear the end of it.

But out of the three of them, Avis is my closest friend and confidante. I am going to miss her terribly. She always has a way of cheering me up without making me feel guilty about being sad. She has taught me that there is a difference between happiness and joy. Happiness is a transient feeling—it comes and goes with your mood. It's hard to be happy and sad at the same time. But you can find joy even in the midst of grief and sadness because joy is a much deeper feeling than happiness. Joy endures because, at its core, it is not an emotion but a gift.

Whenever I see Avis, I remember that joy is a stalwart companion that hasn't abandoned me even though I have been able to find so little to be happy about. The same goes for Margaret and Cooper. They are the only blood kin that I have left, seeing as D.B. never married. Cooper came over after his last day of school, and we talked and talked about his grandfather. It was the first long conversation I've had about Whit since he died (well, except for all these letters, of course), and at first it made me sad. But the more we talked—and the more I saw Whit peeking out from Cooper's smile—the more the joy that lives deep within me reasserted itself. I still love Whit, but it has taken a long time for me to recognize that he still loves me too. We are still connected through the love of God. And even though I can't hear his voice or touch his hand, I know that he never really died. He just walked through a door to find God waiting for him on the other side with open arms.

And yet, believing all that to be true, I still cry more tears than I ever thought my eyes could hold. It's a paradox that I have had to come to grips with. Joy doesn't banish sadness. The thought of heaven doesn't dry the tears. But the love remains, and that is the deepest thing of all.

You can tell that I've been thinking deep thoughts these last few weeks, especially since our anniversary. I've never considered myself to be of the philosophical persuasion, but perhaps Whit rubbed off on me sometime in the last sixty-odd years. His poetry always did struggle with the big questions of life and death. But the beautiful thing about poetry is that it doesn't necessarily try to answer those big questions. It just tries to find more evocative ways of asking them.

The boxes from the attic contained more than Whit's wartime letters. They also contained several journals of Whit's handwritten poems, not to mention hundreds of scraps of paper with verses scrawled on them—you know, napkins from restaurants, sticky notes, the margin from the newspaper. I have decided to start a project and collect all of Whit's poems in one place. Who knows, maybe I'll try to get them published one of these days. Outside of the college's literary magazine, he never thought he was good enough to be published, bless him, and so he never tried. And maybe he wasn't, but he was definitely good enough for me, and if I'm the only one who ever reads all these poems, then that will be fine too.

I'm so glad that he gave you his copy of *Leaves of Grass*, Calvin. Truth be told, I prefer my own Walter over Walt Whitman, so it was no great loss parting with that old volume, especially knowing that you are treasuring it now.

Even so, as the day approaches, I find myself missing certain things that I haven't missed all year, like that book on the bedside table. New things like that add to the things I have missed all along, like the way he used to wait on the front porch for me to come home from Morning Prayer. In a way, he reminded me of my father, who used to sit on the porch and whittle all day long. Except that Whit wouldn't have a knife and stick, but a pen and paper. Mort might have been able to carve angels, but Whit could put into words the soft kiss of the air their wings made when they hovered near you.

As I write these words to you, I feel that same conflict within me that I felt when I was talking with Cooper. The grief feels as fresh as it did a year ago, but at the same time, the joy, which lives in a deeper place than grief, rises to be grief's companion. The two now walk hand in hand, and while I certainly don't feel happy, both the grief and the joy help me to know that I am in God's presence. And so is Whit. And therefore, we are together in a way, as are two distant people who look up and see the same moon.

When you look up at the moon tonight, Calvin, think of me. The next two weeks promise to be hard, even if that joy keeps sneaking up on me from time to time.

Missing you.

Your friend,

Ruby

16

A layer of fog coated the valley floor between the two squat mountains in the early morning of the anniversary of Calvin's first Sunday at St. John's. Calvin stepped out of his car and wiped lines of sweat from his upper lip and forehead. "Fog plus heat means we're in for a humid one," he said to the empty parking lot.

"Sure does," came a voice from around the corner of the church.

Calvin turned the corner to find Carl Sinclair setting up tables in the courtyard. The mayor's sport coat hung from a tree branch, and his face was red with heat and exertion.

"Let me give you a hand, Carl," said Calvin. "Why are you out here doing this by yourself so early?"

"I told the picnic planners that I would help set up, but then Donald Pennyworth put in a tee time for us—he didn't realize today was the parish picnic, after all. So I decided we could sneak in nine holes and be back in time for the festivities."

"Sounds sensible to me." Calvin smiled at the mayor's dual devotion to golf and to God.

The two men finished unfolding the final table and started encircling it with chairs. When they were done, Carl gestured to Calvin to take a seat. "In case I don't get a chance to say so later today, Calvin, let me say this now."

Calvin leaned forward in his chair, concern written on his face. What have I done now, he thought.

"I know I was hard on you when you first arrived. I thought you were just some green kid that the bishop sent here because there was no one else to come."

"Carl, I was just a green kid that the bishop sent here because there was no else to come."

Carl's teethed flashed in the early morning sun, but this wasn't the politician's grin. He wasn't being Uncle Carl, the debate winner. He was being himself. "Granted," he said. "Still, I shouldn't have been so hard on you for no reason. You really impressed me with the way you handled Phil's funeral. And now with the way you're caring for Ruby and Whit."

Carl reached out his hand. Calvin shook it, but when he moved to pull away, Carl held on. He put his other hand on top of Calvin's and said, "You have a good heart, son. Listen to it and you'll do just fine." He let go and stood up. "And listen to your elders too," he added.

"Yes, sir. Thank you for saying so."

"Just don't tell anyone that I'm really an old softy, okay?"

"I'm good at keeping secrets."

"Say, don't you have a baptism today?"

"Yes. Natalie Stewart."

"Excellent. More time for golf."

⸞⸟

"There is one Body and one Spirit," intoned Calvin following the processional hymn and opening greeting.

"There is one hope in God's call to us," responded the congregation as one.

"One Lord, one Faith, one Baptism," said Calvin.

"One God and Father of all," said the congregation.

The opening words to the baptismal service never failed to move Calvin. He made a mental note to go back and read the letter to the Ephesians again to refresh his memory as to where they came from. But no time for that now, he thought. I've got a baptism to do. Carrie Lincoln, the proud aunt of baby Natalie, came forward to read the first lesson. Calvin, of course, had trouble focusing on the words. A sundress again. But then Carrie also led the psalm, and the words drove the distraction from Calvin's mind. Carrie and the congregation passed verses back and forth until they reached the final ones:

> *Hear, O Lord, and have mercy upon me;*
> *O Lord, be my helper.*
> *You have turned my wailing into dancing;*
> *you have put off my sack-cloth and clothed*
>   *me with joy.*
> *Therefore my heart sings to you without*
>   *ceasing;*
> *O Lord my God, I will give you thanks*
>   *forever.*

They were the words upon which Ruby's song was based, the one she sang over and over again at her home, the one that caused Whit to wonder what his new, joyful clothes would look like. There's no such thing as a coincidence, Calvin told himself. Then he scanned the room for Ruby, but he didn't see her. She never missed church, and he knew how much she was looking forward to Natalie's baptism. Something's wrong, he thought.

But there was nothing Calvin could do at that moment because he had to read the Gospel, and then he had to preach his sermon, and then he had to baptize Natalie.

Brad and Rebecca, T.J. and Emily, Esther Rose and Carrie, and Brad's family, whom Calvin had not met before that day, all circled around the baptismal font. Calvin asked the glowing parents and the godparents a series of questions to answer on Natalie's behalf.

"Will you be responsible for seeing that the child you present is brought up in the Christian faith and life?"

"I will with God's help."

"Will you by your prayers and witness help this child to grow into the full stature of Christ?"

"I will with God's help."

The questions continued until Calvin turned to the whole congregation and asked: "Will you who witness these vows do all in your power to support this person in her life in Christ?"

A resounding, "We will," rang through the church, and Calvin felt proud to be part of a community that took such a promise so seriously.

A few minutes later, Calvin poured warm water from a silver vessel into the basin of the font. He prayed over the water, recalling events from the beginning of creation and Israel's deliverance at the Red Sea and Jesus' own baptism in the River Jordan. He touched the water and asked God, "Now sanctify this water, we pray you, by the power of your Holy Spirit, that those who here are cleansed from sin and born again may continue for ever in the risen life of Jesus Christ our Savior."

A second time, thoughts of Whit ran through Calvin's mind. *May continue for ever in the risen life of Jesus Christ.* Is that what's happening today? Is Ruby at home because Whit is in his final hours with us? Again, he pushed the thoughts out of his mind. Rebecca held Natalie out to him, and Calvin gathered the tiny new life in his arms. And for the first time since Christmas, he wasn't afraid that he would drop her. He wasn't anxious. He was at peace holding the baby, and that made Natalie calm as well.

Of course, when the water touched her forehead the first time, she started to whimper. "Natalie Rose, I baptize you in the Name of the Father," said Calvin.

He cupped another handful of water onto her forehead, and the whimper turned into a cry. "And of the Son."

A third splash of water sent the cry into a full-on wail. "And of the Holy Spirit. Amen."

"Amen," echoed the congregation, and a wave of chuckling broke out as Calvin quickly passed the wailing, soggy infant to Carrie. The moment Natalie was safe in Carrie's arms, the wailing stopped, and the laughter increased. Calvin looked at the congregation and smiled. "Sure, make me give her the bath," he said.

The laughter subsided, but the joy it left in its wake remained for the rest of the service. Calvin made the sign of the cross on Natalie's forehead with scented holy oil and prayed over her, asking the Holy Spirit to be present in her life so that she could live days full of courage, joy, love, and wonder.

A moment later, while everyone was shaking hands, hugging, and offering each other the peace of the Lord, Calvin took Natalie back from Carrie and walked her up and down the center aisle. Now that she wasn't being doused with water, she was her normal, burbling, squirmy self, and she charmed every person who shook her tiny fingers and offered her God's peace.

As Calvin walked up the aisle, he surveyed the congregation and realized that Avis Noon was also missing. Since she organized the parish picnic, something major must be keeping her away. Has to be Whit, thought Calvin. But once again, he took a deep breath and moved his anxiety to a holding area in his mind. I need to finish this service first, he told himself.

Chief Stern and Emily Lincoln flanked Calvin as he prayed the prayer of consecration over the bread and wine. When he was finished blessing the elements, he offered the Body and Blood of Christ to his two companions, who then took the wine-filled chalices and moved as one to the altar rail. From the front to the back, members of the congregation filed to the rail and knelt—or stood if their knees were bad, which many were. Calvin went down the line, pressing a piece of bread that was so much more than a piece of bread into each outstretched hand. "The Body of Christ, the bread of heaven," he said each time. The whole congregation of St. John's seemed to have turned out for today's services and the picnic after. The whole congregation, except for two of the faithful and one very sick man.

The service ended and everyone moved outside for the picnic. As Calvin had predicted, the visible fog had turned into an invisible blanket of oppressive humidity, and soon all the men had their sleeves rolled up and their ties loosened. Thanks to Avis's careful planning, the picnic went off without a hitch even though she wasn't there to oversee it. Mary Williams, an able deputy in Avis's absence, stood guard by the punchbowl and made sure no one lacked for anything.

"You did very well, Calvin," said Esther Rose, as she poured herself a glass of punch. She had her yellow legal pad under the opposite arm, but for once it was blank.

"Thanks, Esther Rose," said Calvin.

"No notes from our matriarch?" asked Chief Stern, who was next in line.

"Apparently not," said Calvin. "It appears there's a first time for everything." Calvin helped himself to punch, and the two sat down with the parents of the newly baptized Natalie. "And you, Chief. No uniform today."

"Off duty for the time being," said Chief Stern.

"Do you remember how you arrested Calvin last year?" said Brad Stewart. "That was one of the funniest things I've ever seen."

"Well, Calvin did try to break into his own church," said the Chief. "It seemed justice had to be served."

"It sure was a welcome I won't soon forget," said Calvin. "Whatever happened to Officer Carter anyway?"

"Oh, he's still on the force. Ornery as ever. He's not what you would call a people person. So I tend to assign him beats where I don't want a people person."

"He's not so bad," said Josie Temple-Jones, as she took the seat next to Calvin. "I find him quite charming."

"Josie, you are the consummate people person, so I don't doubt you could rub off on anyone," said the Chief.

"I didn't rub off on Calvin too much this year, though, did I," she said. "One date in a year? We could've done so much better, you and I, Calvin. 'No more setting me up,' he says, and now look at you. Been here a year and have you even had a woman over to your house?"

"Besides Ruby, Mary, Avis, and Esther Rose, no," said Calvin.

"Say, speaking of," said the Chief. "Where are Ruby and Avis? I thought for sure they would be here today."

"Me too," said Calvin. He took a deep breath and found it difficult to speak aloud the thought that came to his mind. He took a swig of lemonade to wet his parched mouth, and the now lubricated words slid out. "My heart tells me that Whit doesn't have much time left. I'm heading over there as soon as I can politely leave the picnic."

"I'm coming with you," said Josie.

Calvin and Josie reached the front door of the house on Lilac Court. The lilacs on either side of the stoop had passed their prime, and the once brilliant purples and pinks were faded and drooping or scattered around the bases of the plants. They could hear the tinkle of the piano from within, and they stayed on the stoop to listen until Ruby had finished the song. "I cried unto you, O God, and you healed me, you saved me and sealed me lest the grave be my bed," came the muffled words.

"She's singing Whit's song," said Calvin. "It soothes him." He knocked on the door. "Heck, it soothes me."

A moment later the door opened, and Josie launched herself into Ruby's arms, nearly bowling her over like a tiger tackling its prey. *Hurricane Josie it is, then,* thought Calvin. He expected her to launch into her frenetic, mile-a-minute talking, telling Ruby all the things that Ruby didn't want to hear just so Josie could feel better. *I shouldn't have let her come. But what right did I have to bar her?*

He waited another minute as Josie kept Ruby in the whirlwind embrace, and still she remained silent. Finally, she said, "Oh, Ruby. I love you so much."

Here it comes, thought Calvin. *The deluge.*

But it didn't. Josie said nothing more. She just held Ruby on the threshold of the front door with Calvin still outside. And then Calvin remembered that, like Avis and Esther Rose, Josie, too, was a widow. *She has been through this before. She knows when silence and touch are the best medicines.*

Finally, Josie broke the embrace, and Ruby ushered them both inside.

"I was so sad I missed the baptism this morning," said Ruby. "But it's touch and go in there right now." She gestured to the bedroom. "And I didn't feel like I could leave him. Not right now."

"How is he?" asked Calvin.

"Nurse Harris told me last evening that it will be any day now. She said there are signs. In his breathing. In what he is and isn't eating. In the look in his eye."

Josie gathered Ruby into another embrace.

"And he doesn't have too many words left in him," said Ruby. "He's always been quiet, but I never thought my husband would be truly speechless. And yet when his mouth moves hardly anything comes out."

Josie guided Ruby to her rocking chair. Avis Noon sat on the couch with a mug in her hands. The mug was empty, save for the dregs.

"You can see him when the nurse is done tending to him," said Ruby. "In the meantime, tell me all about the baptism. Was she beautiful? Did she cry? How did you do, Calvin?"

Calvin opened his mouth to answer, but Josie beat him to it. "Oh, he did very well." And for the next five minutes, the chaotically animated side of Josie surfaced as she told Ruby and Avis all about the service.

When she was done, Ruby said, "Thank you. Now I feel like I was there. I don't know but there's something about that baby that gives me hope even on a day like today." She paused for a moment and collected her thoughts. "Maybe it's because she was born right before Whit got sick. Whenever I see Natalie my heart lifts a little despite itself. I'm sure Whit's would too, if he could see her today. Though I suppose the Stewarts and Lincolns are having a celebration."

"I could call them and see," offered Calvin.

"No. No. I don't want to impose. Let them have their day. And we will have ours. I'm just glad some of the joy of this morning at St. Jack's could spill over here at home. I just hope Margaret and Cooper make it in time. Margaret was here earlier, but she's now on the way to pick Cooper up from summer camp. It will be hours before they get back."

At that moment, Nurse Harris entered the hallway. At once, all four of them turned to face her.

"No change," she said. "But it will be soon."

"May I go see him for a moment alone?" asked Calvin.

"Of course, dear," said Ruby.

Calvin rose from the couch and walked to the bedroom. For some reason, the hallway seemed longer than he remembered. He paused at the doorway and whispered, "God is in this room right now." Then he went in.

Whit lay under a pair of quilts despite the heat outside. He had been a big man when Calvin met him, but in recent weeks, the heft just seemed to have disappeared from his bones, and now Calvin had trouble discerning his form beneath the blankets on the hospital bed. The narrow bed, which had replaced the old king-sized one that Calvin had helped remove from the room, seemed somehow out of place. The dying man went with the shag carpet and the thick dusty drapes and the wood-paneled walls and the women sitting vigil in the next room. But the hospital bed didn't belong in this room.

The hospital bed would have looked very much in place if it had been in a hospital. Everything looks in place in a hospital room, thought Calvin. The gleaming, metal equipment; the monitors with their numbers and lines; the robotic bed—all in pristine order. In fact, the only thing that looks out of place in a hospital room is the patient because the patient is usually dirty—dirty and broken down.

But Whit was in his own house. He was clean, as Nurse Harris had just finished giving him a tender sponge bath. And his body may have been broken down, but Calvin couldn't help but have faith that his spirit was still whole. Maybe even more whole and more holy than it had ever been.

Calvin moved to the side of the bed, and a wave of embarrassment ran through him as he saw Whit's exposed leg sticking out from under the covers. His leg was pasty and spindle-thin with wisps of hair dotting it. The hospital gown didn't cover much, and Calvin could see where Whit's upper thigh met his buttocks. Calvin took the blankets in hand and gave them a gentle tug to cover Whit's leg, and the motion caused the sleeping man to stir.

Whit grunted and gasped. His breath came in ragged gulps as his eyes tried to focus on Calvin. From under the covers, he produced the old copy of *Leaves of Grass*, which seemed too heavy for him to hold. He clutched it like a child clutches a stuffed animal or an old, threadbare blanket. With the fore-finger of his opposite hand, Whit traced the title of the book, then looked up at Calvin, and this time his eyes focused. "For you," he gasped.

"For me?" echoed Calvin. "But . . . "

"You," said Whit, and he lifted the book with what seemed to be all his strength.

Calvin relieved him of the burden and clutched the book to his chest. "Thank you," he said. "I will treasure this."

Whit closed his eyes and settled back into a light doze. Calvin put his hand on Whit's forehead and sent up a prayer to God. It was a prayer without words, of the kind that are too deep for words, for which the Spirit intercedes. Then Calvin bent down and kissed Whit on the forehead. His skin felt like old paper against Calvin's lips.

"He told me he wanted you to have it," said Ruby from the doorway. "I'm glad he could give it to you himself."

"Ruby, I didn't see you there."

"I can't stay away for too long. I needed to come check on him."

"He's resting now."

"I suppose that rest is all that's left for him."

Ruby moved to the other side of the bed, slid her hand under Whit's, and held it gently, as if she were holding a bird's fragile egg. "Fifty-eight years," she said. "Add nearly ten more since we met. Still doesn't feel like enough."

"You'll have more."

They stood in silence for a while and gazed at Whit's ravaged face. Even as he slept, his breath continued in ragged heaves. Calvin closed his eyes, and once again the deep, wordless prayer surged through him. And when he opened his eyes, he saw for the second time the tendrils of liquid gold light reaching from Ruby and Whit to one another. Even with Whit weakened nearly to death, love's radiance spilled forth from him undiminished, unhindered by the cancer, which ruined his body but could not touch the part of him where God stored eternity.

Calvin blinked again, and the vision was gone. But the love remained. And the love will remain even when the grief is at its worst, he thought, because there is no grief without love.

Calvin put *Leaves of Grass* under the crook of his arm and slid his own hand under Whit's other one. "Ruby, why don't you call the others in and we can pray together."

But there was no need, because, as Ruby had done before them, Josie and Avis were standing in the doorway. They silently circled the bed and joined hands with Ruby and Calvin. "But where is the nurse?" said Ruby. "She should be here too."

Josie fetched Nurse Harris from the kitchen, and the five of them circled the hospital bed. Ruby and Calvin held Whit's hands, and the others finished the connection.

"Dear God," Calvin whispered. "We have no words that could possibly match the mystery of what you are doing in this room, but we pray anyway, hoping that you will elevate our humble offerings by your grace."

Calvin paused for a moment and thought, but no more words came to mind. But he found himself praying just the same. "We give to you your servant Walter. Enfold him in the arms of your grace and take his soul into your care, where it has been all along. Lord, you know each of us and you call us each by name. Speak Whit's name now, so he may hear you calling him home to you. Shine the light of your healing on him that he may find the wholeness you desire for all of your creation. Help each of us to know that nothing can separate us from your love. Help each of us to know we are always and forever held in the palm of your hand. Help each of us to know and to share your Son's love so we can find comfort and support in the days ahead. God, thank you for creating Whit just as he is. Thank you for the gift he is to us, especially to Ruby."

Upon saying Ruby's name, Calvin's voice shook and he found no more words welling up inside him. Lapsing into silence, Calvin focused on Whit's breathing and on the warmth of Avis's hand holding his.

After a time, Whit opened his eyes, and his breathing grew faster. But it sounded hollow, like there was too much space inside for it to fill. His eyes fixed on Ruby, and for a moment Calvin felt Whit's hand squeeze his. Ruby must have felt it too because she looked at each person in turn and then said, "May I have few moments alone with my husband, please."

"Of course," said Josie and Avis together. Nurse Harris nodded, and the three of them tiptoed out of the bedroom. Calvin stayed a moment longer, bent down over Whit and made the sign of the cross on his forehead, as he had done to Natalie that morning. "I bless you in the name of the Father, and of the Son, and of the Holy Spirit," he whispered. "Fair winds and following seas."

As Calvin blessed him, Whit never took his eyes off Ruby. Calvin backed out of the room and the last he saw, Ruby was holding Whit's hand to her cheek and Whit's mouth seemed to be forming words. But those words were for Ruby alone.

⤚⤚⤚

June 28, 2010

Dear Rev. Calvin,

I was so overjoyed to receive your letter today that I simply had to write back as soon as I finished reading it. So Anna MacDonnell is the name of your mysterious news, and what's more—you're engaged! Now, my dear, you have only been in Boston for about four months, so you and she must have moved quite quickly. But when you know, you know, they say. It was the swan boats that did it—floating on that idyllic pond. Right?

I didn't realize my heart could be filled with so much joy, especially on a day like today. It is a year to the day since Whit's death, and I woke this morning completely dreading the day. But my friends made it bearable. Avis picked me up for Morning Prayer and afterward, we all sat outside in the courtyard and talked about old times. Rebecca Stewart stopped by with Natalie, who is getting so big. And she's tottering around on her own now, so you have to watch her. We took our eyes off her for a minute and she got all soiled in the new flowerbeds along the courtyard fence. She's a child after my own heart, that one. Rebecca's new bump is starting to show, and soon we'll have another new life to celebrate here in Victory.

Then this afternoon, I got your letter in the mail, and the day went from bearable to joyful all at once. And still, as Avis once said, the grief lives right alongside the joy, so my heart is heavy all the same. But the grief and the joy both spring from love, which my heart still contains in abundance despite its brokenness.

You'll have to tell me so much more about your Anna. I know you must have been excited while writing your letter, so I'll excuse such a short description. As such, I will consider, "She's wonderful and she loves me," as a down payment toward future description. A picture of the two of you wouldn't hurt either. It will go on my piano, the top of which has become over the last months something of a collage of pictures of all the people I love.

And one person in particular. There are pictures of Whit with Margaret and Cooper as babies. There's the one of him in his Navy uniform and the wedding picture with the torn sleeves. There's one from two Christmases ago of him with T.J. and Harry Stern, the three "wise guys." There's a new picture of Josie and Donald from their wedding last month and one of me with Avis, Mary, and Esther Rose. And there's one that Emily gave me of you holding baby Natalie at the baptism. But I need one of your Anna because if you love her, then so do I.

Love is a funny thing, Calvin. It both causes pain and serves as the antidote for it. It is the catalyst for grief, but also the treatment. Whit mentioned that he told you the story of his ship, the *Pittsburgh*. He probably told you that I helped build it, but I maintain I only worked on the stern. This past year, I think I've been something like that old cruiser. I've been split in two, but I'm still floating. Against all odds, I'm still seaworthy. I'm going to make port even with my bow torn away. I can't help but have faith that love is keeping me afloat.

So you make sure you hold on to your love. Don't you ever let her get away. Don't you ever go a day without showing her how much you love her.

And you make sure to write back again soon. I need more details to share with the other ladies. I can't wait for tomorrow morning so I can tell them the good news.

With joy.

Your friend,

Ruby

Epilogue

Calvin Harper put down the letter and blew out a long-held breath. He hadn't thought about Ruby and Whit for quite some time, and now he realized that the second anniversary of Whit's death was in just a couple of days. He sat in silence for a moment holding Ruby up in prayer to God.

If news of our engagement helped her survive the first anniversary, then pictures from our wedding will surely help with the second, he thought. What had she said in the letter? *I need one of your Anna because if you love her, then so do I.*

Thinking back to all the pictures he still had to hang—of the wedding ceremony, the reception, the honeymoon—Calvin knew he wouldn't have a problem finding more selections to send to Ruby to complement the photograph he had sent when he first received her request. It's a good thing your mother isn't around to see them, Ruby, he thought, because Anna bared her shoulders in front of the Lord.

Calvin put Ruby's last letter in its place and wound the rubber band around the collection. Placing them back in the box, he noticed something else within and pulled out an old book.

With his finger, he traced Whit's name embedded in the name of his favorite poet.

Then opening the book to wherever it naturally wanted to fall, his eyes dropped to a line of poetry, and he began to read aloud.

> *O to sail to sea in a ship!*
> *To leave this steady unendurable land,*
> *To leave the tiresome sameness of the streets, the side-*
> *   walks and the houses,*
> *To leave you O you solid motionless land, and entering*
> *   a ship,*
> *To sail and sail and sail!*
> *O to have life henceforth a poem of new joys!*
> *To dance, clap hands, exult, shout, skip, leap, roll on,*
> *   float on!*

"What is that?" came a voice from the doorway.

Calvin looked up to see his new wife standing there with a bag of groceries in one hand and a gallon of milk in the other. He could see packages of flour and sugar pressing against the plastic bag. So *those* are the things that go in the cupboards, he thought.

He stood up and relieved Anna of the gallon of milk. As they put away the groceries, he explained what he had been reading. "That was from a poem called 'A Song of Joys' by Walt Whitman."

"I didn't know you liked poetry."

"I like Whitman."

"But I do know you like frozen pizza. I just couldn't bear the thought of buying it when I can just make it from scratch."

"I didn't know you could make pizza from scratch."

"You've got to keep some mystery for the marriage, hon," Anna said. "I'll make one tonight, how's that?"

"Sounds perfect," said Calvin.

It was the most ordinary moment possible, just putting away the groceries together in their new home. But that very normality took Calvin's breath away. *This* is normal now, he thought. *This* is my life. *Our* life. Together. What had Ruby said in one of her letters? That their story would never make the news or be made into a motion picture, but it was hers and Whit's and that made it special.

Calvin took a step forward and pulled Anna into his arms, and they kissed there in the middle of the kitchen. As the kiss lingered, they started spinning on the spot, and their embrace turned into a slow dance. And Calvin, of course, felt something in his shoes.

Breaking away from the kiss, he whispered, "Have I ever told you that you make my toes curl?"

Anna chuckled. "Your toes curl? Where did you come up with an expression like that?"

Calvin gathered his new wife in his arms once again, and their slow dance continued. "Let me tell you about my friend Ruby."

Acknowledgments

If you were to come to my house and inspect the upstairs closet, you would find a stack of letters that is about knee high. They are letters written to me in the two years after I moved from my first parish to my second. The real Ruby wrote them. They do not tell the story of her life, as do the ones in this book, but they do carry in their pages the affection she had for me. (I hope my less frequent responses returned that same affection.) I knew her for less than four years before she passed away, but a single day with her would have been enough for her to leave her mark of love on me. This book is for her.

So thank you to the real Ruby and to the rest of the Morning Prayer Ladies: Myrna, Shirley, Wilma, and sometimes Verna. Thank you to the people of Trinity Episcopal Church, who nurtured me during my first two years as a priest, with special thanks to Julie. If you see yourself in a character in this book, please know I was writing fiction (especially you, Mr. Mayor). I regret not being able to bring some of the more significant friendships I had at Trinity into the fiction of these pages; I had to make Calvin much lonelier (and less supervised) than I was. You have my eternal gratitude for sustaining me during my time there. (I hope you notice your names making cameos.)

Thank you to my friend Lester and to my grandfather Roy, who both passed away while I was writing this book. Your memories of World War II are in these pages, including the bit about the fruitcake.

Thank you to Kris for setting me straight on several details.

Thank you to the folks at the United Methodist Publishing House for continuing to support me as I develop as a writer: to Audrey and Ron, who probably don't realize that I pitched this book out of thin air the day you asked me to write a second

313

one; to Ramona, for her editorial heavy lifting; to Katie and the proofreaders, for their attention to detail; to Cat, for marketing wizardry; and to Jamie, a freelancer who schooled me in the use of the word "that."

Thank you to my parents for reading the draft and for a lifetime of encouragement. And a special thank you, as always, to my lovely wife, Leah, for more things than could fit on these pages. You always make my toes curl.

Discussion Questions

1. Who is the most influential person for you in your life of faith? Describe that person and the relationship you had or have. Why is it so special?

2. Ruby teaches Calvin to remember that God is already in every room Calvin enters. When have you felt God's presence in an unexpected place? What about that situation made God's presence real for you?

3. Ruby imagines heaven as a place full of sea glass. What images would you use to describe your vision of heaven? Why those images?

4. When have you felt like you were "trying to water the yard with the hose turned off"? What made the "hose" start flowing again?

5. Over the course of the story, Calvin learns that relying on other people is necessary in life. When did you learn this lesson? What happened to force you to learn it? How have you helped to impart this lesson to others?

6. How do you respond to Dr. Pennyworth's notion of the difference between curing and healing? After initial reactions, read a couple of the stories of Jesus healing people in the Gospel. How does Dr. Pennyworth's understanding fit in with the witness of the gospel?

7. Who have you lost in your life? How does it feel to lose someone you love? What happens to your grief? What happens to your love?

8. Calvin realizes resurrection isn't something one can study; it is only something to which one can bear witness. How have you witnessed resurrection in your life or in the lives of others?

9. Ruby and Josie fall on opposite ends of the spectrum as far as seeking the spotlight goes. Concerning the ways you serve God in your life, on which side of the

spectrum do you fall? How would your service to God grow if you were to seek the spotlight more or less?

10. If you were to write a letter to someone who means something to you, to whom would you write and what would you say?

11. Calvin's first days at St. John's were a roller coaster ride. He almost got arrested, his apartment was uninhabitable, and he was alone. How did the parish welcome him into their community? What were their expectations of the new priest? How have you welcomed new clergy into the life your church?

12. While Calvin is the only ordained person at St. John's, everyone has a ministry. How do you see these being carried out? By the Morning Prayer Ladies? The Police Chief? The golfers? Josie Temple-Jones? Others? What ministries are you called to?

Want to learn more about author
Adam Thomas and check out other great
fiction from Abingdon Press?

Sign up for our fiction newsletter at
www.AbingdonPress.com
to read interviews with your favorite authors, find tips
for starting a reading group, and stay posted on what
new titles are on the horizon. It's a place to connect
with other fiction readers or post a
comment about this book.

Be sure to visit Adam online!

http://wherethewind.com

Plan your escape.

What They're Saying About...

The Glory of Green, by Judy Christie
"Once again, Christie draws her readers into the town, the life, the humor, and the drama in Green. *The Glory of Green* is a wonderful narrative of small-town America, pulling together in tragedy. A great read!"
—Ane Mulligan, editor of *Novel Journey*

Always the Baker, Never the Bride, by Sandra Bricker
"[It] had just the right touch of humor, and I loved the characters. Emma Rae is a character who will stay with me. Highly recommended!"
—Colleen Coble, author of *The Lightkeeper's Daughter* and the *Rock Harbor* series

Diagnosis Death, by Richard Mabry
"Realistic medical flavor graces a story rich with characters I loved and with enough twists and turns to keep the sleuth in me off-center. Keep 'em coming!"—Dr. Harry Krauss, author of *Salty Like Blood* and *The Six-Liter Club*

Sweet Baklava, by Debby Mayne
"A sweet romance, a feel-good ending, and a surprise cache of yummy Greek recipes at the book's end? I'm sold!"—Trish Perry, author of *Unforgettable* and *Tea for Two*

The Dead Saint, by Marilyn Brown Oden
"An intriguing story of international espionage with just the right amount of inspirational seasoning."—*Fresh Fiction*

Shrouded in Silence, by Robert L. Wise
"It's a story fraught with death, danger, and deception—of never knowing whom to trust, and with a twist of an ending I didn't see coming. Great read!"—Sharon Sala, author of *The Searcher's Trilogy: Blood Stains, Blood Ties,* and *Blood Trails.*

Delivered with Love, by Sherry Kyle
"Sherry Kyle has created an engaging story of forgiveness, sweet romance, and faith reawakened—and I looked forward to every page. A fun and charming debut!"—Julie Carobini, author of *A Shore Thing* and *Fade to Blue.*

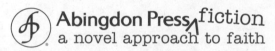

Abingdon Pressʌfiction
a novel approach to faith

AbingdonPress.com | 800.251.3320